SWEET SISTER SEDUCED
by S. B. Hough

*Also available in Perennial Library
by S. B. Hough*

DEAR DAUGHTER DEAD

SWEET SISTER SEDUCED

by

S. B. HOUGH

PERENNIAL LIBRARY
Harper & Row, Publishers
New York, Cambridge, Philadelphia, San Francisco
London, Mexico City, São Paulo, Sydney

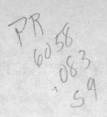

A hardcover edition of this book was published in 1968 by Victor Gollancz Ltd., London, England. It is here reprinted by arrangement with Brandt & Brandt, Inc.

First PERENNIAL LIBRARY edition published 1983.

Library of Congress Cataloging in Publication Data

Hough, S. B. (Stanley Bennett), 1917-
  Sweet sister seduced.

  (Perennial library ; P/662)
  I. Title.
[PR6058.083S9 1983]   823'.914   83-47584
ISBN 0-06-080662-1 (pbk.)

83 84 85 86 87 10 9 8 7 6 5 4 3 2 1

AUTHOR'S APOLOGY

IT HAS always surprised me that people who can appreciate the strict classical form of a Mozart symphony, or the economy of thematic material in a Bach fugue, are disinclined to see those identical qualities in anything so common in our own time as the universal but highly artificial art-form of the detective story.

It will be two hundred years no doubt before the cultural oracles begin to speak of twentieth-century literature in the same terms we now use for seventeenth-century music, but by then we may expect that civil service entrants will be required to make the difficult distinction between the *whodunit* and the *thriller*, while a suitable subject for a university thesis will be the degeneration of Simenon's artistic form whenever he abandoned his detective Maigret.

This book, should any copy of it accidentally survive, will probably add to the confusion.

So to save some poor student the doubt he will inevitably feel on persual of the text, I will give him an authoritative answer: it is a *did-he-do-it*.

S.B.H.

CHAPTER I

'I HAD a very normal and ordinary childhood, Inspector,' Milham told Brentford. 'I don't want to make any excuses of that kind. I am not aware that I loved my mother and hated my father, or indeed the other way round. On the contrary, we were a very easygoing household. We were certainly not well-to-do, but nor were we hard up. My father was the manager of a drapery store. We were officially Church of England, but lax about it. This was in Chester, by the way. I think you know how it is in England when neither beliefs nor standards nor even morals in the least obtrude. There was myself, and my sister Elizabeth who was two years younger, and a baby brother about whom I don't need to trouble you, since he never impinged on me except as a minor nuisance. I think I can honestly say that in my childhood at least I had a happy life.'

Brentford had asked Milham to tell him about himself, but he had not, in the otherwise empty house at midnight, expected such elaborate detail as he was getting.

'I could never have imagined that we were in the least unstable,' Milham said. 'Take our views on religion for example. Officially, as I have said, my parents took the standard Christian view, complete with an actual heaven and an actual hell, a personal God, and very nearly a personal devil. It was only gradually and as I came into my teens that it did occur to me that their views did not quite hold water. Oh, it was true that once a week they dressed us up and sent us off to the Sunday school. But they themselves were most indifferent in their observances. They went to church two or three times a year, and I remember them being mildly disturbed on some occasion, and arguing with one another, because they had not been to a service at Easter, or whatever it is the Church requires. You know what a logical boy's mind is. It was clear to me that either there was a heaven and hell, or there wasn't. If there was, and the alternatives were either an after-life of bliss or an

7

eternity of fiery torment, then it was obviously the most important thing there was. Yet they succeeded in at once believing in it and at the same time treating it as though it was of little consequence. You see what I mean by stability. Heaven and hell and God himself were only minor factors. Ordinariness and the regular progress of life existed above all. I could never have guessed or comprehended, and I doubt if you can, despite the enquiries you have been making about me, the events that were to come upon us.'

'I may tell you now that I have done my utmost not to embarrass you,' Brentford said, sitting back in his chair and wondering why Milham did not trouble to draw the curtains. The house, as Inspector Simpson had told him, was a place like a barn, and though Milham had switched on a bar of the electric fire as they came in, the blackness through the window had the unrelieved and positive quality of the Penlee woods.

'I have gone to almost absurd lengths to maintain discretion,' he said.

'I didn't quite think that when I was waiting for you to come out of the Frazers,' Milham said coldly.

But he did not allow his opinion of Brentford's discretion to disturb him, and he went on with his narrative.

'It is necessary that I tell you something of my frame of mind. I was a moderately bright boy, and I had gone to the grammar school. That is to say I was good at those subjects that interested me, and indifferent to bad in those that failed to catch my interest. I had once, and for some unknown reason, taken an interest in the geometry text book. My ability to run through all the theorems and somehow comprehend them had given me a feeling that I was, or could be, good at mathematics. Translated into my father's language, and as evidence of his reading-for-understanding of my school reports, this meant I was good at figures. It became understood in the household that there was possibilities that I might become an accountant or work in a bank. Even I could see that there was no real actual connection between Pythagorus' square on the hypotenuse and adding up columns of figures at a bank desk, but that, I assumed, as did everyone else of my acquaintance, was the difference between pleasure and interest on the one hand, and work on the other. There was no suggestion that I should go on to the university and really study the theoretical and logical side of mathematics that interested me. There was no injustice about that. I had failed in history and latin in my matriculation examination, and even if I were a genius in mathematics, I still could not win a university scholarship. So when I left school, I went to work in a local office, and went to the night school to study book-keeping.'

'This was in Chester?' Brentford said, since he had reason to believe that Milham had not stayed there.

'To begin with, yes. Unfortunately the firm I worked for went into liquidation. This was at the height of the industrial depression of the nineteen twenty-nine era. To get any work at all, I had to go off into the Midlands, leave my family, go into lodgings, and attend the night school there.'

'I'm sorry. Go on. I only want to get the facts right.'

Milham, neat in his grey suit, paused to give Brentford a look that expressed his opinion about what Brentford called the facts.

'What I was telling you about was my state of mind. A young man, virtually still a boy, alone in a strange town, can easily get into trouble. My parents took adequate care to check up on me. All they learned was that I was going round with other youths, students of my own age, and some of them from the university. I don't know if they were gratified. I hope they were. They can hardly have been disturbed by my taking advantage of the lack of intellectual snobbery in the Midlands, at the same time as, working as a book-keeper, I was also doing my best to qualify in accountancy. That I, being what I was, should mingle with university students, was something that could hardly have happened in Oxford or Cambridge, but they can't have seen a danger in it. My streak of idealism, evident in my unnatural interest in Pythagoras and Euclid, was something of which they were unaware. I doubt if they even saw any danger in 'ideas'. They themselves, as I have pointed out, were very far from taking their own ideas, even those concerned with heaven and hell, at all literally. They had our expertise in the half-belief or the pretended belief, which foreigners always mistake and call our hypocrisy, to a

9

high degree. They were very ordinary pragmatic English people in other words. That was why it must all have been a great shock to them.'

Brentford sat wondering if Milham was the first criminal he had known who had a touch of philosophy. Or an ability to talk. He had been warned about that. 'What was a shock to them?' he said.

Milham smiled a little cynically and sadly, as though that were the point, and something that should not really be revealed until the end of a story of novel length.

'To your way of thinking, Inspector, I doubt if anything "happened" as I feel you would call it, until I had passed my accountancy finals, left my book-keeping employer, and, by diligent perusal of the professional journals and advertisements, obtained a starting post as an accountant down here in the south of England. That was when I first went home after some little time. I wangled, if you will excuse the word, a short holiday between one employment and the next. I had begun to appreciate home comforts after I had left them. And, to be truthful, I had no objection to a certain amount of adulation from my parents, now I had become a professional man. Which I certainly got, from the moment of my arrival.'

Milham stopped, and for the first time since Brentford had seen him, he seemed to pause as though covering some old emotion. It hardly seemed possible that such a man should be at a loss for words, and yet he seemed so for a moment, until he started again, in a drier and more simple tone.

'At first, in our living room, I just gave my father and mother the presents I had brought and accepted their congratulations. I don't think I detected quite the quality of the fuss they made, or the specially adulatory tone in which they asked their questions. After all, I had a lot to tell them. I had not seen them since my finals results came through, and I was just back from a journey down here, to Lockley, where I had seen a man called Follet, of Follet and Follet, who were quite obviously the best accountants in what was to me a strange town. That I had got the job at all, in the face of competition, and coming as I did from places like Chester and the Midlands, was good enough. I had to tell them of the stratagems used to get it, which showed me as a man of the world, dealing with matters they did not fully understand. I even spoke to them in my carefully cultivated neutral accent, which I had adopted in reaction to the affectations of the university men. I had a glow about me, and I suppose I showed it. It was not clear to me at first that there was something panic-stricken and almost tragic in the way they were looking at me and the way they hung on my words. Nor, until I found myself with a present still in my hand, and nowhere to dispose of it, did I think to ask them, "Where is Elizabeth?"'

'Elizabeth?' said Brentford.

'Elizabeth,' said Milham.

CHAPTER II

IT HAD begun when Brentford was digging in the garden. He liked digging. He had not met Milham then, who might have suggested to him that there was something either symbolic or sadistic in the way he liked thrusting the spade home in the soft yielding earth with his foot.

Out of the corner of his eye, he saw Ethel coming across the lawn. In his uncomfortable way, he felt apprehensive about what she was going to say before she said it. He almost knew. 'Telephone for you, John,' she said without haste as she approached him. But her voice had a slight I-told-you-so quality.

Because of her tone, she stood looking a little guilty on the corner of the grass. He was the one who had suggested spending the week-end in the garden, and she had said, with realism rather than cynicism, that if they went to the beaches they would at least be out of the way of telephones. They had been married long enough to be careful how they used statements like 'I told you so.'

'On a Sunday,' he said, leaning on the spade.

'Yes,' she said.

'Who is it? Parker?'

She put her head a little on one side and looked at the patch where he had been digging. 'John, aren't you ever going to move the raspberries?'

It was the raspberry patch he had been digging in. Every year, they grew in all directions, and now they were showing signs of invading the lawn. It was exactly what he had been doing, trying to move the raspberries. He gave her a look.

Then he picked up the spade and walked away with it, to leave it carefully outside and against the side of the garage as he went into the cottage. If she had eyes, she could see what he intended.

'It is Parker,' she called after him. 'You might as well put it away.'

He took refuge in the rear porch of the cottage, and pretended he did not hear her. It was their own cottage, for the police did not provide accommodation for Brentford. He could live wherever he liked, provided it was near enough to Lockley, and the cottage was somewhere they had chosen as far south, and as near the coast and away from the suburbs and centre, as they were able.

In the long, low, converted living room, with its atmosphere, he looked at Ethel's flower arrangement on the telephone stand, and then picked up the phone. He could hear Parker breathing.

'Hello, John,' Parker said in a preliminary way.

Brentford acknowledged that he recognised the voice. He said, 'It's Sunday.'

'Something has come up, John,' Parker said, not cheerfully exactly, but as though it were a law of nature.

'My free Sunday,' Brentford said.

Parker laughed. Brentford must be joking. 'John,' he said, 'do you remember that woman who drowned herself in the river at Penlee at six o'clock in the morning?'

'No.'

'The suicide verdict was only in the papers a day or two ago.'

'You don't give me time to read the papers.'

It did finally penetrate to Parker that Brentford was being like that about it. He paused, and adopted a more serious tone.

'Look, John, the desk called me, even though it is a Sunday.'

Since Parker was a Chief Superintendent, that was very adventurous of the desk.

'Probably the last summer Sunday of the year,' Brentford said, tugging at the telephone cord so that he could see through the window to where Ethel was standing on the lawn.

'A Constable Hebble, at Penlee, has had someone walk into his office and say that the woman was murdered by her husband.'

Unwillingly, Brentford had a mental picture of Penlee, with its white villas on a south-facing bank, the junction of the rivers below, the surrounding tree-covered hills, and the sailing yachts.

'Tell him to call an ambulance.'

'It isn't like that, John.'

'They are very good with those people.'

Someday, though probably not on a Sunday when he wanted him to do something, Parker was going to take Brentford to task for not using the one word 'sir'.

'The person who has walked into Hebble's office,' Parker's voice came very distinctly over the phone, 'is Lambkin, the chapel preacher.'

Brentford was troubled by another mental vision.

Over the scene he could see, of Ethel on the lawn looking at the rose bush, and the one he had imagined, of Penlee with its gardens and woods and the motor cruiser and two ocean-racing yachts at their moorings on the river, he superimposed a third. It was of green-painted windows on Lockley High Street, and gold lettering that said, 'Follet & Milham, Chartered Accountants.'

'Wasn't that the Milham woman?' he said.

Parker had not become Detective Chief Superintendent in charge of the Lockley C.I.D. for nothing. He said, 'I thought you didn't read the account.'

'Only the headlines,' Brentford said.

'John,' said Parker, 'it could be quite a scandal.'

It was only a few moments later that they hung up.

When Brentford went out, to pick up the spade from outside

the garage and put it away, Ethel watched him across the bush she was examining for greenfly.

'I told you so,' she said.

CHAPTER III

IT WAS only necessary to look around the room, at its slightly dusty aspect, and its fruitfully littered quality, to know that it was a room where a family had been brought up, and where a woman had lived who had since departed. Brentford felt he knew it already. An Inspector Simpson had described it to him, what it was like to see Milham, of Follet and Milham, living there alone in Penlee.

'I thought you said you called her Betty,' Brentford said. He liked to get his names and facts right.

Milham looked at him doubtfully from what was evidently still his usual chair in the disordered room. For a moment, he showed a nervous tension.

'So you know? Someone else must have told you that.'

'Oh, possibly.' Brentford treated it with indifference. 'Anyway, it's quite common, or it was in those days, for a family to call an Elizabeth Betty.'

They were away again then.

'The family called her Elizabeth,' Milham said. 'It was part of them. Part of their slight unnecessary pretension as I was telling you. Even when we were talking privately among ourselves, I was the only one who didn't.'

CHAPTER IV

PENLEE WAS specks of colour which were people sunbathing on the riverside lawns. There were private quays and dinghy-landings. The deep-water yachts, seen against the woods from the descending approach road by which Brentford came, looked as though they had lost the sea. the white and coloured sails of the dinghies moved round them. As he had made the journey he had noticed that all the signposts pointed backwards, indicating that all destinations were by the main road. That was one way to keep tourists away.

Penlee meant something special to Brentford, as it did to many Lockley people. Contemplating the scene of blue and green, he forgot he had been interrupted in gardening.

A girl in pink, tight trousers came out of a gate ahead of him. A Jaguar like a sleek, overfed cat moved silently, at least from Brentford's distance, down the narrow lane with the high hedges between the boat yard and the yacht club. The girl, whose minutest shape was meticulously outlined by the trousers, did not look for traffic as she stepped out, but allowed herself to be led down towards the river by a small white dog. Her upper garment was loose, and evidently intended to leave much to the imagination, with various hints. An old man with a bicycle was standing stationary in the middle of the road.

The girl never reappeared in Brentford's life, which was perhaps just as well since in his station in society he was always slightly at a loss what to do with girls of her kind. The old man proved enigmatic. He wore the clothes and had the means of transport of someone's gardener, but as Brentford squeezed his car past, he turned on him a blue-eyed stare, calculated to set even a stranger at a distance, that would have done credit to a retired general. Penlee was simultaneously snobbish and democratic, and Brentford, driving down the hill, passed the turning off to the police station before he realised it. He made no attempt to turn but went on down past the one row of ancient cottages, all of which now had brightly coloured doors and sanitation and water pipes attached to their external walls. There was no real place to turn until he reached the grass, the No Parking signs, the old stone quay and the ship's bell on a pole that marked the point between the rivers.

He was not without a purpose in coming as far as that once he had started on the road. It was not quite true, what he had told Parker about having absolutely no knowledge of the case, and he wanted to look at the lane that ran up the bank of the

15

second river. Unlike the lane up the main river, which passed the yacht club and came to the estate ferry by way of the boat yard behind him, and never got nearer to the water than the breadth of someone's lawn, the lane he could see ahead from the ferry steps ran up and down a little but kept more or less to the bank. For a distance at least it was fringed by minor pebble beaches, and drops that looked like miniature unstable cliffs, and, where clumps of trees intervened, with tree roots that had been undercut and that hung out above the flowing water. It was only in the distance that it left the tidal river, with its debris of water weed and other things less mentionable, and climbed to lose itself in the woods, where house-roofs that appeared through the screen of trees indicated that it still had a purpose.

Brentford spent some time trying to remember whether the house he imagined must lie somewhere up there was called Viewcrest or Crestview, and then remembered that he had two people waiting for him at the police station, and turned the car. He imagined that they must be somewhat tired of waiting now.

Driving back into the village by the second road, up the bank, he caught sight of the white peak of the chapel appearing among the trees, and frowned a little. There had been a controversy about the building of that chapel that had been so widespread it had even affected him. Penlee and Fundamentalism, of whatever variety, hardly seemed to go together, and Lambkin, the chapel preacher, already had much to answer for. The consequences of his building the chapel, and the outcry that had roused, oddly enough from the religious and not the non-religious, had been that the whole area had been declared one of Outstanding Natural Beauty. Aesthetic considerations had prevailed where ethics and theology had failed, and, though too late to stop the chapel, to prevent further incursions there had been a ban on further private building.

But, Brentford thought as he stopped the car, they had not banned the erection of police houses.

The two houses of the Penlee constables were more modern, and certainly more expensive, though the taxpayer had paid, than Brentford's own. Each had a garage, one open and empty at the moment, and the other with a bright red mini-car standing in front of it. Constructed in one block, in ample grounds, they had a small glass-fronted office, over which the blue Police sign hung, between them. One other car, a five-year-old Ford, was parked in the road outside ahead of Brentford's. A child's kiddy-car stood on the garden path and drive on one side, together with dolls and a ball and other toys, though there were none upon the other.

Brentford contained his envy as he got out of his car and opened the garden gate. He wondered if the constables appreciated it, an opportunity to bring up their children in surroundings which a man like himself would have to work all his life to earn, or if they complained about the isolation because they would have to drive nine miles to go to the nearest cinema. Officiously, when he got inside the gate, he picked up the kiddy-car from the path and set it down again on the new lawn of young green grass.

The office door opened, and a young policeman came out, in uniform but without his helmet, moving quickly to intercept Brentford before he reached the office. 'I'm sorry about that, sir,' he said about the kiddy-car before he arrived. When he did arrive, he said, 'I'm Constable Hebble.'

Brentford looked at the glass of the office, behind which an elderly white-haired man could be seen, sitting to a table with an empty tea cup before him and wearing an attitude of patient resignation. Then he looked at the farther, empty garage, and at the red, highly polished mini-car that was on Hebble's side. He said, 'You're on your own?'

'You'll be Detective Chief Inspector Brentford, sir?' the constable said.

Brentford picked up a doll that had fallen off and replaced it on the kiddy-car. 'My fame can't have spread very widely if our own constables don't know me,' he said.

'You see it's only that I haven't met anything of this kind before, sir,' Hebble said, looking back up at the office with a strange expression.

Brentford turned round and looked at Penlee, and the white and colourful sails of the little class boats that were racing round the larger yachts on the water of the river. 'Been here long?' he asked.

'Only nine months, sir. Before that we used to live in the condemned cottages at Lowecreek and cycle over every day. It was pretty there.'

At least they would have ceased to get lost in the lanes by now, Brentford thought. If it had not been for the influx of wealth into Penlee, it would probably never have been necessary for them to make the move.

'My wife and I used to hope to retire here one day,' he said. 'If we'd been wise, we'd have bought a plot and had plans passed for a dwelling before the ban. We didn't, and values have trebled since then on these places, and now I don't suppose we ever shall.'

He was not quite sure if Hebble heard him or understood. The young man was still looking at the office. 'I don't think he's entirely responsible, sir,' he said.

It was not clear if he meant that Lambkin was not entirely responsible for Brentford's thwarted retirement plans, or if he was just not responsible generally.

Partly, Brentford ceased to think of Penlee, though he still looked at it. 'What's he been telling you?' he asked.

'That Mr. Milham murdered Mrs. Milham, sir. He says he pushed her in.'

It sounded clear enough.

'Does he give a reason for his opinion?'

'It was something that Mrs. Milham said to him a day or two before she died.'

'Oh, and what was that?'

'That, he won't say, sir.'

Brentford could not say he was greatly surprised. It had been too much to hope that Lambkin, who was sitting in the office as though about to be crucified, would claim to be a direct eye-witness of the pushing. It came under the heading of Suspicion, not fact.

'All right,' he said reluctantly. 'I'll have a word with him.'

'I'd be extraordinarily grateful if you would, sir,' Hebble said in a relieved voice, and they walked up towards the office.

CHAPTER V

'HAVE YOU ever had, at different times of your life, different ideas of evil, Inspector?' Milham said.

It was as well they had the night before them, and comfortable chairs, in Milham's room.

'I can't say I've ever thought of it like that,' Brentford said cautiously. 'I suppose ones ideas of evil do change from time to time.'

Milham shook his head with an air of being wise after the event.

'It seemed to me the height of evil at the time,' he said. 'You can take it as a reflection of my innocence. That a man, without taking any precautions to help her, should seduce a girl.'

'Look, what are you telling me? That this sister of yours, Elizabeth, had been seduced?' Brentford put it mildly.

'I'm not unintentional in keeping you in suspense about it,' Milham said reflectively. 'If possible, I would like you to feel a little of what I felt, and to understand the length of time it took me to get to know. You do remember the scene I was telling you about, in our family living room, with me giving out the presents, which I had suddenly felt I could afford, and finding my sister missing? We were an ordinary family. When I asked "Where is she?" I expected a direct answer, and I got it, "She is in her room." The question of why she was in her room took infinitely longer. My young brother was with us, for one thing, and he was not presumed to know. I was not presumed to know, or to understand about things like that, either. I am quite sure that if my father and mother could have thought of any conceivable means of keeping it from me, they would have done so. Had I not appeared all but unexpectedly, at only half a day's notice, I'm sure they would have got rid of my sister, by sending her away to an aunt for the time of my stay or something of the kind like that. I was innocent of all these things. I said, "What on earth is she doing in her room, just now? I'll go and fetch her." My mother said, "No, William, you must not do that," speaking quickly and as though I were still a child. I said, "Why, is she ill?" and my mother went pale, and looked from me to my brother as she said, "Yes, she's a little out of sorts," which was the best possible indication that she was lying.'

Milham did not indicate why he was going into such detail about those long-distance family matters. He just sat looking at the single bar of the electric fire burning away through the night in the blank and barn-like yet littered room. The blackness outside the window was something that he completely disregarded, as he did the similar night outside the uncurtained garden door.

'No doubt you regard all this as a farce,' he said concernedly.

'No,' said Brentford. 'My work takes me out among many people from time to time. I've heard of this kind of thing happening to several families.' He considered it. 'It has never seemed to me to be quite a farce.'

For some reason, perhaps due to the hour, the tale Milham was telling him seemed to be one that he could regard with quite unusual objectivity and dispassion. He did not have to believe it for one thing, and that always helped.

'Of course it seemed quite grim to me,' said Milham. 'I had never known anything like it before, not in our family. It was true that one or another of us, ever since we were children, had sometimes been sent up to our room when we had done something really wrong. But I, as the eldest, had always taken it that I had a right to know why. "Why has Elizabeth been sent to her room?" I would ask. "Because she has had another of her naughty tantrums when she couldn't get her own way." That was the way it had always been. But I was a young man now, and Elizabeth was almost a woman. That implied quite a tantrum. Left with her present in my possession, I did not think it wise to ask about it until we got rid of my young brother. It's probably difficult for you to understand how my mind ran. Thinking of adult crimes, I thought that Elizabeth must have stolen something. I have told you I was innocent. That is a quality of innocence. Its capacity to think the wrong things.'

'Was it just wrong? Presumably you knew your sister?'

Milham looked at him gravely.

'She had never stolen anything in her life. Her naughtiness was not that kind at all. She had always been self-willed, but all her troubles always arose because she would not do what she was told. But remember that when I had left home she had still been quite a youthful schoolgirl. I had only seen her during the holidays since then, and I only believed I knew her.'

'Did you eventually guess, or did they have to tell you?'

'The way it seemed to me, I somehow came to it before I got the actual facts. I had the feeling. You know how people are in families. You don't have to say things in words to get the sense of things. It was the special way they were looking at me and offering me anything they could think of. My father offered me a cigar, when in any event I did not smoke them, and at that time of day was quite ridiculous. My mother wanted me to take the chair by the fire, her chair, making the excuse that I must be feeling cold and she didn't want me to catch a chill. They weren't treating me well, they were treating me extravagantly. It suddenly struck me that they were almost fawning on me. I got it right then. I was their wonderful son, whom they couldn't make too much of because he had done the right thing, though what I had done was after all quite ordinary. Even my young brother somehow got in on it, and it was horrible. I could not think what had come over them. Because there was I being treated well, too well, almost as though I were a stranger, and there was my sister, who would have been the first to welcome me, with her impetuous nature, shut up in her room with everyone trying to pretend, once the first questions were over, that she did not exist. I don't know how you can describe it, except as a family thrown. They were doing all the wrong things, and they must have known, whatever my sister had done, even if she had committed murder, they were still the wrong things.'

'Have you told this story often?' Brentford said.

It was a question that Milham did not answer. It was his silence that seemed to suggest that he had never mentioned it to anyone. Now he had told it, it would never be the same again.

21

'Foreigners are right, when they accuse us of hypocrisy, due to our habit of half-believing things,' he said. 'If my family had really believed in sin and hell-fire, and all the things they said they did, they would have known what to do. Elizabeth could have been shown the door and sent out into the cold, cold snow. But they were too liberal for that. They did not in fact believe in the physical maltreatment of unmarried girls who were going to have a baby. In theory they didn't. In theory, sometimes, I imagine, because of the kinds of things they sometimes said, they imagined those girls as more sinned against than sinning. That was, of course, someone else's girls, when it happened to someone else. I discovered what their feeling was when it happened to them. They were incredulous. They did not want to face it, any more than they wanted to face the fact that if what they believed on Sundays was true, then there really was a hell. That was the idea. Even when my brother went out they wanted to banish her from their minds, as they always did with nearly everything. I told you I had been mentally sharpened and was pretty rigid in my own views, didn't I? I said, "What is the matter with Elizabeth?" And my mother, without hesitation, said, "Oh, don't let's talk about her; let's talk about you." I just got up and went to the door. I knew I was being cruel. I think it was the first time in my life I practised deliberate cruelty on anyone, and I had to begin on my own parents. I said, "You'd better tell me, or I'm going right up to see her." I intended to do that anyway, but after what they had done to me, I intended them to crawl first. My mother treated me as a child. She said, "You don't understand these things, William. You're a boy. Your sister is going to have a baby." It was filthy. I felt as though I had been smeared by some particularly viscous kind of glue.' Milham waved a hand. 'I mean my parents' behaviour, of course.'

They contemplated the behaviour of parents from the point of view of midnight.

'I think you are laying it on too thickly,' Brentford said.

Milham's eyebrows went up on his expressive face.

'You think, or imply, that on recollection I hate my parents? You are wrong, I assure you. My criticism, even at the time, was precisely because I loved them. I was like a man who condemns his own country. Scrape such a man, and you will find a hidden patriot underneath. I felt that my parents, just because they were my parents, should behave better than the average, and of course they didn't. It was that which I felt, that I was implicated in their behaviour.'

It was possible, Brentford thought, barely possible. At least he himself sometimes felt uncomfortable in the presence of those who were too loud-mouthed in the praise of their country. But he did not see that if Milham had decided to praise his parents it would have been to praise himself, which was the implication, if any, of the other thing. 'If you feel you must go on,' he said.

Milham nodded to him as though he had said something gracious.

'I went upstairs as I told you, to see my sister. My parents forbade me, and I was half expecting to find her door locked. It wasn't, which surprised me. I went in, and noticed they hadn't followed me. I found Betty curled up on her disordered bed. She hid her face and cried when she saw me. "Bill, don't you come near me." She had adopted my parents' view, I saw. That she had done something unspeakable, and let our family down. She wept. I knew she did have a tendency to go overboard in her emotions. It took me ten minutes to get a coherent word out of her, and in the middle of it, too obviously quoting my mother, she said, "Bill, I don't want to sully your great success." I said, "Say that again, and I'll pull you out of bed, take off your nightie myself, and slap your bottom." I made her smile a little, momentarily. But she only yielded to despair again when I attempted our usual unarmed verbal combat and tried to get it out of her what unknown man, a married man as she said it was, hated and despicable, and either completely without remorse or helpless, who had done this to her. I shared her view of him, but that only made it worse, I saw. She was far from looking up at me defiantly and saying, "I did this, all right, it can't be helped, I did it." On the contrary, what affected me was to see her broken like that, and accepting a set of standards that none of us actually believed in. It was that that really made me hate the man. The insult of Betty and her humiliation and degradation. I saw it against the background of our family life, with its petty deceits and its half-lies and its self-evasion. I think I was the only one who actually hit Elizabeth. It was when she wept again and said, "Don't stay with me, Bill. Go down and be with the family, who want you, and enjoy yourself." I smacked her face.'

'You what?' said Brentford.

Milham looked at him as though he ought to understand.

'To put some spirit into her,' he said. 'To get her to start to think and see herself. It was better that, than wallowing in a luxury of self-pity, which was what all of them were doing, till I came home.'

CHAPTER VI

PRECEDING CONSTABLE HEBBLE through the glass door from the garden, Brentford discovered that there were some disadvantages to the otherwise architecturally attractive Penlee police station. For one thing the office was small, and the sunlight pouring through its glass front made it hot. The admirable view of the river and the boats sailing under the woods outside began to have something of the aspect of an oasis in the desert.

Having allowed him precedence through the door, Hebble had to push past him. Also, Hebble wanted to close the door, while Brentford decided he was going to have it at least a little open. As soon as he entered the office he began to have doubts about how soon he would be able to get out again. There was a moment of confusion at the door before Hebble got round him and was able to begin to perform the introductions.

'This is Mr. Lambkin, sir.'

Lambkin proved to be a slight, somewhat undersized man in a neat blue suit who had risen from his chair in a faintly alarmed and guilty way when Brentford entered.

It was wrong, Brentford felt, to feel he might discount a proportion of what Lambkin had to say merely because he was a chapel preacher, but Hebble showed the same tendency.

'Mr. Lambkin,' Hebble said in careful tones, 'this is Detective Chief Inspector Brentford, who has given up his Sunday afternoon to come over from Lockley specially, to hear what you have to say.' He treated Lambkin as though he were a child, or slightly mental.

Lambkin rallied fairly well under their assault.

He had eyes that would have been suitable for a martyr in a religious painting, but at least he did not turn them up to heaven immediately. He used them to look at Brentford. 'I have prayed every night for a week, and asked God's guidance before I came here, Inspector.' He used a controlled voice, with just a trace of fulness.

'Well, an accusation of murder is a serious business, Mrs. Lambkin,' Brentford said agreeably, and saw to it that they all sat down.

The usual problem of procedure arose then, as they sat around the little table. Hebble produced a sheaf of handwritten papers and handed them to Brentford, to fill the time. Brentford looked at them and saw there were a lot of words. 'I took this statement from Mr. Lambkin while we were waiting, sir,' Hebble said, and Brentford, turning the pages, wondered what Hebble had meant when he said Lambkin was uncommunicate. He feared he guessed.

Across the table, he expressed his doubts unfairly.

'Perhaps if you hadn't taken quite a so long to pray, Mr. Lambkin, we might have received all this before the inquest.'

Lambkin looked to a degree alarmed, as was perhaps to be expected.

'I didn't want to name Mr. Milham,' he said. 'I did not wish to name anyone. I hoped to say only that I suspected murder. But God guided me through prayer to see what you would suspect innocent people if I said that. It has come to me that I must tell you all, except for the confession.'

Glancing at Lambkin, Brentford found it a slightly remarkable statement, and held his comment.

Lambkin looked afraid.

Brentford sorted through the papers. They would take as long to read as a chapter in a novel, and Brentford felt discouraged. He did not see why he should read them. It was possible that Lambkin did not know the police procedure, and he could always read them later.

'What's this about a confession, Mr. Lambkin?'

Lambkin looked down at the table and said, 'Do you know the Sunday evening meetings of our chapel, Inspector?'

Brentford said, 'No.'

'We are not like other churches,' Lambkin said, explaining. 'On a Sunday evening we meet together to discuss a bible text. We don't sing hymns or rub up a religious fervour. We have an address by our speaker. After that, we discuss the moral among ourselves. When necessary, we confess its application to our private lives.' He endeavoured to sum it up in a well-used phrase. 'The truth emerges.'

Brentford's reaction was to look out of the window and think that the chapel was not such an anachronism at Penlee as he had thought. He could well see that there would be lonely people in Penlee who would like to partake in that kind of social game.

It was better than he had expected when he left home. Then, preparing himself while departing, he had asked Ethel, 'What is the chapel at Penlee?' She had said, 'Fundamentalist.' He had said, 'What are Fundamentalists?' and she had said, 'They believe the bible is a magic book.' It had sounded far cruder than Lambkin's Pharisaical attitude to the other churches, and the idea of truth emerging like a Prime Minister at a conservative party conference.

He brought his attention back. Who had confessed? He thought wildly for a moment it might be Mr. Milham.

'You mean Mr. Milham—?'

'Mrs. Milham.'

'Mrs. Milham confessed? To what? Look, if it happened as you describe, other people too would have heard a confession in these circumstances?'

Lambkin pointed to the statement he had made, and which was a pile of paper lying on the table. 'It was not like that with Mrs. Milham,' he said. He indicated Hebble. 'I told him.'

Brentford broke the news to Lambkin. 'You are going to have to tell it all to me again,' he said.

Whatever Lambkin's sect was, it was at least Christian. Brentford could tell that by the resigned sorrow under pressure that came into Lambkin's eloquent eyes across the table. It did not explain the slight tinge of fear, however.

'If you will read what I have written,' he said.

'I will read it,' Brentford said. 'In detail, later.' He picked up the statement and passed it back to Hebble. 'In the meantime he will check it, from what you say now.'

Lambkin looked as though he had become involved in a conspiracy of some kind. It took a visible effort for him to look at Brentford with Christian charity. He appeared to think that Brentford was getting at him in some way.

'You make it very difficult for me. I don't know where to begin.'

'Begin with what you know of Mrs. Milham, how you came to be acquainted with her, and that kind of thing.'

Lambkin looked subdued at Brentford's apparently unexpected grasp of relevant detail. But he did not refuse to speak or collapse into incoherence. Brentford had guessed he would not, for Lambkin was a professional speaker.

He told a straightforward narrative with an air of being forced to do so, but he did not lose the thread.

'I first knew Mrs. Milham when she joined the chapel two years ago. I must point out that I did not approach Mrs. Milham, or ask her to join the chapel. She just appeared in the congregation one evening. I gave her our usual welcome, and she came again. Her attendance was irregular at first. In a few months she became one of our most assiduous members. By the end of a year, Mrs. Milham had come to me and given me, of her own accord, a sum of over a hundred pounds towards the chapel funds.'

'Of her own accord?' said Brentford. He did not want to be impolite to Lambkin, and he was well aware that in the Lockley area almost any kind of exponent of almost any religion was held to be immune from gross suspicion.

Lambkin looked at him directly. He was not evasive. 'I did not persuade Mrs. Milham to give the chapel money. Not at any time. On the contrary, though I gave Mrs. Milham a key, I remonstrated with her when I heard that she was coming to pray at the chapel early in the morning and sometimes late at night. I told her that it was what was in the heart that mattered, and not where the praying was done, or the outward show.'

'What's this about a key?'

Lambkin looked out of the window. 'Although we have built a chapel here, I personally cannot afford to live in Penlee. Admirable as the police are, they do not appear to be able to guard a building that is left unlocked. It was therefore necessary to have keys made, and to distribute them to those of our more earnest members who wished to come to the chapel from time to time for their private prayers.'

From the way Lambkin was looking at Penlee it might have been thought that he considered that it should be possible to leave a chapel open there, even though it had not been.

'All right,' Brentford said. 'I understand about Mrs. Milham now, and your connection with her.'

Lambkin turned to look at him as though he did not think he did.

Brentford thought he might ask Lambkin how much more money Mrs. Milham had given him, but refrained.

'It was three weeks ago that Mrs. Milham came to me in a state that seemed to be one of some distress,' said Lambkin. 'It was at the end of our evening meeting, and one or two among us, following a reading about the woman taken in adultery, had seen fit to make confessions that were more or less unexpected. Mrs. Milham told me that she had something on her mind, and for a long time she had been wondering if she could confess it. But it was too terrible, she said. She did not know if she should or could. She felt she ought to see me first, and tell me in strictest confidence, and ask for my advice.'

Despite some curiosity as to what Mrs. Milham had to say that was worse than adultery, Brentford looked at Hebble. He asked the constable, 'Three weeks ago?'

Hebble took out his notebook and consulted Lambkin's statement on the table. He said, 'This was the Sunday evening of the twenty-second, sir. It was just after eight o'clock on the morning of Wednesday the twenty-fifth that the ferryman found Mrs. Milham drowned in the river, after she had set out for the chapel at six a.m.'

'All right, Mr. Lambkin. What did Mrs. Milham say to you?'

Lambkin looked at Brentford and looked afraid. He said, 'I am not going to tell you that.'

Brentford looked at Lambkin coldly. 'Mr. Lambkin,' he said, 'I have come over from Lockley to hear you. But if you are accusing Mr. Milham of having murdered his wife on a basis of what Mrs. Milham told you, and if you are not going to tell us what she said, I don't really know why you and I are here at all.'

'I swore to Mrs. Milham that I would never tell anyone unless she gave me her permission,' Lambkin said. 'As you well know, she never did give me her permission. She died instead. That makes my solemn promise to her not less binding, but more so.'

'I might point something else out to you,' Brentford said. 'It is all very well, Mr. Lambkin, to make an accusation of murder against a respected man like Mr. Milham, who is a business and professional man in Lockley and a householder in Penlee, but unless you can substantiate your charges, you run a very grave risk, which it is only right that I point out to you, of a charge of slander.'

'It was possible that God did not wish Mrs. Milham to make her confession,' Lambkin said. 'As she pointed out to me, it would have dire effects on her husband and her grown up children if it was said in public. I have looked at it this way. God was quite satisfied that Mrs. Milham should be truly repentant and confess to me. He did not wish her to harm the innocent. He took her to Himself instead.'

It looked as though they had reached a deadlock. Brentford did not feel himself capable of disputing with Lambkin when it came to Theology. He tried to get a grip on the conversation from another angle. Somehow it seemed to him that the interrogation, which had started out so normally, had gone off the rails at some point. He surveyed the small man across the table from him. 'Mr. Lambkin, if you have come here to accuse Mr. Milham of Mrs. Milham's murder, and if you don't tell us what Mrs. Milham said that makes you think he did it, don't you see that you are letting Mr. Milham off?'

Lambkin looked resigned. 'That may be God's will,' he said.

Brentford was more pointed. 'I don't see that it is God's will that you should waste my and this constable's time,' he said.

Lambkin looked at the table for a little time.

'I don't think I am wasting your time,' he said. 'What Mrs. Milham had to tell me was a story of sin and crime almost beyond belief. I have heard many confessions. You will understand that I do, in my profession. Not all of them are true. When other people are confessing, some people feel they have to invent sins, of an even more lurid nature, if they have none to tell. But what Mrs. Milham said was true, I can tell you that.'

He seemed convinced of the substance of what he was saying, and unshakable.

'Also she gave me facts and times and dates and places,' he said. 'But for sheer wickedness and awful unredeemed obscene sin, it was beyond anything I had ever heard before, either true or false. I cannot tell you what Mrs. Milham said. It may come out; but as she rightly saw, to bring it out voluntarily would cause too much damage. But after she had finished telling me, we had a little conversation, and I can tell you that. We were in private, in my private room in the chapel and everyone else had gone home. She said, "These are the awful sins on my soul, mine and William's. I know I ought to confess them publicly, but how can I? Think of my grown up son who is a doctor in London. Think of my married daughter, and the second one who is at the university. Think of William and his work. I know I should confess myself publicly, and perhaps to the police, but I have not dared to do so, and that is why I have come to you, to tell you first, in confidence, and to ask you for your advice."'

CHAPTER VII

BRENTFORD WAS not sure how much of the night he should spend listening to Milham's problems with his sister, which after all had happened a very long time ago. But he thought that on first hearing, whatever the official statement said eventually, he ought to get the whole of it.

'I don't understand what, in practical terms, you were trying to do,' he said. 'Or for that matter what your family had intended either.'

'I'm not surprised you don't,' Milham said, 'since my family did not know, or were not facing what they were going to do, either. It was that that moved me to begin with. The fact that my mother and father were downstairs, and supposed to be deciding what to do, though you can guess how long that took, and how nearly impossible it was for them in their state of mind, while Elizabeth stayed upstairs, just waiting for them, expecting them to tell her, with a patience that seemed to me incredible, what she had to do. The two sides were not meeting. They were not, intellectually or practically, in any kind of contact. The decision was with my parents, who had virtually, all their lives, shown themselves quite incapable of any kind of decision whatsoever. Elizabeth, who had always shown herself so capable of decision as to be impetuous, had given up the ghost. Her sin, as she was calling it, was looking so vastly large in her eyes that she had abnegated, abdicated her total personality and her mind. She took it that she had no right to make decisions, that she had no say at all. I was confronted by a peculiar female passivity that I, being what I was, and at my age, did not try even to begin to understand. It was foreign to me, alien, and less comprehensible to my mind than any possible behaviour of a man from another country, and I set out to change it, to stimulate Elizabeth into some kind of thought at least, since she was the one who was most affected.'

'I am not sure you were not up against something physiological there,' said Brentford.

'You mean the difference between the sexes? Do you think I don't know it now? For God's sake, Inspector, you don't have to explain a thing like that to a man of your or my age. Do you think I don't know what it's like to try to explain to a woman why you aren't even enthusiastic, if you want to put it that way, about her taste in hats? But I was young then. I had met girls from the university who were as clear and intellectually free in their thinking as any man. Or more so. It was true, and I was aware of it, that many of the girls did better in their examinations than many of the boys. I had thought once, and wondered what happened to those girls in later life. Why they did not run industries, research departments, and rule the men. I was innocent. It never crossed my mind that they really were different, and might not want to. All I saw was that my sister, herself, ought to come to some kind of decision, or at least help in the making of it, about her future. And that was how I made my fatal mistake. I put some heart into her. I insisted that she come down, at meal times at least, and instead of having her food sent up to her, take her regular place at meals at the family table. And then, when we really talked about the thing, not on one night but on several nights when my young brother had gone to bed, I insisted that she be there too, or else I would leave the house, I said, never to return again, while we decided what millions of families must have had to decide, and probably were deciding in their thousands even then, what to do when the daughter of the house was pregnant.'

'There are only about three things you can do,' Brentford said.

'Until,' said Milham, 'I found a fourth.'

CHAPTER VIII

BRENTFORD LOOKED out at the boats sailing on the Penlee river. He felt it was somehow still hot and airless in the glass-fronted office, which was surely a stroke of misplaced modernism for a police station, despite the partly open door.

The boats were strung out on the river. They had tacked up, taking infinitely long about it, against wind and tide, and now they were running free, and opening out with wind and tide behind them, on another leg. Sailing must be like every other human sport, Brentford thought. They just went round in circles.

But he had to take Lambkin seriously. Or he had to appear

to take him seriously. Heaven alone knew whether there was anything at all behind his story.

'Mr. Lambkin,' he said across the table. 'What advice did you give to Mrs. Milham?'

Lambkin looked at him with tortured eyes. The surprising thing was that they were tortured. Lambkin did actually feel it. It was a far more difficult problem to decide what he felt. It could have been sympathy for the woman in the pitiful tale that he was telling, since he seemed to think it was a pitiful tale, or it could be that Lambkin only felt his own position.

'What I said to Mrs. Milham was, 'Whether you tell all this at a chapel meeting, Mrs. Milham, is between your conscience and your God.' And she, who had been praying, got up and said, "Thank you, Mr. Lambkin. I knew you would say that. I'll tell my husband. I'll tell him I'm going to tell all."'

Brentford looked at Hebble, who looked back at him with a confirming and pained expression.

'That's what Mr. Lambkin said before.' Hebble referred to his statement. But he thought it well to read it out. 'Mr. Lambkin told her, "It's between your conscience and your God," and she said, "Thank you. I knew you'd say that. I'll tell my husband. I'll tell him that I'm going to say all."' Hebble looked at Brentford.

Lambkin also looked at Brentford.

'There seems to be some misunderstanding,' Brentford said to Lambkin. 'If you said that to her, and she said that.'

'No,' said Lambkin. 'That's how God works, Inspector. I gave her a statement which she could interpret in the light of her conscience, and God showed her how to interpret it.'

Brentford looked at Lambkin for a moment. He wanted to ask him various things, but refrained. Lambkin looked back at him as though he were ready to answer all Brentford's questions about God's workings.

'So you just left it like that?' Brentford said.

Apparently Lambkin hadn't. He shook his head.

'I remonstrated with her. I said, "You aren't going to tell your husband that you have said all this?" She said, "Oh, no. I won't tell him I have told you. That would spoil the plan I have in my mind, the way I see it." I asked her, "And what is that?" She told me. "You know my husband disapproves of the chapel," she said. "He has never been near it, and he has disapproved most strongly of the money I have given you from time to time. But now the way is clear. I shall tell him what I am going to say next Sunday. For the first time in his life, he will come here and go down on his knees with me next Sunday, and find true repentance. It is his only hope," I must admit that, in view of what she told me, I was apprehensive. I could not see her husband doing it. I said, "Mrs. Milham." She said, "My mind is made up. Thank you, Mr. Lambkin. With God's aid, you have shown me the way." And she went out.'

Lambkin sat back as though he had concluded his story now, and they could make what they could of it, though he seemed to view them with some apprehension as they did so, especially Brentford.

Brentford found himself staring at Lambkin. He said, 'For Heaven's sake, or God's sake, man, if you knew all this, why have you waited until now to tell it? Surely you know the right time would have been at the inquest. What do you think an inquest is for?'

Lambkin looked at Brentford as though there was something he only now realised that Brentford did not understand.

'But I did go to the inquest,' he said. 'Both of them. The original one when evidence of identity was taken, and the resumed one a week later. Do you think I was not shocked by Mrs. Milham's sudden death? I heard it in the bosom of my family, in the radio news, and I went down on my knees to pray. "Foul play is not suspected," they said. How could they know that? Mrs. Milham had died on her way to the chapel, and what evidence would there be if her husband had just come up behind her and pushed her in? I went to the inquest expecting to hear the husband most severely cross-questioned about where he was, and how he could prove he was there, at the time of his poor wife's death. Then I would come forward with my testimony. But the inquest was not like that.'

Lambkin paused for a moment, and Brentford wished that Lambkin had been to inquests before. They rarely were like that.

'The whole atmosphere was entirely different,' Lambkin said. 'There was Mr. Milham being treated with the utmost respect and solicitude by the court. He was the bereaved husband, and the whole proceedings seemed designed to make him happy. Far from being questioned about where he was at six o'clock in the morning, which was the time his wife died in the river by that narrow lane, he was only asked what she was doing, going to the chapel at six in the morning, and if she was eccentric. It seemed to me that the whole inquest was designed to malign the dead. Mr. Milham said that his wife had recently been giving large sums of money to the chapel from their joint account. A doctor appeared, who said that Mrs. Milham had been coming to see him for her nerves, until two years ago when she joined the chapel. Witnesses were produced who said that Mrs. Milham was a most religious woman, but it had come on suddenly, late in life, and recently she had gone in for a wholesale excess of praying. They did not think it wholly natural, and someone said they blamed the chapel.'

Lambkin looked at Brentford with scared eyes, and then down at the floor.

'The whole atmosphere of the proceedings was changed after that,' he said. 'Or if not changed, it was made worse. It was not an inquest on Mrs. Milham any longer, but a trial of the chapel. You may remember what the coroner said in his summing up. "Rash evangelism" was one of the phrases that he used, and "In a free country it is doubtful if it is possible to prevent even dubious amateur tinkering with the human soul." How could I come forward at that point? It was I, who was silent in the public gallery, who was on trial. A verdict of "Suicide while the balance of the mind was disturbed" was the one recorded. If I had come forward then to say that the husband murdered her, they would have laughed me to scorn or worse.' Lambkin looked up at Brentford. 'Just as you will tell me I am a liar now,' he said. 'I don't expect anything else. And I expect to be sued for slander. I know what the feeling is, among those who don't go to the chapel, among the people here in Penlee.'

'Just a moment, Mr. Lambkin,' said Brentford firmly. 'I'm

afraid you're going to have to excuse us for just a moment.' He looked around to see how they could do it, and met Hebble's eyes.

Hebble got up. There was, it was true, a door of the the office into the house, but he did not use it. He moved to the front garden door, so Brentford went ahead of him. The front garden of the police station at Penlee after all was big enough, and a relief, so that Brentford took out his handkerchief and mopped his brow when they got out in it.

'I suppose the garden is the best place to talk,' Brentford said, looking at the unoccupied adjacent gardens and the empty road.

'Well, we could use my living room, sir,' Hebble said. 'But we'd have to turn my family out.'

'No, no. We couldn't do that,' said Brentford, and looked back at the police buildings as though the county architect had made other mistakes besides the glass front, such as not including an interview room, or even cells.

'I mean, sir,' Hebble said with difficulty, 'that at two-and-a-half, my little girl is too young to hear about the kind of things that Mr. Lambkin is hinting at.'

Brentford looked at him to see if he was serious. It seemed he was. They stopped right in the middle of the lawn to look at the one and only flower bed, which contained nasturtiums, the only flowers that Hebble and his colleague had successfully grown since they got the site.

'What exactly is Lambkin hinting at? Do you know?'

Hebble gazed away at the river, where the boats were heading round the buoy for a second time, then shifted his gaze up to see the hills.

'What he was hinting at, sir?'

'Black magic?' Brentford said explicitly. 'Necrophily? Child murder? The torture of dumb creatures?' He looked at Hebble. 'You live here. You ought to know.'

Hebble looked at the pleasant Penlee houses and the row of cottages by the river as though, if anything of the kind did happen in his district, it was quite outside his knowledge. His expression changed slightly. He resented that Brentford should suggest it did, and was prepared fervently to deny it.

'It seemed to me, sir, that what Mr. Lambkin was really saying was only that Mr. and Mrs. Milham weren't married, and that all their children were illegitimate. After all, it would be quite a facer for the children, to say nothing of the husband in view of his place in business, if Mrs. Milham were to announce it publicly, as part of her confession in the chapel.' He was satisfied with that.

Brentford looked at Hebble as though he were stupid. 'It can't be so simple. Even he must have heard of that before. He couldn't possibly make such a fuss of it as all that.' He looked at the office. 'Not what he said.'

Hebble took on an injured expression, but not one that was prepared to admit that, in the atmosphere of Penlee, people could find sins more subtle, or more attractive anyway, than those of fornication.

'I sometimes think I've been sheltered, going into the police and marrying young, sir. I'm not very *au fait* with the sins of the world.'

Brentford glanced at him quickly. 'You're not a member of the chapel, are you?'

'No, sir.' Hebble's expression became staunch. 'I'm strictly C. of E.'

'Then in view of what he said, and before we tell him what to do about it, you'd better tell me a little about the case.' Brentford added. 'If there is a case.'

Hebble cleared his throat and fiddled with the pocket in which he kept his notebook a little. But he did not actually produce the notebook. He seemed to infer that Brentford would not want it, or that it would be out of place to be seen reading from his notebook while they were in the garden.

'Mrs. Milham was aged about fifty, sir. You'd see her about the village. Five foot five or six, dark clothes, and a rather long face, but not bad looking. I wouldn't say she was particularly noticeable.' Hebble looked back at the office. 'But despite what he says, sir, she was eccentric.'

'In what way?' said Brentford.

Hebble thought for a moment, then said, 'Well, there was her hats.'

All the women of fifty that he knew were eccentric in that case, Brentford thought.

'Mr Milham?' he said.

'Tall, sir. Grey suits. Looks rather like his wife, the way long-married people do. But drives an M.G. car, sir. Not the sports, the saloon, but all the same. Has a keen look, and was sharp the only time I've spoken to him about his car. I'd say he was very different.'

Mr. Milham, alive, seemed to come through at least as clearly as Mrs. Milham deceased, but Brentford thought that all he had derived so far was that they were a wholly normal married couple of their age, fairly well-to-do, with a background of business and a profession, and able to own a house in Penlee. They had educated their children well too, he thought. You did not turn out both a doctor and a university student without some kind of background. He was finding it distinctly harder to believe Lambkin's allegations.

'All right. Now tell me what, of your personal knowledge, you know yourself.'

Hebble felt the lack of his notebook, searched for it, and eventually took it out.

'It was half past eight, sir. I was ready to go out on patrol, and Hunter was having breakfast. The phone rang and it was Mr. Lamont of the boat yard. The ferryman had found a body in the river and he didn't know what to do with it. Mr. Lamont said it looked like Mrs. Milham. I went down to the yard while Hunter phoned Lockley. When I got there, the body was laid out on trestles. Our Dr. Hargreaves was leaning over it, cleaning it up. The ferryman and his passenger, a Mr. Halford, were there, and all the workmen. I asked Dr. Hargreaves if she was dead, and he said she was, so I told him to leave her alone.'

'You say this Dr. Hargreaves was cleaning the body?' Brentford felt a morbid fascination.

'Yes, sir. I asked him why, sir. He said Mr. Lamont had been phoning the husband, and he expected him to turn up at any moment. In fact, that was a mix-up. Mr. Lamont had phoned Viewcrest, Mr. Milham's house, but got no reply. He'd phoned Mr. Milham's office and left a message with an office cleaner. But the body was in a fair state. Its eyes and its mouth were open, and there was some waterweed or similar hanging out of its mouth.'

There had been a convincing death, Brentford thought.

'Also, when Mr. Halford and the ferryman found it,' Hebble said, 'when Mr. Halford was crossing from his cottage to catch the bus, it was drifting near the mud flat. So they'd hauled it out onto the mud to give it artificial respiration. That mud is soft. So they and it were covered in mud. Things were like that, sir. Dr. Hargreaves said that the Milhams were his patients, like everyone else in Penlee, and he didn't want a fainting Mr. Milham, which he was likely to have, when Mr. Milham turned up at any moment.'

Things were like what, thought Brentford?

It sounded like other occasions, or most instances of drowning that Brentford had sometimes known. People did not leave a drowned body alone, as they did when it had an axe-wound. They removed it, un-ended it, tried artificial respiration on it, and took it from place to place. If a murderer contrived a convincing drowning, he was already one up. They thought of that. But who said there was a murder?

'What did you do?' said Brentford.

He had great difficulty applying his mind to it. He did not want to face it, on a Sunday in a garden, that kind of thing.

'I cleared the shed, sir. I told the ferryman and Mr. Halford to stand by. Mr. Halford wanted to go home to change, and I thought to let him go, but then I couldn't without the ferry.'

'Quite right,' said Brentford.

Hebble looked pleased. 'Constable Hunter said Lockley was sending an Inspector down. Dr. Hargreaves said "Where is Mr. Milham?" Hunter went to the phone to find out and got Lockley to send a police car to pick him up when he reached his office. Mr. Halford said they shouldn't have taken the body on the mud. The ferryman said they should, because they didn't know then that it was drowned. Mr. Halford said the way it was they were more likely to have drowned it than make it breathe. They argued. Then Inspector Simpson turned up. Very quick it seemed to me, sir. Then they sent me out to watch the gate, because I was the youngest there.'

Brentford felt relieved. 'I don't suppose you saw or heard any more after that?'

Hebble looked insulted. His evidence was valuable. All people thought their evidence was valuable. It always was.

'That was when Mr. Milham came, sir, looking very pale. Then there was getting the body off in the ambulance. And then there was the search.'

'The search?'

'Sergeant Cranston came out, sir. He said he and me and Constable Hunter were to search the river. The river bank, that was, between Viewcrest and the village.'

Sergeant Cranston? Brentford wondered how many police they had had, or who had turned up of their own accord, to look after Mrs. Milham.

He did not ask about the search, but Hebble told him.

'Mr. Milham had told Inspector Simpson, sir, that his wife should have a handbag. We were to find it, sir. Or find it missing. Or find it there, but with her money and change and the chapel key all gone. That was it, sir. She was on her way to the chapel. But that would be at six in the morning, and that is a lonely road.'

'Look,' said Brentford. He knew he had the inquest and the verdict against him, but he said it all the same. 'I've seen that lane. You don't think she was walking too near the edge, and she just fell in?'

Hebble looked from the office to Brentford as though they were now both guilty of heresy.

'Now why would a woman of her age walk too near the edge, sir? You know they don't.'

The trouble was, it was true.

'Of course we did find the handbag, sir,' Hebble said thoughtfully, 'on the rocks in the river bed, all wet, but with the money and key still in it.'

Brentford had an overwhelming feeling about that. It was the one fact that was right. When women committed suicide by jumping somewhere, they always took their handbags with them.

'What did Inspector Simpson say?'

'He said it was right, sir. When a woman commits drowning

for suicide, you always find her handbag with her in the water.'

It upset Brentford. He looked back up at the office. 'I suppose we'd better get back to Lambkin.'

'I tried to phone Inspector Simpson today, sir,' Hebble said in an aggrieved tone. 'He was out. When the Lockley desk heard I wanted him for a murder allegation, they put me onto you, to the C.I.D.'

Lambkin, in the office, was sitting in profile. From his expression it could be gathered that he was a heretic who had just confessed himself to the Inquisition, and who was now waiting for the more interesting part, with whips and the rack and red-hot pincers and boiling oil.

'We aren't getting anywhere,' Brentford said. 'We might just as well go back to him.'

All the same, it took a moment and a considerable effort before they left the nasturtiums and crossed the lawn and the path and went back into the office.

It did not seem to have become any cooler in their absence.

'Well, this is a bad and complicated business, isn't it, Mr. Lambkin?' Brentford said as they sat down. It was not his fault, he reflected, if he seemed to have retreated to the simian level of understanding.

'I did not come to you without thought, Inspector,' said Lambkin sententiously and as though that, now, was the only kind of thing he had to say.

'You did very right,' said Brentford. 'We appreciate it. I want you to know that. It's just that it is like—well, you know how it is when a body has to be exhumed.'

'Exhumed?' Lambkin looked lost. He looked as though Brentford had got hold of the wrong end of the stick in some way. 'I wouldn't have thought, I mean, after drowning, with Mrs. Milham?'

His bewilderment increased instead of decreased.

'Like if we were to go round the village asking questions,' Brentford said. ' "Did you see Mr. Milham on the morning of his wife's death?" It sticks, you know. And since they can't clear themselves unless you bring them to trial, he might have grounds for action.'

Lambkin went pale.

'I'd have thought,' he said, 'a few discreet inquiries—'

'About what?' said Brentford. 'We might inquire about whatever it is Mrs. Milham is said to have done. Or was it her husband, what she confessed to you? But you won't tell us that.'

Lambkin looked sick.

'I thought, I wondered if malefactors should be punished in this world,' he said, 'since they will be in the next.'

'Oh, I think they should be,' Brentford said seriously. 'You see, they don't always believe in the next.'

Lambkin looked at Brentford as though Brentford did not believe in it either.

'Inspector,' said Lambkin, 'do you believe I invented this story, just to try to shift the blame for Mrs. Milham's death, so people wouldn't blame the chapel?'

'Now I didn't say that, Mr. Lambkin.'

'No, but your attitude. Inspector, do you intend to keep me here?'

'Why on earth should we do that, Mr. Lambkin? I assure you that you are free to go.'

Lambkin did not look delighted on hearing he was free to go. He almost looked as though he would rather have been kept a prisoner.

'I suppose now I will be sued,' he said.

'Not if I can help it, Mr. Lambkin.'

Lambkin looked as though he would get up and go if only he could believe that.

'Not that I am concerned about it,' Brentford said. He looked at the door and the window. 'I'm thinking of the inconvenience to other people. But it will be what people will say, you know, that you only said it to shift the blame from the chapel.'

They watched Lambkin's head bobbing up and down as he walked down the garden path.

CHAPTER IX

'WE DIDN'T, in the family, consider whether Elizabeth should have an abortion,' Milham said. 'That was the kind of thing that was unspeakable, fortunately, because otherwise I think my parents might have advocated it, and she, obediently, might have done it. We just sat around and talked. My father said that he had never imagined that any daughter of his, and all that kind of thing, for some little time. My mother wept and said, "When I think what your grandmother will say," and all the things of that kind. Elizabeth said, "I'm going back to my room," and turned on me and said, "I was better there." I said, "Oh no, you're not, because I've got to go off to this place called Lockley at the week-end, and I want to know what's happening here before I go."

'What puzzled me and made me hate them was their shift-lessness and apparent thoughtlessness in time of crisis. My father said, "This is no business of yours, William," and my mother said, "If one word of this gets out to the place you're going, I don't know what I'll do, I don't." I said, "You can't keep Elizabeth in her room for ever, and you might as well face that now." They just didn't answer. "You should tell everyone, neighbours and friends and members of the family, that Elizabeth is going to have a baby now," I said. "Don't wait for rumours to start. Don't give them a chance to run round telling one another and discussing you behind your back. Just tell them. They'll have seven months to get used to the idea. By the time the child is born, it will be an accepted thing." My father said, "This is silly talk." My mother said, "William, you're just so young, you don't know." I said, "All right, what's wrong with it?" I couldn't get a coherent word out of them for half an hour, and then my mother let slip, "Elizabeth will have to go away." Elizabeth then made her one and only contribution to the discussion, "I want to keep my baby."

'I was appalled. I thought at first my parents must have a plan. It appeared they hadn't. I kept saying, "Go away? Go away where?" and my father said, "There are homes for unmarried mothers, and the babies are adopted." That was as far as they had got, to think of that. It wasn't the baby they were concerned about. It wasn't having it, and it wasn't Elizabeth. It was that the knowledge, the news, might slip out, and that the home for unmarried mothers might not take Elizabeth before her shape became visible and the knowledge of current events became apparent to all who were unconcerned.

'I said, "Look. I don't agree that Elizabeth has to go away. It seems to me immoral. And as to what you propose for the child, it is your grandchild." That did not have a good effect. My mother wept, and my father seemed to take it as a slur on his honour that he should have a bastard grandchild: that I had said it, that was, not the fact of it. "But if she has to go away," I said, "then for heaven's sake not to an institution where she will be prayed at. What do you think Elizabeth is? Why not to Auntie Flo?" They looked at me as though I were mad, even Elizabeth. "What's wrong with that?" I said. "You're always saying what a good woman Auntie Flo is, and she lives in the country where no one knows Elizabeth, and this will give her a chance to perform a Christian act." My father said, "You're crazy." My mother said, "In that village?" and Elizabeth became hysterical and said, "What, with her friendship with the Vicar?"

'The thing about this discussion, which went on going round in circles, and never getting any nearer all the time I was there, was that it had to be conducted in a cloak-and-dagger fashion. It had to stop dead the moment my young brother came into any room where it was going on, and start up again the moment that he went out. It had to be like that, my mother said, because he was not of an age yet when he ought to know how babies were born at all, even naturally, which was the opposite to what she meant, which was in wedlock. But of course my younger brother did know, though Elizabeth and I had not the heart to disillusion her, and he too missed most of his sleep, though he went to bed earlier every night so we could start, because he would come down in his pyjamas after he had gone to bed, and listen outside the door, with the result that he got a cold as well.

'I suppose you think all this is amusing, and I suppose it is, but I assure you it wasn't for we who took part in it. It was a nightmare just precisely because we had not realised, any of us, until it happened, that we lived like that.

'I can't tell you the complications, or I won't. Elizabeth came into my room, *en négligée*, at dead of night, in a new role, that I did not know yet, of an abandoned woman. I had done something, apparently, in my effort to put life in her. She put on and off her roles more quickly than she could change her clothes, and as though she were trying them on for size, and I wonder we did not wake my father and mother by our talking, as I imagine we would had they not slept the sleep of the dead from pure exhaustion. "I am going to run away," she said to me, "Can you lend me any money?" I asked, "Where to?" and, "I thought you wanted to keep your baby?" "I'll go on the streets," she said. "You can't," I said, with more certainty than in fact I felt, "in your condition." But she had caught my words. "I won't be prayed at," she said. "I won't go to one of those places." She had never been away from home before. "It will be horrible." Then she threw herself in my arms and wept. "I'm a Fallen Woman."

'This was very awkward, considering she was my sister, and in view of what came later you may see some significance in it, but I assure you you would be wrong, and I had some difficulty in getting her out of my room again, in time, before the morning.

'The next night with my parents I tried things backwards. It was unfair in a way that I should use my position to try to enforce my own views, and particularly so as Elizabeth and I could sleep and doze in the daytime while my parents had their work to do, but my idealism just would not accept it, that despite all the advances of liberal thought, and the fact that my parents were easy-going, Elizabeth's position, and that of her child, were still what she said they were, that it was to be a bastard, condemned before birth, and she a Fallen Woman.

'I started on them as soon as I could. "Look," I told them. "Have you no pride or honest family feeling? This child, when it is born, will be your grandchild. You can't really condemn it to an institution life, or to foster parents whom you will have

45

to think of as impossibly ghastly because you won't even know. And as for Elizabeth, she is your daughter. You brought her up, and if family ties mean anything at all, you must stand by her." They looked at me as though I were mad, of course, and my father embarked upon a speech. He had been thinking too, it seemed, and it was about his position in the town.

'It was not only the various committees he was on, he said, such as the Parent-Teachers association, with which he had some connection, and the fact that he was in the Rotary. He could resign from those. His pride, he said, was humbled, though to me it did not seem that he was talking of pride at all, but saving face. But there was his work, he said, and though I, in my new high position, would not think of it, there was still the drapery store, and the fact that he was the manager. Oh, it would become known, he did not doubt that, that his daughter had had a child. But that he might get away with, on consideration that his own actions were strict and right. It would be a different matter entirely, and would have heaven knew what consequences, were he to flaunt it.

'I saw what he meant, I think, but I turned on my mother then. "Mother," I said, "This will be your grandson." I got what I expected, tears. But it should have the effect I hoped for, I thought, the insistence on the family connection and the fact it was a defenceless babe. Instead, she said, "What would your Auntie Flo say?" And it was that, I think that finished me. I had known that our English life was hollow, but not that hollow. Not so that even family relationships depended on the power of the person concerned to say, and that they would not be effective at all if the one concerned were dumb.

'What made it worse was the effect my arguments had had upon Elizabeth. I discovered then why Elizabeth should have been kept in her room, out of it, while we argued elsewhere and came to a united front downstairs. For she was the only one I had succeeded in convincing, about the future horrors before her baby. At first, her statement "I want to keep my baby" had been only an idle and romantic gesture. It was romantic still, but after my descriptions of foundlings' homes, which I had used upon my parents, it was now, "I'll drown myself if I can't keep my baby." I don't know why she chose drowning, but that too is something in which you may see significance.'

'What did you do?' said Brentford.

Milham turned his head to him and spoke in careful words. 'I went into Elizabeth's bedroom that last night I stayed in my parents' house. She sat up in her best pretty nightdress, and since I was fully dressed, she looked at me as though I were some strange young man whose intentions she could not decide. "Get dressed," I said. She pulled the bedclothes up, and said "Why?" and "What?" I said, "We're leaving here." She looked amazed. She looked as though she had never seen me before. "Oh, Bill," she said. I turned my back as I pulled the bedclothes from her, then went to her dressing table and began to pack her clothes quickly into a suitcase that I had brought. Instead of dressing, she came to me and clung to me trembling. "What are we going to do?" she said. "You know I've got to go to Lockley tomorrow," I told her. "I start work there on Monday. I shall set you up there somehow, and you will have your baby." She clung to my coat, and said, "Bill, can you afford it?" I told her, "No. This new employer I'm going to work for seems a mean old bastard. I don't know how we'll manage, but in some way we're going to have to." She looked at me for a while, and then she began to get dressed. She looked at me again, and said, "I never thought I'd elope with you." We got packed and dressed and out of the house completely, without waking my father and mother, and we only left a note.'

CHAPTER X

FROM PENLEE, Brentford went home to his cottage to the south of Lockley, and they had tea there on the lawn, with two chairs and the card table, which they brought out to sit in the September sunlight.

'Follet and Milham?' Ethel said. 'Aren't they the accountants with the office up on High Street?'

'Milham is the junior partner, although he's fifty. Follet is retiring soon.'

'What do accountants like that do?' Ethel said. After hearing the story and speculating on the evil things Mr. and Mrs. Milham might have done, she displayed a curiosity.

'Audit books mostly. Income tax for people who have that kind of income. Or businesses. Commercial.'

'Pass the jam,' she said.

Brentford looked around by habit to see that none of their neighbours were near enough to the hedges to hear. 'I doubt if they even handle particularly large sums of money.'

'It is absurd, isn't it?'

He was inclined to agree, but wished he could dismiss it as easily as that. And Ethel was none too sure.

He was thinking of the problem of the handbag. Despite what he had said, he had a visual image of the murderer pushing the woman into the river and then seeing the handbag on the ground where she had dropped it. Would he throw it in after her? It was not a logical or likely act, but the picture was compelling. He tried it on Ethel.

'Her handbag was found in the river. It is presumed that when she committed suicide, she took it with her for use in the next world.'

'Women do that,' Ethel said. 'I've noticed it in the newspapers. When they jump over cliffs, they take their handbags with them too.'

No result. He never would know about the handbag.

'But I think I'd better go out again.'

Ethel looked across the lawn. She had known before he had. 'I noticed you didn't bring the car in.'

So Brentford went out again.

The housing estate to the east of Lockley had covered its countryside slowly, in the course of twenty years. Brentford drove slowly. The houses were close-packed, to the maximum permitted. A child chased a ball across the street, and Brentford thought there were too many children, as well as other things. He had difficulty finding the number because there were only pretentious names upon the house gates.

When he got out and left the car, the front doors were

mostly open to the vestibules and so he still could not see the numbers. He chose by calculation and a close-cropped lawn. The bell produced an elderly woman. 'Do you want to see Harold?'

'Inspector Simpson? Yes.'

'He's expecting someone.'

'It's probably me. I'm Detective Inspector Brentford and I phoned just now.'

In the small sitting room the furniture was too large, having come from a larger home, and there were stags in Highland scenes on the walls. Inspector Simpson, who was at ease and out of uniform on a Sunday, said, 'I hope you survived my mother.'

'We all have mothers.'

'Yes, but not everyone lives with theirs.'

'There are worse things to do with them.'

They got down to business. Taking the easy chair Simpson offered him, Brentford said, 'You were on the Milham case?'

'Yes, what about it?'

Parker had used the best words. 'Something has come up. Would you like to tell me how it looked to you?'

'What has come up?' Without making an undue point of it, Simpson said, 'You're C.I.D.'

'You wouldn't like to tell me about it first?'

'With all due respect, I like to know what I'm dealing with.'

'A man called Lambkin, the chapel preacher, has come along to say that Milham, the husband, pushed his wife into the river. He thinks he did.'

Simpson thought about it for a moment, and then said, 'You can bet your boots that something like this is sure to happen, whenever you do the decent thing.'

'The decent thing?'

'There were some points that didn't come out at the inquest. But then you know that. There almost always is.'

'Look. Are you sure you want to tell me, or would you rather make a new and separate report to Superintendent Croxton, while I make mine to Parker?'

'If I tell you, it may save a deal of trouble.'

'It won't necessarily by-pass Croxton, you know. And that won't be up to me. I don't want to put it too pointedly, but Parker doesn't love you.'

'I'll take a chance on that. I don't want to be the first to make a thing of it.'

'What happened?'

'You know the location, down in that boat yard?'

'Vaguely. Not to really see it.'

'There was the usual shemozzle going on when I got there. Lamont, the manager, had made the mistake of letting them put the body on trestles in the main boat shed. He was just getting round to wondering when, if ever, he would get work started again. There was a ferryman who wanted to run a ferry, and a man called Halford who had had a mud bath. I just caught a Dr. Hargreaves. He said the body was a clear case of drowning. That was gratuitous. He was on his way, but before he went he said there were no major lacerations or significant injuries that he could see.'

'I know a little of this. I got it from Hebble, the Penlee constable.'

'Oh, so you've talked to Hebble, have you?'

'Don't think he didn't try to phone to warn you. He did, but you weren't in.'

'I've been taking my mother to see her sister,' Simpson said, and sucked his lip as though he were really feeling the lack of that call from Hebble.

He was not really improving as he told his story. The more he got into it, the more difficult he seemed to find it.

'That's why I looked at the body myself and saw this item I was telling you about,' he said. 'Because it had already been seen by one doctor, who seemed quite sure. I mean, the next thing was to get it from the boat shed to the morgue, and it would be far more convenient for McIvor to see it there. You see what I mean. He would be doing the P.M. anyway. It was only the interval, during which I might have been scouring the country for a rapist or a murderer, and apart from the handbag, which I cleared in due course, it didn't seem likely since the woman was nearly fifty. So I just confirmed the doctor.'

'Anyone see you lifting the dead woman's skirts?' said Brentford.

Simpson gave him a hard look. 'That's not as funny as it seems for a man who isn't married and lives with his mother.'

'Sorry, I was only joking.'

'Yes, but you won't be too happy too when you hear about this. Doctor Hargreaves had said it was all clear, and I hope you remember that. Because what I found were two bruises, slight but distinct, one on each wrist, and a mark on her face as though someone had slapped her there or hit her cheek. And those are the things that were never mentioned at the inquest.'

Brentford thought about it and said, 'Not as though someone had seized her wrists when she was on the road, and then put a hand over her face to stop her screaming?'

Simpson gave the point due thought.

'Naturally, I gave time to that. The marks were slight. If anyone seizes even an old woman like that, he's likely to do more damage than that to her. Especially if she kicks. You may know, you're married. My own experience with women is that if you try to hold them against their will, they can even cause you an astonishing amount of damage. This was more like minor bruises, you know, the way a woman will mark if you indulge in a little gentle horseplay.'

Brentford wondered if Simpson's experiences with women, and the things he did with them gently, did not have some relevance to why he was not married.

He also wondered if death had happened very soon after the events supposed, whether the woman would have shown marks at all.

'I suppose you're going to tell me why all this didn't come out at the inquest?'

'What do you think I'm doing? But look, don't imagine that it was just me. All this was known to the Coroner, McIvor, Hargreaves and the lot of us. I first ran into it when I got hold of Hargreaves again, around lunch-time, and asked him whether he'd seen the marks, or whether I was not to believe my eyes, since due to what he said I'd arranged not to call the police doctor in to see the body as it lay in situ.'

'You mean he gave you an explanation?'

'He said, "Inspector, do you have to make a lot of this? If you want to know how those marks happened, why don't you ask the husband?"'

'I see,' said Brentford.

He remembered the evidence he had heard had been given at the inquest about the woman's state of mind.

'I told him,' Simpson said. ' "Mr. Milham, after he identified his wife's body this morning, wasn't in a state to answer anything." It wasn't quite true. I'd had to ask him about a handbag, and when he last saw his wife; but it was near enough. They had been married near enough to thirty years, it seemed, and their family had grown up and left, and they were alone together. They take it hardest when it is like that. I said, "If you know anything, Doctor, you'd better explain it to me. It is your duty."

'He told you a story?'

'He said, "You will have to make up your own mind, Inspector. If I tell you that when I saw the body this morning I was not entirely surprised, and that my own private assumptions were that it was a suicide, and not an accident or anything else, you'll ask me why. I'm not in a position to give you concrete evidence. The woman hasn't been to see me for two years, since she started going to the chapel. Under the circumstances, you will be the first to say that any evidence I give will be quite out of court." '

'At least he knew what is evidence. It makes a change.'

'I pressed him. Apparently she was his patient. She was still on his books, and that was something. You know what doctors are, even the best of them. When I asked him what he was treating her for before she joined the chapel, he said, "her nerves." If the words are not intelligible to a five year old, the lay public can't be expected to understand them. Had he considered her cured when she stopped seeing him? He answered, no. I said, "You must know something." He said, "Her husband has continued to see me. He is my patient. He talked to me about his wife. That's what he came for. That's not evidence, is it?" I said, "Look, Doctor, when I'm trying to find out what I'm dealing with in a case like this, I don't apply the Judge's Rules. You don't need to be such a tight-mouthed doctor, either, between the two of us." I asked him: "Why did Milham come to see you about his wife?" He told me in confidence, whatever that may mean. "Milham was concerned about his wife's mental condition. Not least because she wouldn't come to see me. All this praying and getting up at six in the morning several days a week to go to chapel, on her own at that, for he'd found out there was no one else there."'

'It isn't exactly certifiable,' Brentford said.

'Of course it wasn't. And so he said he'd told the husband. He'd soothed him down. His own opinion was another matter. Not even all psychiatrists would agree it was a classic symptom when a woman suffering from nerves suddenly refuses to see her doctor and takes up excessive praying instead. Milham took a different angle. His wife had always been an intelligent and clear-minded woman, he said. He's been able to talk to her about all kinds of things. Now he said he felt there was a mental deterioration. I suggested that if Milham was an agnostic, say, of the kind who considers himself intelligent, he would be liable to say that, just on the grounds that his wife had taken up a strict and Fundamentalist religion. He said it went a little deeper than that. She'd always been a good housewife. At least she'd always kept the place clean and tidy, and prepared his meals on time. Now she didn't. Her excuse was that she no longer considered those things important. These cases become infinitely complicated when you go into things like that, Hargreaves told me. You can go on "he said", and "she said" for ever. The only thing to do is to take some outside opinion, and Milham had something there. His wife was beginning to be considered eccentric around the village, and he felt it. A neighbour's wife had asked him, "When your wife goes to the chapel, to pray for two solid hours in the morning, doesn't she make your breakfast?" In other words, people were beginning to talk, and he was getting sympathy. It touched him to the quick.'

'This is a long way from the marks on the body,' Brentford said.

'Hargreaves told me that he'd told Milham he could do nothing for him about all this, except certify her if it ever came to that. Milham was on his own as to how far he tried to restrain his wife and maintain an appearance of normality about her actions. He should be gentle, and not argue, and at the same time not use violence. If he could be firm, it might help to avoid ever having her certified. "I'm only a G.P., Inspector," he told me. "I couldn't tell Milham how to do all this. I couldn't do it myself. A man needs years of training as a nurse in a mental hospital to know how to handle patients." '

Brentford had taken Simpson's point. What went on between Milham and his wife was something that could not be known to the doctor, but he could guess.

'Lambkin thought this story of the wife being mentally ill, and at the same time falling under the influence of the chapel, was just put out to blacken the chapel's name.'

Simpson looked shocked. For a moment, his eyes looked blank, and then they looked angry.

'You don't think it's the other way round, and he has only put out this story of Milham murdering his wife to clear the chapel?'

'It did occur to me, and I have that in hand,' said Brentford grimly.

'You know the Coroner was right, and some of these self-appointed preachers don't take anything like the responsibility they should for what they do?'

'So that's what he said, is it? Can you tell me this? Did Hargreaves actually suggest, in so many words, that Milham might have hit his wife, or maltreated her in that way?'

Simpson looked uncomfortably at Brentford for a lengthy moment before he got back to the point.

'He ended quite specifically, as he began. If I as a policeman felt I had to take notice of those little marks, then before I roused the county and started a hue and cry for a murderer, he thought I should ask the husband.'

'And so you did?'

Simpson looked at Brentford in a smouldering way, and then looked away at the small tiled fireplace of the little room.

'I've had to do some pretty unkind things as a policeman, but I hope I don't have one like that again, to go round to ask a man like Milham whether he had been hitting his sick wife,

54

on the same day she'd been found, and when he'd been so obviously cut up and had taken it so to heart, about her death.'

'Is that how you put it?'

Simpson's eyes came back. 'You know damned well it isn't.'

'What did he say?'

Simpson relaxed a little, or seemed to do so.

'You know that place Viewcrest? It's like a barn. He must have bought it when he had a family, and had need of it. It looks isolated, too, from inside. From the window, all you see is the bend of the river, and the trees around. He was alone. I asked about his family, but of course they hadn't had time to come from London, or wherever it was they had to come from.'

'No neighbours?'

'No. That is a bit of Penlee. His wife's friends were chapel people, and they'd stay away from him. It seemed he'd been just standing around at the time I got there. I asked him hadn't he anywhere else to go, and he said, yes, but he preferred to come home. Then he said, "I'm glad to see you, Inspector. It's coming back to an empty house that gets you." He, a professional man, and at his age, had been too innocent to realise it would be like that. You aren't interested in what I was feeling. I said, "There are some marks on your wife's body, Mr. Milham. I don't know if you know what I mean, but we have to explain them. Otherwise, the police being what they are, we might have to look on it as a possible case of murder." He just looked blank, of course. Then he said, "What do you mean?" "Some marks," I said. "Some bruises." I'd tried to make him sit down. He wouldn't. Now he did sit down. He put his head in his hands and said, "My God."'

'Can you remember what else he actually did say?'

Simpson looked at Brentford as though asking him if he thought he was sufficiently inexperienced to need a notebook.

'What do you think he said? He said nothing for about two minutes. Then he said, "Will this have to come out at the inquest?" I had to keep it cool. I tried to keep it that way. I said, "Why? Why do you ask that, Mr. Milham?" He looked up at me. His eyes were wide. "You know what they'll say," he said. "They'll say I drove her to it. I did. You think I haven't been thinking about it? I was the one who killed her." I remembered it was evidence I wanted. I always do. I said, "What do you mean, Mr. Milham?" He said, "Because she wouldn't make my breakfast." I persuaded him and told him he'd better tell me. He said, "I argued with my wife last night, Inspector. I did something. I believe I took her by the wrists and shook her. I slapped her face." I asked him why. He said, "I told her she was to stop it. She was not any more to get up early and go to the chapel in the mornings. When she wouldn't promise, I shook her and I smacked her. I made her a martyr." I said, "I don't understand, Mr. Milham." He said, "I told her what I'd do to her if she went to the chapel again. This morning when I awoke, she was up and out. I'd told her that I'd wait, but of course I didn't. I went to work. The next thing I knew, I heard that this had happened. Don't you see? She hadn't dared come home. People will say I drove her to it, when this comes out at the inquest, and they'll be right. It'll finish me." But it wasn't that. He only looked blank when he said that. It was after that that his face crumpled and I had to get up and put a hand on his shoulder. He said, "The truth is, I loved her." '

It was an hour later when Brentford went out to his car and drove home from Simpson's.

He drove back through the town, since it was Sunday evening and traffic was light. All the same, there were a number of people on High Street, girls in high heels, and boys in their Sunday clothes, and cars. He turned off and made his way out homewards by a short cut, among the little houses and back streets by the upper river, which, in the Lockley area, was little better than an urban ditch. When he came into the kitchen, he was blinking in the transition from the darkness to the light. The dinner smelled as though it had been kept waiting some little time.

Ethel looked at him twice. She said, 'You're later than you expected.'

When they sat down to the meal, she waited until they had started. 'How was your Inspector Simpson?' she asked.

When he answered, 'He was well. He lives with his mother,' she looked at him again, then passed him the *Radio Times*.

They watched television for the rest of that evening, which was unusual.

CHAPTER XI

THE SILENCE in the house at Penlee was such that water could be heard dripping from the trees in the mist outside the window. If Brentford had made any move to go, he did not doubt that Milham would have welcomed it. The man did not seem even to be brooding as he looked away from Brentford and as though through the wall.

Brentford wondered if it was the same for everyone, that what had happened at home, and in the original home before it was left, seemed most important.

'At least you took one of them with you,' he said. 'You did not cut yourself off from everything. There was your sister.'

'I wonder what they thought?' Milham said. 'My parents. I suppose they said it, that they could not forgive us for going off like that. But did they really think it? Could they really disguise it from themselves, the relief that they no longer had to think and plan? We left a note. Knowing them as well as I do, I still can't think how their minds moved.' He winced. It was a tragedy.

'You came to Lockley,' said Brentford.

'After two years, I got a letter from my father,' Milham said. 'He enclosed a little money and said that all was forgiven.'

'Lockley must have been a strange town to both of you.'

Milham took a little time to face it, that neither Brentford nor anyone else was interested in his parents, nor how they lived or how they died.

He looked at Brentford for a moment, as though wondering if he could tell him how he visited them, and what he said and what they said, until recent years. But people did not live against a background of public approbation. Their sufferings were their own.'

'It is perceptive of you to say that.'

'These inquiries I have been making about you. I have had to guess to try to get to know you.'

Brentford thought of the first inquiry he had made, at noon on the Monday. The regular channels, he thought. How you began to inquire about a man.

It was Parker who had seen clearly that the inquiry was necessary, when Brentford had reported to him in his office on the Monday morning. Listening to Milham, Brentford felt that he had almost known him better then, when he and Parker were talking about him, than he did now. Except that they had not known or guessed the truth then. But that was not now, and the truth was almost credible as he listened to it.

'When you have lived in a town for some time, it is difficult to see it as a stranger sees it,' Milham said. 'I first noticed that in Rhyl in north Wales, where our parents used to take us for our holidays. It is only a small and flat town, and easily understood, but I remember its strangeness when we first went there, and the different shape of the buildings, and the streets that seemed to lead away in all directions. Later the town was so fully understood and comprehensible that when we came back to it I had only to stand in any part of it to feel thoroughly at home. I could hardly believe it was the same place from which we had set out from the railway station, luggage in our hands, to find accommodation, with everything new and strange around us and every step an adventure. I could never quite reconcile that first vision with the later ones, and it was like that, even to the tingling of a slight terror, which heightened the awareness, when we first came to Lockley.'

He was still harking back to childhood, images, Brentford noticed. He was still explaining things in terms of a child's thoughts, and as he had seen them before he left his parents. He did not truly know himself. Or did he?

'It can't have been the same. You can't have set out with your luggage in your hands when you first arrived here in Lockley.'

'I remember arriving and arguing with Betty among our suitcases on the strange station platform. I had been to Lockley once before, for the interview. I was able to show her where the refreshment room was, and it was only when we went there, to talk about what we should do in a strange place, as though we had not had ample opportunity to discuss it on the train, that I admitted to her what I had not told her before. "I shall have to find you somewhere very cheap," I said. What I had not told either her or my parents was that this work I had got in Lockley was primarily an excellent opportunity. To get work as an accountant at all was something in the nineteen-thirties, when newly qualified. There were many book-keepers with accountants' qualifications, who never expected to rise at all, unless trade grew better, which in those days was as remote as flying to the moon.'

'You mean the salary you were to start on in Lockley was very low. I understand that.'

'Yes. You probably do understand it. But Follet, of Follet and Follet, the firm I was to work for, had made it clear to me. He had told me that if he was to introduce me into his firm as a new young accountant, following his father's death, then I would have a position to keep up. It would be all I could do, on the money he was giving me, to appear as I should in behaviour, dress and manner. He was frank in the way accountants are frank. He and his father had been partners, but the firm could not really afford the salary of another full accountant, of the responsible, married kind, although they had the work for him. My qualifications were a nominal asset. Our future, both his and mine, depended on how we could work the business up, and in the meantime I would have nothing to spend on extras whatsoever.'

'Yet you had brought your sister to Lockley, knowing that, and also that she was going to have a baby?'

'What else could I do?' I have told you that.'

'I imagined you would know what you were doing. Or are accountants reckless of their own position, like doctors with their own health?'

'It was a matter of principle. I've told you my frame of mind. My sister was to be sent away as though she had acquired a disease that was contagious. She was to lose her baby. I was seething with indignation. What I confessed to her in the refreshment room of Lockley station, which seems such an absurd place to do it now, was that I had only thought and determined that we should manage somehow. "After all," I told her, "Suppose I was married, and my wife was expecting a baby, just as you are." It was my youthful idealism that I tried to recreate for her in railway surroundings over a cup of tea. I did not tell her that Follet had carefully asked me if I were married, and I had told him no. Instead, we just decided to put our suitcases in the left luggage office and set out on foot to find accommodation for her.'

Milham paused as though Brentford should reply to that.

'In Lockley?'

'Where else? We came out of the station and went across towards the High Street.'

'If you had gone on towards the coast, you would have found landladies in the resorts. In all the country around Lockley, you would have seen signs saying Bed and Breakfast and Teas with Hovis.'

'I know that now, but that is what I was telling you, that I did not know it then. I was just a young man who was setting out, so far as my sister was concerned, to change the world. Any young man like that is a strange combination of strength and weakness. I was right and accurate, cruelly just, in a god-like way, about everything that happened in my parents' house. But when it came to dealing with the outside world, I was completely hopeless. My father, whose weakness and self-deception so much appalled me, would have done much better. My mother, whose mind was a seething muddle, would have done infinitely better: she would have been successful. I just took my sister walking through the streets of Lockley, and you know what they are. It took us far longer than we thought to find the few streets where there were "Accommodation" signs. We did not dare to ask, least of all a policeman, for we were in a sense running away from home, and it was just possible that our parents would make some attempt to find us. I went to the first front door, and when I confronted the first landlady I was feeling sick. "I want accommodation for my sister," I told her, "And it's only fair to tell you she's going to have a baby, since it will be for several months." She just stared at me and said, "You have a cheek," and closed the door in my face. I was demoralised. For all I had said to my father and mother, I had not known it was going to be like that.'

'She must have been exceptional,' Brentford said.

'You're right. The next three all wanted our full story before they told us no.'

'They didn't believe you?'

'Oh, I think they did. But they didn't think anyone else would. That is the same thing, I have come to think, in most women's minds.'

Brentford did not find it necessary to reply or comment. He was quite sure that Milham would not leave the story there.

'We tried another district,' Milham said reflectively. 'A far more disreputable one. It was getting late. I had stopped saying my sister was going to have a baby. I knew by then that we were not going to find her permanent accommodation that day, and I was realising that it would take us a few weeks to find it. The woman named a price. Even when I realised that it was for the two of us I still did not get over my shock. I had not allowed for the price differential between the north and south of England. I began to realise that when Follet had given me that talk about maintaining my position on the salary he offered, he had meant every word he said.'

'But you took it temporarily?'

'No. The woman was clearly regarding us as a young unmarried couple who were having difficulty in finding a room for just that reason. Betty said no. We wondered what time the railway left-luggage office closed, and went back to the station to get our bags. We found it closed. Then we had not even luggage to bring to demonstrate our respectability, but only a tale to tell about it. I was also beginning to realise the impression we were creating, and the way I was getting known in the town to which I had come to live and work. Anything less like what Follet had required of me it was impossible to imagine. We were literally out on the streets in the end, at ten o'clock at night, in the dark, with no luggage and nowhere to go. We should have gone to the police but did not dare. If I solved the problem in the end, it was from sheer necessity. I was already a long way from the young man, full of confidence, who had gone back to his parents home.'

'You'd tried the hotels?' said Brentford.

'That's what I'm telling you. I understood by then that we

were going the wrong way about it, looking for cheap accommodation, at a moment's notice. We tried the Royal.'

'The Royal?' Brentford's eyebrows went up.

'I told you we went about it the wrong way. We went from one extreme to the other. I had to do something, and it could not cost the earth, I wrongly thought, to go there for one night. I insisted we straighten ourselves up and go boldly in, to be paralysed by the bright lights and the suavity of the night desk. "We require accommodation for the night," I said, or some such pompous statement from a young man. Then I got into a panic over the fact we had no luggage, and to explain it asked the clerk if he could get it for us from the station as soon as the office opened. He looked us over and gave us the book to sign. I wrote W. Milham, and Elizabeth, who was just following my actions, and who didn't know she had no need to sign at all, wrote "E. Milham". "We only have a large front room, sir," he told me, "With a double and a single bed." He looked at Betty's gloved hands with some significance. "I am sure you and your wife will be very comfortable." I didn't intend it. I believed what he said about the one room that was available and didn't dare to argue. We could not afford two rooms. It was not until we reached the room, with its two beds and its spacious, central-heated comfort, that I realised I had begun my married life in Lockley.'

'Oh, come,' said Brentford.

CHAPTER XII

PARKER'S OFFICE in police headquarters had a large window, one of the few large windows, and it gave a view of a cross-town street. The office differed from Brentford's, which had a small window and a view of the car park, in that it had wooden cupboards, room to walk round the desk, and a strip of carpet on the floor.

People usually had to wait outside Parker's office on a Monday morning, but Brentford was inside, looking out of the window, and it was for him that the people outside were waiting.

'So what did he do?' said Parker.

It had been going on a little time.

'You can't really fault him.' Brentford watched the traffic. 'After Milham, he drove back to Lockley. He had a learned discussion with McIvor in the autopsy room in the morgue. They talked about bruises and blood penetration beneath the skin and coagulation. Very technical, and McIvor said he would give him confirmation of Milham's story.'

'You mean he told him Milham's story first, and then McIvor made up his mind and did his examination of the body?'

'It wasn't intentional.' Watching the traffic, Brentford found himself thinking of Simpson's decency and Simpson's mother. 'It was just a question of when and where and saving time for doctors.'

'I can fault him all right,' said Parker.

Brentford knew the tone and felt for Simpson.

'Now look. You can't blame Simpson exclusively. There was McIvor. It was his responsibility; he had his own mind. The Coroner was old Tapman. You know Tapman wouldn't let anything go, if he thought it was relevant and created the slightest doubt. It's true Simpson had to tell Tapman. Tapman likes to be put in the picture, and not merely get an answer to a question about how long an adjournment the police want in open court. But he swears he didn't try to influence Tapman about the relevance of bruises, and how far they should appear in evidence.'

'You mean they whitewashed him?' said Parker, flatly.

'I didn't say that. It's not as though there was the old school tie network or anything of that kind. I doubt if any of them went to a Public School. Look.' Brentford pointed out of the window. 'You know where it is as well as I do. Go down to the traffic lights and turn left, up the street. Everyone knows those green-painted windows with Follet and Milham on them. They're a fixture, and the firm's been there, under one name or another, since the eighteen seventies. Dammit, it's not as though he were a city father. If anything, they did no more than try to cause embarrassment unnecessarily to another professional man.'

'You mean they didn't want to make Milham have to say he'd shaken and slapped his wife the night before she died?'

Brentford looked gloomily out of the window at the heavy vans that went perpetually past the police headquarters and wondered how he could communicate with Parker.

'Be reasonable,' he said. 'How often does an inquest go out of its way to pillory the husband of a deceased woman? They just don't do it, and rightly too. Every time a woman drowns herself you could make out a case that the husband didn't treat her rightly, or she wouldn't have drowned at all.'

His discomfort increased, and he knew Parker was watching him and wondering why he did not sit down before the desk. 'It's the kind of thing that could never be disproved,' he said. 'Any newspaper reporter who wanted to make a headline could do it just by pointing to the woman's death. Q.E.D., he did the wrong thing. And in fact those bruises could have been about as relevant as if she'd fallen down stairs and cut her knee the night before.'

'So,' said Parker.

'What do you mean by that?' Brentford was apprehensive.

'What you're telling me is that Simpson went to see Milham virtually with evidence of a murder in his hands. When he came out, he was convinced not only of Milham's innocence, but also that there was no murder. He forgot that he'd just been talking to the only man who was likely to do the murder. And Milham only had to convince him. When it came from the police inspector in charge of the case, it was convincing to other people.'

Brentford left the window. He could go to the visitors' chair before the desk and sit down now that Parker had followed his usual habit of saying the most uncomfortable thing that he could think of.

But Brentford too had a facility for making cases.

'She was mad,' he said. 'Hargreaves was willing to go on the stand and suggest that, on a basis of what he knew two years ago. She chose the chapel and Lambkin as opposed to the doctor and medical science. When she met Lambkin, she had

64

a feeling for him. She gave him money. The time came when she took Lambkin privately to one side and said obscene things to him. Then she committed suicide. How are you going to see the obscene things she said to Lambkin, which he won't repeat? As a basis for a legal case, or as just an aspect of her madness? A defence counsel would slay you and say that Milham had never a whiff of a case to answer.'

Parker watched Brentford sit down before him and thought.

'I'm not satisfied.' Parker added: 'You're not.'

'Why not?' Brentford frowned. 'Simpson saw Hargreaves before he saw Milham. It was Hargreaves he believed, and Milham only confirmed a story that Hargreaves told him.'

But he was dubious, and Parker saw why.

'You think Hargreaves really does remember what he thought of his patient two years ago? A lot of water has flowed under that bridge since, and much of it has been Milham, going to have little confidential talks with his doctor about his wife. Have you ever tried looking up a few classical symptoms and telling them to a doctor, John? He believes you invariably because he can't conceive you already know them.'

Brentford said sharply, 'That is far-fetched.'

Parker had a kind of smile Brentford did not like. 'Where did she die?' he asked. He also had a grasp of facts. 'It was in the river virtually opposite Hargreaves' door. At six o'clock in the morning, on her way to the chapel, which was bound to point up the question of her mentality. Also at a time Hargreaves was sure to be in, and there. Could it have been any different, given the time and place?'

Brentford stared at Parker.

'If a man is educated and intelligent enough to set up a murder in a way like that, I'm not sure he shouldn't get away with it. He has to know people too.'

Parker was not listening. He was thinking. In Parker's business nothing Brentford could say would be likely to affect him.

He said, 'You can't close it. It is an open file, John.'

'Oh, hell,' said Brentford. 'Why should this be a black mark against me?'

Parker just looked at him over the pad he had picked up, and on which he was writing a note to remind himself to see

Croxton about Simpson. If Parker complained that Simpson had not called the C.I.D. in when he should, it might go hard with Simpson.

'If you feel the Chief Constable may look through your list of unsolved crimes, why don't you go ahead and solve it?' Parker asked calmly as though it were Brentford's case and Brentford's duty.

Brentford had to think hard to realise it was his case now, and no longer Simpson's.

But that was what Parker was saying. It was Brentford who had started to go into details and question them, not Simpson nor Tapman nor McIvor.

'Look,' he said. 'This is what I told Lambkin. If I go down to Penlee now, and start asking the neighbours when they saw Milham get up in the morning, and the milkman and farm workers whether they saw Milham on the lane at that time, it'll be as though I exhumed the body.'

Parker looked at him blankly. 'You want me to tell that to Superintendent Croxton too?' He made a note on his pad. 'Give him a list of all the things Simpson should have done before the inquest, but that it appears in fact he didn't?'

'I'm only pointing out that if I talk to Milham's business acquaintances, in the hope of getting a line on him that way, it'll be about that that I hear from the Chief Constable. Persecution by investigation of a Lockley business man, after an inquest has already cleared him of any suggestion of any crime.'

'You shouldn't get yourself into these things, John, if you don't know how to get out of them.' Parker seemed to forget that it was he who had sent Brentford to listen to Lambkin in the first place. But he looked at him curiously. 'You think he will complain?'

'If anything like we suspect is even partly true?' Brentford looked at his superior gloomily. 'A man of that ingenuity? You can be damned sure he will.'

He went back to his own office, with its narrow view of the car park, and left Parker to his other callers.

CHAPTER XIII

'I'M NOT used to having you home for lunch,' Ethel said. 'I don't know if you realise, but if it weren't for yesterday's cold meat, I'd have nothing in the house for you.'

'I phoned to warn you.'

'At twelve o'clock, yes, saying that you might be here by half past. What do you expect me to buy and make in that time?'

There was in fact a perfectly good green salad in the bowl on the cottage table. There had been lettuce in the garden Brentford knew, because Brentford grew them, and the tomatoes in the little greenhouse were ripening successively before the autumn. Any talk of a lack of food in the Lockley area at that time of year was purely academic.

'Officially, I'm thinking,' he said.

'Thinking?'

'Yes. Parker handed me a difficult assignment this morning. I shall do what the detective sergeants do. In my private log book which I keep in my office I shall enter "12 noon—2 p.m. Thinking." They do their thinking in the local pub.'

'You don't all really enter up your times like that? I don't believe it.'

'You can believe it or not as you like,' Brentford said, playing with his cold meat and salad and admiring the reflections from the view from the window on the polished table. 'There's no charge for believing.'

'What are you supposed to be thinking about?'

'The Milham case. I have at least a dozen other things I could think of, but I have chosen to think of that. That should teach Parker.'

'You wouldn't talk about it last night.'

'No.'

'Did your Inspector Simpson do something wrong?'

Brentford stopped eating with lettuce in his mouth and looked at his wife. 'Now why should you think that?'

'I've noticed that the only cases you don't talk about are those that reflect on the police.'

'Do you ever realise that I shouldn't talk to you about any of my cases? I'm always telling my men, when I have any, that. That all police inquiries are official, and all of them are confidential.'

'It's as well you don't enforce it. If the village constables' wives didn't chat constantly with the neighbours over the backyard fence, the machinery of justice in this country would grind to a standstill.'

'You have an exaggerated idea of the duties of village constables' wives. They are only supposed to answer the phone, run the police station and answer inquiries while their husbands are away, hand out first aid and call ambulances, deliver children and comfort the dying, and occasionally hold one prisoner in custody while their husband goes out to catch the next one.'

'Just think what I missed by not marrying you sooner.'

'What are you doing this afternoon?' Brentford said, having already changed the subject away from Simpson.

And from Tapman and McIvor and all the other people who might be involved were Lambkin suddenly to take it into his head to preach a sermon condemning Milham. Brentford's thinking had had a little purpose so far. He had begun to see that there was such a thing as Parker's point of view.

Ethel was too wise to attempt to over-ride her husband's heavy-handed tactics. 'Mondays and Fridays are Red Cross days. You ought to know that.'

'Oh yes. Mondays are bandages, which is First Aid, and Fridays are parcels, which is Relief.'

'The other way round,' she said.

'Do keep your ears open if you hear anyone talking about Milham,' he said. 'Even if you never were a village constable's wife, in a place like Lockley it's not too late you know.'

CHAPTER XIV

BRENTFORD HAD a busy afternoon. He had already begun
it in effect before he came home to lunch. He had consulted
Lloyds Register of Yachts.

There was virtually no danger in going to see Colonel Baker,
he thought as he drove on from his home to Penlee. Colonel
Baker was the kind of man who was accustomed to it, and who
always was consulted. Gentlemen with names like Smith came
down from London, worried police headquarters for a while
asking who was who in Lockley, and then went out to Penlee
to talk to Colonel Baker. That was when someone in the
Lockley area had applied for a position, of a kind that was
known as sensitive, and whose nomination had something to
do with the higher civil service. It was also as well, if you
wanted to be a J.P. in Lockley, to know Colonel Baker and a
few other people. Brentford drove down the lanes thinking he
had a low opinion of M.I.5. M.I.5., so far as Brentford could
gather, believed a thing when someone of known political
opinions said it, while the things that Brentford believed had
to be proved, with infinitely more difficulty, in a court of law.
He smarted at times about it.

It was not the same thing, in Brentford's estimation, but
there proved to be a striking similarity, at least to begin with,
about their methods.

He found Colonel Baker working in his garden. dressed in a
pair of old trousers, a shirt that had seen better days, and with
naked bony feet in sandals. The Colonel's garden was peculiar.
Situated on the riverside and between the water and the land
that ran from the boat yard to the yacht club, it consisted
entirely of banks and beds of flowers, and it had the perpetual
look of being just about to become one of the most colourful
gardens in the whole of Penlee. There were many crates with a
London florists' agents name on them by the shooting brake
in the Colonel's garage, and when Brentford found the
Colonel he was busily cutting his flowers in large quantities,

just before they came into bloom, and packing them into boxes.

From the look of Colonel Baker, it might have been thought that he was an object lesson in the working of English democracy, since a man who had such *mana* in the district should have to make his living or eke out his meagre pension by growing flowers. But the three larger yachts, the two ocean racers and the ten-ton cruiser, lay to their moorings not far from the Colonel's garden, and that was why Brentford had consulted *Lloyds Register of Yachts*. The larger and better of the two ocean racing yachts, it so happened, was the Colonel's.

'I've been wondering,' Brentford said, watching the Colonel, 'how to retire in Penlee. And now I know.'

It was true. He saw it as a revelation, and he doubted if he would even need a yacht.

It was surprising what things came of simply doing your duty. He felt quite warm to Milham.

The Colonel said, 'Who are you?'

'A policeman,' Brentford said. 'Detective Chief Inspector Brentford of the county,' he felt it necessary to add. The Colonel might love such things.

They walked up to the house.

With the cynical foreknowledge that he applied to all classes other than his own, the Colonel said, 'I suppose you want a drink?'

Brentford did not deny it, and while he looked at the cane chairs and the view of the yachts from the verandah, the Colonel's wife came out and stayed long enough to get a drink in her glass. She questioned Brentford to discover that he did not belong to the Surrey Brentfords, and then lost interest and left them.

'A nice place you have here all the same,' Brentford said as they sat down. 'Thank you. Hold it.'

'I have to work like a dog to keep it up,' the Colonel said.

Bentford looked at the yachts and said 'Which of them is yours?'

The Colonel told him. 'I don't know how long I'll be able to keep her in condition to win her races.'

'You're still Commodore of the yacht club, aren't you?'

'Timothy Evens is Secretary. Lives up at the back there. If you want to know anything about the club, you should ask him.'

Lloyds Register of Yachts had its uses. Brentford already had that information. The book had only been acquired when a yacht was reported missing, but it had not succeeded in its objective of enabling the Lockley force to distinguish one yacht from another.

'Do you know Milham?' Brentford said idly. 'Chap who lost his wife recently?'

The Colonel gave him a lengthy and sideways look. 'No,' he said. 'I don't think I know him.'

Brentford was surprised. It was almost a beginning.

After thought, he showed it. 'I'd have thought everyone here would be a member of the yacht club, if only to use the bars.'

Flatly, the Colonel said, 'He's not.'

'Oh, well,' Brentford said, wondering if Timothy Evens could have given him the information in so little time.

'If you don't sail,' the Colonel said. 'Why don't you own a motor cruiser like that one? She's owned by a chap called Tankerton who keeps a garage.'

Brentford looked at the motor cruiser. She had chromium plate and a curved mast and a kind of flying bridge above the main deck, and she looked a little out of his class.

'So you do have someone who keeps a garage in the club,' he said. But it was not that he meant.

'Yes,' said the Colonel. 'He's on the membership committee. He collects the dues.' He took a look at Brentford.

Brentford drank his drink. He was reflective and took a little time over it. Then he stood up.

'Thank you Colonel. I'm sorry to have taken up your time, apparently for nothing.'

'You take up the time anyway,' the Colonel said, and went back to his gardening.

Brentford went back to his car. He looked back once, at the Colonel's house and the yachts in the river, in a puzzled way, and then he looked at the Point and up the other river towards

Viewcrest. Then he drove back thoughtfully to the main road just short of Lockley and found a garage.

It was a large affair, with a wide forecourt and lines of pumps, a white building, a plate-glass show-room with new models, and a parking lot at the back for second-hand cars. Over the covered forecourt was a sign, Imperial Motor Sales Lockley, and then, in small print, which was only likely to be read if it was looked for, was the name, R. Tankerton.

Brentford sat in his car for some time, lying off the forecourt, looking at the complete range of family cars in the showroom and mentally arguing with the Colonel about the definition of a garage, until an attendant came across and asked him what he wanted. Then he said, 'All right,' and drove the car in, got out at the showroom and said he wanted to see Mr. Tankerton. He might be sacked, he thought.

It was not easy to see Mr. Tankerton, and he had nearly been sold a new car, which he very much wanted but could not pay for, before he changed his mind and brought matters to a conclusion by saying he was Police.

Tankerton's office was nearly as big as the showroom and Brentford had an interesting talk with him about the recent incidence of car thefts and the difficulties the police were having in identifying the stolen cars before they turned up in second-hand car-dealers' yards like Tankerton's. Tankerton, who was a heavy man whom Brentford could just visualise driving his power yacht among the smaller fry of the Penlee river, was able to advise him on the point. 'Why don't you take it up with the manufacturers?' he said. 'What you want is a really sound number, inscribed indelibly in some vital portion of the chassis, and forget all this business of exchangeable engine numbers and little tags.' He sounded calmly helpful.

'The trouble is that the cars aren't made in the county,' Brentford said after listening with careful attention to Tankerton's dissertation. 'Being what we are, and in view of our limitations, we've only been able to go about it a different way and check up on people like you.'

'Like me?' Tankerton was shocked.

'You see someone told us that some dealers weren't very particular where the cars came from that they took in part exchange,' said Brentford. 'After all, you people have the workshop facilities, and once the thief has a new car on his hands, to which he has a proper title, he can take his profit.' He hoped he was ingenious.

'Listen.' Tankerton said. 'I've only had two stolen cars in here in the past twelve months, and I've reported them both. Your trouble is that what you want is for the dealers to do your work for you, and take the losses too.'

'Oh, don't let's be like that about it,' Brentford said. 'You're all right, or at least they tell me so, from what I hear.' He admired Tankerton's physique.

Tankerton did not look at all pleased at Brentford's gratuitous description of his character. 'You mean you've been checking up on me?' he said. 'You've got a cheek.'

'The Penlee yacht club is a useful organisation,' Brentford said. 'There are at least some people who will vouch for you, those who are in the club.'

'My God, they better had,' said Tankerton. 'Considering I live just right behind it.' He seemed appalled.

Brentford wondered it it would be worth while buying a few shares in Tankerton's when he eventually did become a limited company, and decided it probably would. From Tankerton's accent to a place behind the yacht club and on its membership committee was a long way already. 'Though what have you been doing to some of the people who aren't in the club?' he asked with interest, mildly.

'Look.' Tankerton was breathing heavily. 'Have you been talking to a man called Milham?'

'Milham' Brentford said not quite innocently enough. 'Who's he?' It was important not to be surprised.

'An accountant, and you damned well know it. That man is a dirty piece of work. I can tell you that.'

'Careful,' Brentford said. 'You are talking to a police officer, and I might insist that you substantiate that kind of statement.' He used a serious eye.

Tankerton looked in a smouldering way at Brentford, as though for two pins he would do more than substantiate, except that he was a businessman first, and one who kept his balance on the credit side.

'Speaking unofficially,' Brentford said, looking out of the window, 'it isn't only cars. I'd be glad if any tip you can give me in that line or any other.'

Tankerton looked nonplussed. 'Oh, I don't know. I don't know it's anything from the police line.' But he took another look at Brentford.

'We could try,' Brentford said, turning to look at Tankerton. 'You don't use us enough. We can always try.'

Tankerton's jaw was down and his lips were open. But he reached across his desk for his pad, thought for a moment, then wrote a name and address on it and passed it across to Brentford.

'Ask him,' he said. 'But don't expect me to vouch for him. I don't know his information is reliable.'

Brentford was puzzled when he left Tankerton's.

That was two in a line, he thought as he went back to his car. The Colonel said he did not know Milham, which perhaps required a little translation from the Colonel's language, and Tankerton said Milham was a dirty piece of work.

The case could not go like that, crumbling at a touch. It was not possible. He looked at the name and address and tried to visualise where the place was. It was in Lockley, and the wrong part of Lockley.

It was difficult to conceive that Milham's private life had any connection with the street where he was going, and when he drove the last two miles into Lockley and found it, it proved to be a shop.

He could not even see that Tankerton would have much connection with that particular kind of shop, on a street off the wrong end of High street, despite a few spanners and screwdrivers and precision tools in the window. Tankerton would already have those, and there were galvanised pails in the doorway, and a few dusty plastic bowls as well.

How did he approach the unknown without telling him what he had come for? He might have to tell him.

The penalties of speaking out grew less as you descended the social scale, he thought as he entered the shop. Credibility also grew less, until you could say anything by the time you entered the underworld, since no one would believe it. The light was poor in the shop, and the assistant was serving a man who wanted a three-eighths eye-bolt with a chromium-plated head, and who, to Brentford's surprise, looked as though he was going to get it. Brentford watched the box-searching operation for a moment, then nodded to the assistant and went through to the store-room behind the shop as though he owned it.

'Mr. Hall?' he said to the older man with the grey apron who was inside. Hall looked at him without surprise and nodded. Commercial travellers often came in like that.

'I'm Detective Inspector Brentford of the county,' Brentford said. 'You have an old-fashioned black-iron door knocker in the window. Can I have one?'

Hall nodded again. He was not surprised by that, either. He seemed to take it for granted that if a Detective Chief Inspector wanted anything from a shop, he would go in the back and talk to the proprietor. He went to get the knocker.

When he came back, he said, 'Seven-and-six to you.' And Brentford said, as an afterthought, 'There was something I wanted to ask you. Is there somewhere we can talk?' They went into a little partitioned office, with a calender nude on the wall that made it appear that either it was an all-male sanctum or the women who entered it must be broad-minded.

'How's trade?' said Brentford.

'Not bad,' said Hall.

'Not getting trouble from competition of the chainstores?' Brentford said, thinking of the plastic bowls outside.

Hall pointed simply to Brentford's door-knocker, which he had placed on the desk. 'You won't buy that in a chain store.'

Brentford's opinion of Hall rose. Outside the little office he could see a section of the store that contained precision tools. There was more value in that side of the stock than he had supposed.

Almost casually, he remarked, 'Have you ever had dealings with a man called Milham?'

Hall examined Brentford and said, 'Accountant?'

Brentford nodded. 'That is the man.'

'No.' Hall seemed to study his words carefully. 'I didn't.'

Brentford wondered what to do about it. There was something enigmatic about the negative and the way Hall looked at Brentford.

He thought, why not?

'We have you on the list,' he remarked.

'What list?' Hall said evenly.

'People connected with Milham.'

'Then you can take me off it,' Hall said in the same tone. 'I wouldn't play.'

In Brentford's work surprise was a luxury he could not afford. It could only be allowed to come afterwards if it came at all.

He tried to think what the game was that had not been played.

He said, 'Look, Mr. Hall, I'm not necessarily disbelieving you, but I should think you ought to convince me of that.'

Hall shook his head. 'I'm not going to tell you who introduced me to him. He meant it as a favour. I don't do it, not to anyone.'

It was not the first time Brentford had run up against a brand of ethics, and a lot of time could be wasted in the attempt to overcome it. He said, 'What happened?'

'Someone gave me a note to him,' Hall said, 'and told me have him do my income tax.'

Brentford wondered what Hall's income tax could possibly have to do with Milham's private life, but he said, 'Of course.'

'Well he wasn't so keen, and I wasn't so keen either,' Hall said. 'He said, "How much do you pay?" and then, "Even if we claim a rebate for the past five years, it isn't worth it." And I wasn't sorry. I wouldn't want to put in a claim, not sign it and have it put in for me by a man like that.'

Brentford was lost, so he said, 'Why not?'

'Well, it would be me that would sign the claim,' Hall said with a lift of the voice that from him was melodrama, 'and he could always say I'd given him the wrong figures. I'd be in his power.'

'I see,' said Brentford, resisting the temptation to hold hard to the desk. 'Well look, Mr. Hall, I'll try to keep you out of this. If not, you won't mind if I come to see you again?'

'No,' said Hall. 'I'll tell you what I know, but there isn't any more.'

'Except who sent you to Milham in the first place,' Brentford said.

'Oh,' said Hall. 'But I won't tell you that.'

Brentford did not even try to find out.

He went out of Hall's shop, where the assistant was now trying to tell a woman that to supply a washer for a bathroom tap you had to know the size. Hall followed him to the shop and gave him his door knocker and said, 'Seven-and-six,' and Brentford gave him three half crowns. But instead of walking up with his parcel to where he had left his car, he walked down to the end of High Street.

He could not actually see Follet and Milham's green-windowed office, looking up among the traffic. Or if he could, looking far away up round the Woolworth's corner, it could only be a tiny glint of green round a double-decker bus. But shame, he thought. The certified accounts fraud, and the gold letters said, 'Estd. 1871', and Hall, of all people, had been afraid he might be blackmailed if he even tried it.

Supposing, that was, that the whole thing was not a product of Hall's fevered imagination, due to sitting too long under that calender in the windowless office and the airless stock room. What an accountant could do legitimately for someone's income tax, if they had always done it themselves before, might be enough to spark off a train of imagination in a man like Hall. He shook his head. It was off, he thought.

But he went back to his car and drove to his office, in what was still not late afternoon, to do his thinking there.

If he had found out anything about Milham, he was sure of one thing. That it was not the right thing, and not what he had been looking for, that he had found out. He would have another talk with Parker, he thought, for at least it might be a handle.

CHAPTER XV

'You are claiming this was innocent,' Brentford said, 'you and your sister in a twin-bed hotel room, as man and wife without a wedding ring, in the Royal Hotel in Lockley?'

'You must have a warped sense of humour,' Milham said, 'if you think it was anything else but that.'

'It's not me who has a sense of humour,' Brentford said. 'I thought you had.'

'If you think it's funny, I don't,' said Milham. 'Not after what people have been saying about me. We couldn't even go down to the dining room for breakfast, since Betty didn't have a ring, but had to have it sent up to the room, which was another item on an already outrageous bill, as well as the fact that I had asked the clerk to have our luggage brought.'

'I have heard that the Royal does tend to overcharge guests whom they don't regard as quite desirable,' Brentford said. 'I don't know that they actually turn anyone away. I've never heard of that.'

'It made our problem not merely difficult but insoluble by the time we had paid the bill,' Milham told him. 'This was on the Saturday, the Saturday of the week-end I had given myself to become acquainted with the town and settle down in Lockley. I was due to start work at Follet's on Monday morning. I needn't tell you I was in a state of despair and panic. I had about five pounds left in the world, a new job to face that demanded that I present myself and be presentable. With me I had a sister who was not yet too visibly pregnant but who would soon require medical attention, maternity clothes, a pram, and all kinds of things. I had not a hope of keeping two homes going, which was what, in some dim way, I presumed I had supposed. I reached my nadir of despair around mid morning, when we gave things up as hopeless and went to sit on a bench in Lockley park. A bird sang on a tree over our head. It seemed to me symbolic of the unfeeling nature of all life, not merely human. I gave in and collapsed at that point. I asked Betty if, after all, and in view of what was happening to us and our desperate straits, she did not think that she had better, after all, give me up and go back to mother.'

'It does seem a reasonable and sensible suggestion,' Brentford said.

'You wouldn't think so if you heard how Betty replied to it,' Milham told him. 'I had thought we were in tune with one another, Betty and I. I had thought that my reactions were her reactions. It was news to me, as she told me in round phrases, that in fact they weren't. How could I suggest it, she said, when I knew that mother in fact simply would not have her? I spoke as though she had a home to go back to, but in fact she hadn't. All mother would do would be to lock her in her bedroom again and then send her off to some kind of redemption home. I had quite mistaken her mood, you see. To me, our journey to Lockley, our wanderings around a strange town, and our eventual disastrous episode in the Royal Hotel, had been a kind of increasing nightmare. But she did not see it that way at all. As I have told you, she had never left our home town before, except as a guarded girl, though she had longed to do so. Family holidays in North Wales, with everyone around her, had been the extent of her journeys, and she must have had a love of travelling. The whole journey had been an excitement to her. To wander a strange town, at large, just to see what lay down the next street, was the kind of thing she had wanted but never dared to do. I had forgotten that her spirit was such that, despite the way she had been cared for, she had somehow got herself attached to a married man, and let him get her with child. As for the Royal hotel, she had loved it, every minute of it, and taken it as a kind of present. Go home? Go anywhere else, surely. She had not a thought of it.'

'She had to face the fact of your finances.'

Milham spoke carefully. 'I never really did get Betty to face anything. To her, that was always something that other people did.'

Brentford was silent in admission that there always were difficulties in a case like that.

'I tried to explain to her,' Milham said, 'sitting there on the park bench. I spent an hour doing it, when we might have been doing what we had been doing the previous day, still searching for rooms. I went into it with her in pounds, shillings and pence. I quoted to her what the landladies had asked for, for any of the kind of rooms we were accustomed to. It was not that we could not afford two, one each, for the next month, until I got my salary cheque. We could not even afford one, and still eat and live in the style to which we were accustomed. And that was quite apart from the fact that the landladies would not have her at all, not even temporarily, when they knew she was an unmarried mother. It was not that they were heartless, I believe and still believe. It was just the opposite. That they knew that once they got a girl like that in the house, in that position, they would not have the heart to turn her out, even when the money stopped. For the sake of their own salvation, and for the businesses by which they ran their lives, they could not have had her in the first place. And as for them letting us take one room, as brother and sister, which Betty seemed to hint, they simply could not allow it. And you know what she said to that?'

'I simply can't guess,' said Brentford.

'She said, "We managed all right last night, now didn't we?" Then she met my eyes with her big ones and said. "You know you told me before we came away. You would find some way to do it, just as though I was your wife, and we were married, and I was going to have a baby. And now you say it's not like that." That was her response to my suggestion, my admission rather, which I had only covered up by my explanations, that I had attempted the impossible.'

'You had been unwise in what you said.'

'Unwise? I who had just qualified as an accountant had just made the most elementary mistake an accountant can make, which was not realising that all things, human emotions, ideals, and the most elementary sense of justice, all have their strictly cash value, which must be accounted for somewhere, in the books. Either you can afford them, or you can't. That was what my father had been trying to tell me, about his position and his job, but I had been too young to see it, and he had been too inarticulate to express it. I saw it now, when we sat on he park bench with our luggage round our feet and the birds flying down to the grass and expecting us to feed them.

'"What do you suggest?" I said to Betty. I made it sound desperate, which it was. "That we take one room, in the most awful street we can find, because that is all we can afford, and live there in poverty, pretending to be man and wife?" I thought she would blench at that. I was sure of it, and I made it sound something quite impossible. Instead, she was thoughtful "They do say two can live as cheaply as one," she said, and, "Oh, William, will you?" She was nothing if not practical; I have never met a woman who wasn't. It was just that she had no sense of the consequences, or of the ultimate outcome of what she did. And what could I do? Pick up my suitcases and walk away from her? If I did, she would follow me. I just sat there looking at her. And then I thought, all right. It would not last, of course. It was just my hope that it might last a week or two, while I earned a little money. Because we would need a little money, to tide us over, because as soon as my employer Follet found out, I would need another job.'

CHAPTER XVI

FOLLET, BRENTFORD thought. He had just come into his office, and was sitting down at his desk, looking out of the narrow window at activity in the police car-park, and considering picking up the telephone. If there was any truth at all in what Hall had told him about Milham, he thought, then Follet, that old and respected citizen, either could or should know about it. If he did not know, and unless, incredibly, he was involved in some kind of fraud himself, then, if this was the kind of thing people were saying about his junior partner, he should be told.

There was a little muddled thinking there, Brentford perceived. He would have to sort it out before he did anything so rash as consulting Follet. He looked out of the window to where the one and only county radar detection van had come into the car-park, and where a sergeant and two constables were getting out. They wore benign expressions, suitable to men who had had a short and easy, fruitful day, catching speeding motorists on the Hapton road, which was the only road in the district that was suitable and safe for speeding, and Brentford picked up his telephone and tried to make an inter-office call to Parker.

'The Chief Superintendent is out, Chief Inspector,' Gladys told him. Gladys was the middle-aged woman who did a day-time spell of duty at the police switchboard in business hours. 'Your wife's been calling you.'

Parker would be out, when for once he might have been useful in consultation, Brentford thought. He said, 'What did my wife want?'

'Your wife asked me when you would be home for dinner,' Gladys said. 'When I asked if there was any message I could leave for you, she just rang off.'

'My wife must be mad,' said Brentford, and put down the phone. He did not know when, or if, he would be home for dinner himself.

Follet, he thought. Was it possible that a man like that known and respected in Lockley since his father's time, and almost basic to business life in the district, yet self-effacing as accountants were, could know that his partner was indulging in nefarious practices, and not do a thing about it? Worse still, was it possible that he could not know? The unlikelihood of both contentions raised forcibly the question of the credibility of the story that Hall had told him.

Brentford thought that he was thinking, practically, and not merely officially now. To aid the process of thought, he drew his note pad towards him across his desk and drew a match stick man upon it. That was Milham, he thought. The drawing became difficult because he had never consciously seen Milham, and did not know his features for the cartoon-type head he used. He put a skirt on the model, and decided to call it Mrs. Milham, but ran into the same difficulty, with the addition that she was also dead. He might have put a beard on it and called it Follet, but Follet, he was fairly sure, would not wear a beard, and it was the thought that he had not seen him

82

either, not knowingly and knowing who he was, that decided him.

This case was far too abstract, he thought. Due to the impossibility of approaching any of Milham's neighbours about him, with the inquest over, or of approaching the people with whom he did business, except at the remotest distance and with the utmost circumspection, he felt a dire lack of direct knowledge of Milham. He had no feeling for the personalities of the people most concerned. He had no idea of the kind of mental universe that people like Milham and Follet inhabited. And that, he thought, was an excellent reason for seeing Follet.

Brentford, sitting at his desk, might have thought that the physical universe itself lacked either meaning or significance, except in the minds of the men who caused or reacted to events in it; he might have considered that reality itself, being an invention of the minds of men, did not exist unless he knew the minds of the men concerned. He did not. He only felt uncomfortable, with a sense that events, all disconnected, had got in a sense beyond him. And he saw very clearly that what Hall had told him might be true or false, but that strictly did not matter. It gave him a legitimate approach to Follet.

He picked up his telephone, unaware that it was not so easy to get in touch with Follet as he supposed.

'Gladys, will you make a call for me? I want you to do something, but do it with discretion.'

'As long as it isn't too cloak-and-dagger, Chief Inspector,' said Gladys calmly.

'I want you to call Follet and Milham, the accountants. Don't say you are police. There are people in that office I don't want to get to know about this. Just ask for Mr. Follet, and if they want to know who's calling, tell them that it is a Mr. Brentford.'

While he waited, at the mercy of Gladys' discretion, he wondered what Parker would say about it. Parker would say he was rash, he presumed. Hall's story should be investigated in a way that would not alert Follet or anyone in that office. But Follet had distinct advantages from Brentford's point of view. Follet must necessarily know Milham intimately, and he

83

was the one person Brentford could think of who would not spread it about, to the detriment of his own business, that the police had become interested in William Milham.

It was too bad, in Brentford's estimation, if Follet and Milham were alerted and had time to hide their fraud. What Brentford wanted to do was to get out of the murder investigation with his skin intact.

'Hello, Chief Inspector.'

'Hello?'

'I'm sorry, Chief Inspector. Mr. Follet is retiring and doesn't come to the office on a Monday any longer. Do you want me to try to get him at his home?'

'No, thank you, Gladys.' Brentford put down the phone, thought a moment, then went to his shelf, looked at his own telephone directory, and prepared to leave the office.

He had only come into the office quarter of an hour before, but now he was leaving it again. It had occurred to him that Follet, if he proved to be at home, might be more susceptible to a sudden and chance call, particularly if it were unannounced. The local directory had contained only one G. Follet, and that at an address that seemed likely, in Fairfield, the suburb of large old grey-stone houses to the west of Lockley.

Brentford, setting out to see Follet, was quite prepared to find him dead on arrival, and be faced with a second murder, but he knew that things never happened as simply and easily as that in his life. He got the hard ones, who only murdered once, or who were careful not to murder provably at all, and who were careful to think that that probably was enough.

He was getting through town before the rush-hour, he noticed when crossing High Street. How could he phone Ethel to tell her when he would be back for dinner when he did not know if Follet would be in, or whether a talk would last five minutes or five hours providing that he was in? He caught a glimpse of the Follet and Milham offices because he looked for them. They were still there. A little farther on, he saw a woman with a small brown dog at a lamp-post. She was not looking at the dog, but was standing away at the far end of the outstretched lead, looking into the distance, and, by her expression, saying 'Tt, tt, tt,' to it. By the time he got to Fairfield and was driving under the trees down Coronation Road (Fairfield was like that: the address he was going to was Acacia Crescent), there was a schoolboy wandering dolefully homeward with his schoolbooks, and a schoolmaster beyond him getting out of a large car, necessary because schoolmasters had large families, and going into a house on which he must have been carrying a heavy mortgage.

There was a slight temptation to go home, give up for the day, and arrange to see Follet in the office in the morning, but Brentford persisted to Acacia Crescent, through the iron gate after he had parked his car, and had a dark, slim, fiftyish housekeeper woman look at him as though he might be selling brushes.

'Mr. Follet is retiring,' she said when he asked for him by name. 'He isn't taking any more business now, and not from callers here.'

Brentford was being impressed by the size of the house, and an old-fashioned bell-push, let in the stone, with a large white eye marked 'Press', of a style that seemed to date from the days when people used to pull at bells, and that reminded him of the Leyden jars of his early years, mouldering away in butler's pantries.

'Tell him that Detective Chief Inspector Brentford would like a word with him,' he said. He tried to remember what private detectives did in American novels, but reflected that Americans were easier of access than men who lived in Lockley. It was still a large house for an accountant, though, like Milham's, not exactly ostentatious.

The room had a large front window that looked out on the clump of trees that was circumnavigated by Acacia Crescent, and wallpaper that emphasised its proportions with Grecian pillars. The house was centrally heated, and better inside than out, and the furniture, though old-fashioned, was done in a kind of golden plush that must be expensive. Follet was a thin man, grey and bald, pedantic and officious in a blue suit, and Brentford had the immediate impression that he had seen him many times in many places before he ever met him.

'What is it, Inspector? It is "Inspector"? This is a surprise.'

Follet seemed prepared to hear that some minor employee

had been discovered helping himself, or more likely, these days, herself, from the cash desk in the office. Or perhaps thieves had broken in in the night and got the safe.

'This is a little difficult, sir,' said Brentford. 'Do you mind if I sit down?'

'Sit? Oh yes, by all means sit. There. Will you be happy in that chair, or do you want a table?' Follet himself sat reluctantly. Far from showing signs of retiring at his very advanced age, he looked as though he thought that things would always be better and quicker if he was on his feet.

'I am sorry to have to bring this to you at all, sir.'

'Bring what?'

'We have some awkward duties to perform sometimes, sir.'

'Yes. Yes, I understand that. What is it, man? Get on with it.'

'The police, Mr. Follet, occasionally get allegations against notable people from time to time.'

'Eh? What's this? I must confess I don't understand this—is it "Chief Inspector"?'

Nor did Brentford himself quite understand it, Brentford reflected. He had Hall's story up his sleeve, to explain the line that he was taking. But it was not his business actually to give information, and he felt he ought to tell Follet that. It would be nice if he could continue to speak in general terms—in terms so wide that they would cover anything that Milham had done, of any kind, and, if it was not necessary to define more closely, then Follet too.

' "Inspector" will do nicely, sir.'

'Inspector, what are you trying to tell me?'

'Of course it's mostly famous people who get these allegations, but sometimes in a town like this it's others.'

'Who? Inspector, are you suggesting—Who has said what?'

'Ah, that we don't say, sir,' said Brentford heavily. 'We don't spread these rumours.'

Follet's expression recorded the fact that he was certainly under the impression that something dire was happening.

'What rumours? Inspector, really—'

'We only try to pin the people down, and so disprove them.'

'Who—?'

'Mr. Milham.'

Follet sat silent for a moment. It was as well that he had got him seated first, thought Brentford. The old were always in a state of uncertain health, and a rush of blood to the head, or a fall, was always possible when they were taken aback quite literally. The old man opened his mouth like a fish for a moment. There were several things, on the evidence he had been given, which he might say or think. Brentford wondered if it was by chance that he chose the right one.

'Inspector, do I understand that you have come here to talk to me about my partner, Mr. Milham?'

'I did wonder if you would tell me a little about him,' Brentford said. 'There have been some allegations about Mr. Milham, as I have told you.'

Follet showed signs of getting up. 'Inspector,' he said, and then again, 'Inspector.' He looked at the clock on the marble mantlepiece. 'I must get Mr. Milham here,' he said. 'He will be leaving the office, and I must tell him. He must be present at this interview. Of course, he must.'

CHAPTER XVII

'THE DIFFICULTY we had, as we took our suitcases with us and worked down the town, was that the bed-sitting rooms we were offered had a double bed. Also it was Saturday morning, to begin with, and the women were out shopping in the morning, and in the afternoon we found one who was out at a football match. Even Betty, I am glad to say, drew the line at a double bed. She had, after all, learned the consequences of that kind of thing, and even if I was her brother, she must just have been realising, at that time of her life at least, that in some things it was possible to go a shade too far. We exhausted what you might call the passable places, and saw, and were most taken by, a two-room flat. Betty was all for taking it, when, as we argued about the rent, the woman said, in passing, that she would want a five pound advance. Betty knew we had five pounds, but I remembered that we had to eat as well, and hissed at her, and said what we really wanted was better rooms, and got out quickly, and that was that.

'We descended the town, and I'm sure you know how it was then in Lockley. The housing estates were not yet built, or the outer suburbs. There was just Fairfield at the top, where the gentry lived, and then the streets descending, in an almost stratified class-structure until you reached the cottages down by the river. We saw a steady deterioration as we descended. Houses became smaller, and streets became narrower. Pubs became more frequent, though we could never tell down which street we might or might not find a "Rooms" or "Apartments" sign, except that signs of any kind, or those that demanded literacy, were getting rarer. We began to see children, partly clothed, playing in the streets and on the doorsteps. Sometimes I think we forget what a change has come over English life in thirty years. It was possible to see barefoot children then, at the height of the depression, or an infant crawling out of a doorway into the cobbled street dressed in nothing but a dirty ragged shirt. We could not mistake where we were going or being forced to go: the people were either shouting or yelling at one another or very cheerful. You would have to go to the west of Ireland or the south of Italy to see that kind of life today. It is true that, coming from the north, we had seen it, but all the same it was a surprise to Betty, who pretended to take it in her stride, and there is a law about landladies, of the kind we were visiting, that I don't know if you've discovered.

'One woman said she would be glad to give us house-room, but unfortunately she already had her boarders. We did not want board anyway, since although it certainly looked cheap enough, we could not afford it. But there was someone she knew, she said, in the street below, who might have a room to let. It was true enough, but the room was let when we got there, and she told us to try someone in another street, some distance away, who told us to try a fourth. We were carrying our suitcases all this way, for it is the only way if you are a young couple and wish to appear respectable. But the law about landladies is this, that they will always send you on somewhere, but always to a room or house worse than their own, and never to a better. Perhaps they think that if they send you to a better place you will never come back to them, while if they send you to a worse, in fullness of time you will. So we were descending the town, and still descending, and we had already walked enough the previous day. I could see the river below us, and I was beginning to think we would soon be in it, and that was the way it was when we came to the last two streets.'

CHAPTER XVIII

AFTER ITS unpropitious start, Brentford's interview with Follet proved easier than expected.

'I wouldn't do that, Mr. Follet,' Brentford said in the gracious room with its view of the trees and Acacia Crescent as they sat in the golden chairs. 'I wouldn't call Mr. Milham.'

'Why not, Inspector?' Follet looked doubtful. 'Surely you don't imagine that I'm going to talk about my business partner to the police behind his back?'

'It isn't quite like that, sir,' said Brentford amicably.

Follet raised his eyebrows, but he did not immediately fly off to the telephone.

'What is it like?'

'It's always awkward, this matter of investigating allegations. We don't like going round asking all the sundry about the man concerned. As you know yourself, sir, that kind of thing can do a great amount of damage. On the other hand, just to go to the man concerned, and put it to him and let him deny it, would hardly be an investigation at all. So we adopt a middle course.'

'A middle course; I see.' As Brentford had hoped he would, Follet looked judicially as though that were probably the right course for anyone to adopt.

'It's far better for us to approach someone of undoubted probity like yourself, sir.' Brentford said engagingly. 'Someone who both knows the man concerned, and whose knowledge and opinions can be respected. Then, when we do go to the man, if you have been able to assure us that he is a man of honour, we can attach far more weight and substance to his denial, and that is that.'

'Ah, I see,' said Follet.

Brentford hoped he did. He certainly looked as though he did, for the moment. But would it last when Brentford left? An almost instinctive reaction for the man questioned was to pick up the telephone after the police had gone and to tell the man concerned all about it, and in the greatest detail.

'What we want, sir, is your cooperation. It's essential, as you must see, sir, that I should talk to you, for example, today, and then talk to Mr. Milham tomorrow without his prior knowledge. I must ask you for that amount of cooperation, sir, or I shall have no alternative but to take the allegations more seriously and start what on the face of it would be the more obvious procedure of asking questions of all the sundry.'

'Oh, all right.' Follet obviously did not like it, and it was possible that he was going to have second thoughts, but he said, 'I suppose so. I suppose I have no alternative but to cooperate with you, Inspector.'

It was the best Brentford could do. He could not say he was completely happy. He could not guarantee Follet's actions after he left the house, but after the way they had started he was glad to have got as far as that.

He started with his questions.

'When did you first meet Mr. Milham, Mr. Follet?'

'Thirty years ago.' Follet evidently saw no need to be reticent about that. 'My firm was Follet and Follet; that is, it consisted of my father and myself as principals. My father died. I took charge myself, and took his place, but I obviously needed a qualified assistant to take my place and do my own work.'

'How did Mr. Milham come to you? You advertised?'

'Yes. If you will recall the date, Inspector, you will notice that this was at the height of the Great Depression. A great number of qualified people were unemployed, and I had no difficulty in getting applications.'

Brentford noticed the addition to the question he had asked. It was possible that Follet, though abrupt in his manner, might also, like many old men, have a tendency to loquacity when talking about the past. Brentford set out to cultivate it assiduously.

'Things were bad at that time; I remember it myself,' he said sympathetically. In fact, it was unlikely that Brentford would ever have entered the police if it had not been for the Great Depression, but he did not say that. He adopted a reminiscent tone. 'How did you choose Mr. Milham? It must have been a little difficult, from what you say.'

Follet looked a little suspicious for a moment, but he showed signs of being seduced by what he regarded as an account involving his own shrewdness.

'It would have been difficult had I not been methodical. I made up my mind about the kind of man I wanted in the first place. I did not wish to bring a mature man into our family firm, since he would have his own methods, and his salary would be higher. I preferred to take a young man, as my father had taken me, and train him in my own way. That disposed of half the applications at a single stroke.'

Brentford looked impressed for Follet's edification.

'For the rest,' Follet said, 'I told my secretary to send regretful letters to all those who applied from over a hundred miles away.'

'I see. So that means that Mr. Milham must have come originally from this part of the country, sir?'

'No. Milham was working in the Midlands. He was one who received our letter, but he wrote back by return saying that he appreciated what he had been told, but he hoped that none the less I might still consent to see him, and if I would, he wished to make it clear that he would travel for the interview entirely at his own expense.'

Brentford was not so sure that he would have gone for a young man who was importunate, but he did not say that to Follet. He gave Follet deference. 'That was good?' he asked.

'The point about the train fare was noticeable. It was an accountant's letter. I told my secretary to reply that I would see him on the basis that he indicated.'

It would not have been suitable for Brentford to comment on Follet's meanness.

'Perhaps that also helped him to impress you at the interview, sir?'

Follet demurred. 'We are spending rather a lot of time merely on my first contact with Mr. Milham, are we not, Inspector? After all, I may point out that he was my assistant for ten years, with an interval for the war, and my partner for nearly twenty since.'

It was true that Brentford had thought he would be more concerned with those events until Follet said so. It was possibly the sheer perversity of his method of conducting an interview that made him say, 'First impressions are important, sir, especially when dealing with a shrewd man like yourself.'

'Oh.' Follet looked at the same time disappointed, if not a little wary, and yet a little pleased. He was evidently not aware of Brentford's dictum that the older a man got, the more susceptible he became to the grossest flattery. Centenarians could even be complimented on their beauty without rousing the slightest suspicion in their fading minds. 'I can tell you this,' said Follet, 'that he stood out among the other candidates as a personable and clean young man. You asked me if Mr. Milham was a man of honour. He seemed to me just that.'

Brentford would have passed on, but there was something in Follet's expression that he had learned to notice. He merely waited.

As he expected, when he did not speak, Follet began to explain himself.

'It isn't often these days we hear people speaking in such old-fashioned terms,' said Follet. 'Even then, it was perhaps unusual for me to think in them.' His eyes became fixed on the wall beyond Brentford. 'I remember thinking to myself, "This is a young man who will do the decent thing." As it happened, I shortly had proof he did, but you won't be concerned with that, Inspector.' He turned to Brentford as though expecting him to wish him to go on again.

It was unlikely, even if he had not been fishing, that Brentford would have left such a remark alone.

'"A young man who would do the decent thing"?' He remembered Simpson, speaking of a much later contact with

Milham, talking in almost identical terms. Tankerton, equally clearly, had said the opposite.

Follet looked straight at him. 'That is how he struck me.'

'And you say you very soon had proof that he was like that?'

Follet's face seemed to close. 'From what I have understood, you will not be concerned with Mr. Milham's personal life, Inspector. And the point to which I was referring was very personal. It concerned his wife.'

Brentford could hardly agree with Follet that he was not concerned with Milham's wife. He only marvelled slightly that Follet did not guess it. That he did not do so, though Brentford had not told him at all what the allegations were about, made him think more of Hall's slightly dubious statements than he ever had before.

But for the moment, he was concerned to keep Follet to the subject, which he himself had raised, of Milham's wife.

'I didn't know he was married then,' he said simply.

Follet frowned in the way perfectly innocent citizens did when their own explanations, as almost invariably happened, got them into the position of having to give still further explanations, about matters they did not want to talk about, to the police.

'He was not supposed to be. At the interview, I had asked him particularly, explaining that I had no wish and was not in a position to pay the salary for a married man. He had said he was not married. Then, hardly more than two months later, when he had been working for me for about three weeks, I found he was.'

Brentford had a vision of the late Mr. Milham adrift in the Penlee river, floating half submerged to the mud bank and going around there, lapped by the receding tide. It was not a mental image he wished to describe to Follet.

'That doesn't sound very honourable to me, Mr. Follet,' he said, 'To tell you that he was not married, to get the job, and then, so shortly afterwards, for you to find out he was.'

Follet looked like a man whose explanations had gone wrong, and who found himself in the mire. 'I can see I shall have to tell you the whole thing, Inspector.'

'It might have been better if you had done that in the first place, Mr. Follet.'

Follet looked unhappy. 'He was in fact perfectly honourable,' he said. 'It was just the things that happened. That is, he was as honourable as a man could be, who had once made a young man's mistake.'

Simpson too had found Milham's conduct honourable, and that it was only the circumstances that were at fault, and Brentford was interested in the mistake. He looked patiently at Follet.

'He was such an exceptional worker,' Follet said. 'That was his undoing. I had told him most particularly that the young man I engaged would have to live on the salary I gave him, and have nothing over for frivolities, since he would have to maintain a good appearance, for our firm, and live at a good address. If he had not taken work home at the week-end, I would not have found out at all, or else not for a long time.'

Like many another person, he seemed to find that a story which he had indicated had a simple explanation proved the hardest kind to tell. He looked at Brentford as though Brentford might try to help him.

'He took papers home to work on through the week-end, the third week-end he was with us, you understand,' he said. 'He had proved to be like that. A most indefatigable and industrious and competent worker.' Follet stressed the words, which hardly seemed necessary in the context. 'I suppose you can call it his misfortune that I needed those same papers. I picked up the phone to call him and ask him to bring them round to my house, when I discovered that I did not have his address.'

Brentford allowed it to be seen that he was paying acute attention. 'That was odd, wasn't it? I should have thought you would have asked him about where he was staying, and that kind of thing, when he had moved, as I presume he had, to Lockley?'

'I had asked him.' Follet looked surprised at the recollection of it, after thirty years. 'He had told me, I remember thinking quite distinctly, that he had got good accommodation, and that he had left his address with the girl in the outer office. So

I phoned her, of course, since fortunately her parents, with whom she lived, were on the phone. There was some difficulty getting the address then. She had it somewhere, she said, but she would have to phone me back. I explained why I wanted it, and when she phoned me again I understood the reason for her attitude. She herself volunteered to go and get the papers. I was not blind. In the short time he had been with us, she had formed an attachment to our eligible young bachelor, our Mr. Milham, and she was glad to go to meet him and see him out of office hours.'

'I think I begin to see,' said Brentford.

'No doubt you do,' said Follet, who had what seemed an unnecessarily grim look about that part of his story. 'You will gather that when she got round to Milham's address she found that he was living there, not alone as we thought, but with his wife. I need not say that I had no difficulty getting the story out of her when she came to me. She was angry as though he had misled her, and spoke with indignation. It was not customary in those days for young girls to speak so freely about a woman being pregnant, but she certainly conveyed to me that Milham's wife was that, which hardly indicated a very recent marriage. She also told me why Milham had not given me his address: he was living in a single furnished room in Lower River Street, which you will be well aware is hardly the best address in town. It would be difficult to think of a worse or cheaper.'

Brentford could see that Milham had had some explaining to do, but he remembered Parker's comments on the way he had explained, in possibly even more difficult circumstances, to Simpson.

'Needless to say I had him on the mat in front of my desk on the Monday morning,' Follet said.

He seemed to think he had expanded enough on the dramatic background of his story and could now begin on the simple, logical explanation.

'He could not have behaved better,' he said. 'He was straight and clear. Yes, he told me, he was married. But no, he had not been married at the time of the interview. I was impressed, but found it necessary to point out to him that I had heard his wife was pregnant. That that should be visible hardly indicated a very recent marriage, I said, particularly a sudden one, and I could not abide lying. At that, he rose from his chair and said that if that was what I thought of him, he could only tender his resignation. I told him I was still listening. It had happened after his interview with me, he said. He had telephoned his old employer, told him he had got a new job, as a qualified man this time, and demanded that he be given a further day's leave, since he was away, to go to see his parents on the way home and acquaint them with his movements. Then, in his home town, it happened. It was true he had a girl there, but he had not intended marrying her. In fact he had not seen her for three or four months, since his holidays in the summer. Her letters had been over-possessive, so he had disregarded them. But now she fell on his neck, told him she was pregnant, and demanded that he marry her.'

'In short, do the decent thing,' said Brentford, who was fascinated by the tale.

Follet looked hard at him.

'Exactly,' he said, 'and in short, he did, while he was serving out his notice with his old employer, and before he came to Lockley. And you should not think that was a little thing for a young man, Inspector. Remember his situation. He had already handed in his notice to one employer, and his work with me was explicitly based on the fact he was a bachelor. It would have been very easy for him to move off to Lockley without telling her. And what he had done in Lockley was not to deceive me. On the contrary, his aim, he told me, was simply to accept his position with Follet's on the basis that I had given it to him, and not make new demands on me. He had got himself into difficulties through his own fault, he said, and he was not asking anything from anyone, only doing his best, with it.'

Brentford remembered what Parker had said about Simpson's interview with Milham. Simpson had gone to Milham with evidence of a murder on his hands, and had come away convinced not only that Milham was innocent, but also that there was no murder.

'What did you do about the way he was living and Lower

River Street,' he said. 'I gathered you wanted him to maintain a position and use a good address.'

Follet, who had been telling his tale with an air of triumph for Milham's virtue, looked embarrassed. For a moment, for no particular reason, he looked out of the window at Acacia Crescent, which was being used as a car park for the cars that were coming home. 'I thought it over when he made his explanation. I didn't want to lose him. I gave him a minor loan.'

Brentford wondered if he were doing Milham an injustice. He must have gone into that interview expecting to be dismissed, he thought. 'Minor?' he asked.

The old man's eyes came sharply back. 'It doesn't cost much more to rent an unfurnished flat, with proper references, than a furnished room. Obviously their main lack was capital. And you don't have to ask if he repaid the loan, Inspector. I paid his salary, and could make deductions in the years before the war as I saw fit.'

There was something in the way that Follet said it that made Brentford wonder if relations between Follet and Milham had been quite consistent throughout that time. He did not pursue it, however. Follet's glance at the street must have reminded him of passing time, and Brentford himself remembered Ethel's call to the office.

The remainder of the interview was much more normal and brought nothing new. Milham emerged as a businessman who both worked and had ability, who neither drank to excess nor was known to bet on horses.

'There is one thing I want to draw to your attention, Inspector,' Follet said voluntarily and without being asked by Brentford. 'Mr. Milham has been a loyal colleague over many years. But he has had no need, if he did not wish, to stay here in Lockley. As I told you, he was away on national service during the war, and when the war ended, I know for a fact that he had several offers. The situation was very different from when he first came to me during the Depression. After five years of war, young qualified and experienced accountants were in short supply, and he could have gone anywhere in the country. I was distinctly pleased and happy when he came back to me. His efforts, quite as much as my own, have built up Follet and Milham's. I was glad to give him a partnership, on a strict financial understanding of course, and you may add personal loyalty and a liking for this part of the country to his other virtues.'

When they reached that level of platitude, Brentford thought at the time, it was time he went home. He reminded Follet of something as he got up from his golden chair and looked again at that wallpaper with its Grecian pillars.

'Thank you, Mr. Follet. You will be careful not to mention this to Mr. Milham until I have a word with him? It is to your advantage and his, and especially to the firm's, to do it our way.'

Follet, getting stiffly to his feet to see him out, seemed genuine when he said, 'I shall be very anxious to hear what these allegations are, Inspector, and if I do as you say, it will be on the assumption that you will have the earliest possible talk with Mr. Milham.'

They went to the hall. Follet would say that anyway, Brentford thought, whether or not it was what he intended to do in fact. He had to think all the time that his questions might well be transmitted to the man they were about.

None the less, when they were in the hall, and just as he was leaving, he did ask another. He tried to make it sound not so much like an afterthought as like something so unimportant it had almost been forgotten. 'Since you mentioned Mr. Milham's marriage, would you say it was, on the whole, a happy one?'

Follet, opening the door, looked at him as though he were either slightly mad or asking something in bad taste.

'You can hardly expect me to be a judge of that. But yes. On the whole, I should think it was, Inspector.'

There were an awful lot of holes in that, Brentford thought as he slipped down the path into Acacia Crescent.

In the car, he started and drove out of town by the nearest road. By the shortest out of the traffic, that was, though not the shortest home. He only hoped for home.

He did not know then that he was going to see that interview with Follet from a different angle.

CHAPTER XIX

AFTER TWO midnight hours of it, Brentford wondered if Milham knew if his eyes were sometimes as sad as the trees that dripped in the darkness outside the garden door they had come in by.

'So this is what you are telling me.' He fought to control his scepticism. 'That when you came to Lockley, you just had to move into one room with your sister, and to do that you had to say you were man and wife?'

Milham seemed to have grasped the dangers of a voice that went on and on. He looked distinctly worried.

'You put it too baldly,' he complained. 'How could you understand it if I didn't tell you all the detail?'

'Detail. . .'

'I worked for Follet,' Milham reminded him. 'I believe you've met him.' He showed signs of going on.

While Milham went on, Brentford thought that when he had seen Follet he had not known it would be like this.

'Yes,' he said.

'I don't have to tell you how I felt,' said Milham, 'when I left our wretched furnished room and walked to Follet's office on our first Monday morning here in Lockley. Follet had told me that I had to be a presentable bachelor to work for his firm. Well, I was presentable, and I was a bachelor, but that could only last as long as no one found out about us or discovered our home address. All I could do was to tell myself to work, to work as no man had worked before, and keep up a smoke-screen of sheer efficiency, to keep things going as long as possible, until I saved some money. At least I must somehow keep things going until the month-end and my salary cheque, and I don't need to tell you I was nervous. I could only hope it would work, and it might have worked. It would, if Follet had been a normal employer. I could have kept things going at least until I had some cash in hand, and then either shifted Betty out, to another town, or, if I thought I might be recognised someday, as the man who had been married once in Lockley, I could have left suddenly, and started again elsewhere.'

Knowing Lockley, Brentford thought it would have been the latter. But it was not that he questioned.

'You say Follet was not a normal employer? In what way was that?'

'Follet? Surely you know. I found out in the first ten minutes of my employment in his office. In Follet and Follet's he had always been first an employee and then a junior partner to his own father. He had got the idea that a paternalistic attitude was normal for an employer to his employees. The first thing he did was to call me into his office and ask me all kind of personal questions, had I got good accommodation, what was my landlady like, and did I like Lockley, in answer to which I could only lie or be evasive. I told him I had left my address with the girl in the outer office, and had to do it later, a paper folded in an envelope which I hoped she wouldn't open, to keep up with the lies I had already told. I got off on the wrong foot, and could only try to make up for it by work, and by asking him about the firm's business and what I could do for it, every time he came in sight of me. But that didn't succeed. My apparent efficiency and dramatic keenness only increased his curiosity and that of everyone around me.'

'Yet you did keep it up.'

'He set a trap for me. I could see it coming, but I could not do a thing about it. He talked about some urgent work until I had to offer to do it through the week-end. But it was his work, and I knew he would get a call about it. It was just an excuse to walk round to see me, to get the papers. I could only rely on the fact that he did not have my address, and the girl I had given it to had dropped it in a drawer, and, I hoped, forgotten it. But I did not allow for her curiosity too. When he called her for the address, she did not have it, but instead of just saying so, she temporised, slipped round to the office, got it, and called him from there and suggested that she should go to get the papers, pretending she was still at home. It was like a damned conspiracy, or one of those nightmares in which, whatever you do, sheer circumstances will immediately outface you. She had glanced at my address once, I believe, and immediately thought there might be something. Under the guise of trying to find us, she saw our landlady first and pumped her, and of course got our story about being a young married couple with a coming baby, and it was that that I was faced with, and which I had to explain to Follet on the Monday morning.'

'Why didn't you tell him the truth?'

'I didn't dare. My nightmare feeling was that if I admitted that we were brother and sister, living as man and wife and with a coming baby, there would be a charge of incest. At least I could see one thing, and that was that a man like Follet would be shocked to the core. The fact that my relations with Betty were perfectly innocent, and could be proved so, was quite irrelevant. He would be horrified at the proving of it, and the scandal would be the talk of the town of Lockley.'

'What did you do?'

Milham thought before he answered.

'Nothing. I took it for granted that he would dismiss me and I would have to leave Lockley. So why explain? I could not look forward to explaining to the landlady, the office, and the neighbours. It was better to be dismissed and get it over. So I just said, "Yes, Mr. Follet; it's true I'm married." I waited for the blow to fall. He said, "Tell me why you lied to me." It took a moment to realise he was asking why I had said I was not married at the interview. I had lied saying I was married, so I had to invent something. "I got married since the interview, sir." "Why? If you intended that, you must have lied in spirit." "No sir. It was forced upon me." By then I had forgotten why I was lying. I think I was only concerned with making sense. I did not hope to convince him. I was only concerned with getting out. But he said, "Forced? How?" I said the obvious thing that came into my head. "She was pregnant, sir." He stared at me, and ummed and ahed. I wished he would get it over with. He said, "That was decent of you, under the circumstances, wasn't it?" "It was only what I would expect to do, sir." I hoped he would pay my salary if I said that. He said, "I like that, Milham. I think I like that."'

Brentford shook his head. The normal muddle and confusion of human life was not new to him, but the interview with Follet was exceptional. 'He let you stay on?'

Milham shook his head.

'I suddenly got the wild idea he might. Only almost immediately, he introduced conditions. He did not know they were conditions. He was helping me, like a good fatherly employer. "Let me see what we could do if I were to forgive you, Milham." "Oh, I would do anything if you were to forgive me, sir." I meant it, too. I must have sounded most convincing. "I'd have to give you a loan, you understand. Get you out of Lower River Street." I must have gaped. "A loan, sir?" He was sharp. "You don't think you can live in Lower River Street and work for me, do you?" "Oh, no, sir." "Then we will have to calculate, won't we, to see how much you need to furnish and establish yourself in a proper flat." Helplessly, I must have said, "Oh, yes, sir." "Come on," he said. "You're supposed to be an accountant. Work out the figures." So I did. I had to. He remembered items like a child's cot, a pram in proper style, maternity clothes, and conversely new clothes for Betty to go to church for the christening. It came to a staggering total. "Oh, you can't do this, sir," I said faintly. "Why not?" he asked me. "I pay your salary, don't I? I shall charge you interest. Regard me as your hire-purchase company. I shall stop it out of your salary, instead of increases, for the next three years." I was staggered. Three years. Desperately, I said, "I'll have to talk it over with my wife. It is a lot of debt." "Yes," he said. "You do that."'

Milham looked at Brentford as though he were again facing that point of agony.

'That's when you should have left,' said Brentford.

Milham looked helpless. 'To what?' he said. 'And where? Do you think I could have done better with some other employer, if I had gone to try elsewhere?'

Brentford would not have it. 'It was one thing,' he said, to move in with your sister, and tell a foolish story, to get a roof over your heads, for a night or two. But three years. You must have seen it was something you would have difficulty getting out of.'

'Difficulty!' said Milham, as though Brentford had not grasped it.

He stirred and shifted in his chair, which he had not done before. 'I was foolish enough to talk it over with Betty,' he said, like a dire confession.

In the silence of the night, Brentford made a sound that was half a sigh and half a wolf-whistle.

'Now don't run away with the idea that Betty wasn't solemn about it,' Milham said. 'It was just that the month we had been together had given her a new idea of companionship, of something higher, of facing life side by side, as she pointed out. She pointed it out, anyway. And her pregnancy was becoming noticeable, if not to other people at first glance, at least to herself. It made her feel different, she said, looking at me with big eyes. It was a change in her constitution, she thought, but she had previously only known in her mind that she was going to have a baby, and now she really felt it. And we must be practical. She was going to need all kinds of things now. She had got around to seeing it. A place to live, for a start, and bring up her baby. A place of our own, security, medical attention, comfort, maternity clothes for herself, and clothes for the baby, a high chair, a pram—she supposed that people did live without those things, somehow, if they had not got them, but she didn't know how. She had been feeling it rather desperately, she said, that she didn't know how. And now I was telling her that all these things were being offered to us, wonderfully, just as though we had been right to trust in fate or providence, knowing that something would turn up because it had to. But if we didn't take it—it wasn't that we actually had to do anything for it, was it, she said, not that we weren't doing already?—then could we feel that something would turn up again? Or did I really feel it? Could I really see any way out for us, she meant, practically, apart from this?'

'Women,' said Brentford, 'can be persuasive.'

'A woman facing the birth of her first child,' Milham said, 'can be very persuasive.'

'And so you succumbed?'

'Not at first, naturally. What do you think? I replied to her. I was sensible. I was more than sensible. I was scared. Also I was selfish enough to see that I too might have a point of view. I'm sure I said everything, or almost everything, that you could say to me now. Look, I said, all this was all very well. But *three years*. I managed to catch a glimpse of what it meant. Three years of living with your sister, as though that were not bad enough, in the same house, but living as man and wife! We might be arrested. We couldn't hope to keep it up. "Oh, really, Bill," she said, using her big eyes again, "how many married people have you met, even if they look more alike than we do, as many of them do, have you started wondering about, and thinking if they were brother and sister? It isn't that. You know there isn't the slightest danger that people will guess. If we sound alike that's only because we come from the same part of the country. It isn't that at all." Then she had an inspiration. It would be so much better in a flat, she said. Really. We could have separate rooms. And if we didn't take this chance, how could we get that? Or was I so tired of her company already, she said, with tears coming into her eyes, that I could no longer bear even that proximity? Did I want to get rid of her? Was I going to cast her out, was that what I really wanted, after all my promises? Her mood changed again. She would be good to me, she said. She would look after me as no young man had been looked after before. She wouldn't get in my way. She would see her baby didn't get in my way. It would be a good life for me. She would see to it that it was. And even from my own selfish point of view, unless I wanted to marry in the next three years, young as I was, how could I possibly do better?'

'That wasn't a good idea of hers,' Brentford said judicially, 'to mention that.'

'Oh, I don't know.' Milham seemed more dubious. 'Have you ever known any young man who thought of marriage in that way, as a prospect, like buying a new car, until he actually falls in love and decides to do it? And I was not thinking of marriage just then, believe me. I had too much on my plate already. I think it was a shrewd move. Not that Betty worked it all out, I'm still convinced of that. There was no theorising behind it, and hardly any thinking. That was to come later, when we had accepted, and made the great move into the flat, and life seemed one hundred per cent ordinary, the way it always does after six months of anything. Then she may have thought she had been right, which to all appearances she was, and started to do some thinking. But Betty was just my sister using a sister's knowledge of what I was thinking, feeling, and reacting to it. And she was right, you know. I was feeling the close physical proximity to her in a single room, and I didn't see any way out of that, not after I had taken her on, unless we took the flat. At times it made me quite uncomfortable. I was bound to feel that the flat was a kind of haven, at least some kind of a solution, and that was what I really felt, I think, when I saw Follet again, with my heart in my boots, the next day.'

Milham seemed to expect some expression of 'yes' or 'of course' from Brentford, but he did not get it.

On the contrary, Brentford sat silent in the room, studying the electric bar, as though noticing how it had become effective in the long run and slowly warmed up the air around them. Or perhaps he was thinking quietly that Milham talked too much.

It did seem, when Milham said he had accepted Follet's loan, as though he thought that things had come to a turning point, and that when Milham said 'six months' he might have said 'six years' or 'thirty years', though they had not talked of that yet.

'You accepted,' he said.

Milham said abruptly, 'Yes.'

'I suppose you are going to tell me,' Brentford said, 'that when the three years were up, or when your debt was repaid, since I can see that that might be a hindrance, something else arose, some other circumstance, equally binding and involuntary, that you could not escape from.'

Milham looked at him for a moment, then spoke with ironic grimness. They had reached a point now.

'It's kind of you to pass over those three years for me,' he said, 'the time I lived and worked, in debt to Follet, keeping my sister in the flat he arranged for us to get. It does save a lot of talk of practical details, such as how I was congratulated like any young husband, and teased in the office about my first-born. Or about how I talked with the neighbours about babies' nappies, and walking the floor at night with a crying child, and baby-foods. You don't exactly want to be harrowed with it, do you? Such things are done, as I know since I did them, and people survive even three years in a flat in Calwen Row, but I don't think you should take so much for granted.'

It was noticeable to Brentford that his voice had taken on a note of active bitterness, and one that had not been there before.

'What are you telling me?' he said in a voice he could only hope was not too unfeeling. 'What was the next step?'

Milham did not alleviate the tone that he was using.

'We had worked it out this way. Betty did the housework, of course, before and after the birth, in our flat in Calwen Row. I kept up a front at the office, having to appear to be the concerned and worried husband. It was not so difficult. You don't live in the same flat with a woman, before and after she has her baby, if she is your sister, and remain indifferent. Far from it. When we made public appearances together, with baby David in his pram, my pride was genuine, foolishly, as time went on. After all, if the child was not mine, the pram was, and its and its mother's clothes. I paid the rent.' His voice became top heavy.

'I only had to work hard at Follet's all the time, to pay for those things, and the loan, and live an impeccable private life. Not marry, as you said, and respond to Follet's paternalism and all his questions. And it was nearer four years than three, day to day, until I could see the end of it.'

Brentford said suddenly, 'You did see an end?'

'I lived for it,' Milham declared. 'After three years, you do. Four years, with the loan partly repaid and the child old enough to go to a nursery school, so that Betty could go out to work. Not in Lockley, of course. The time I dreamed of was when we could leave Lockley, I assuring Follet that I had got a better job, in London I hoped, but I would repay the rest of his loan in no time. While Betty went to Glasgow, or some point equally distant to the north or west or south. Just so long as Follet did not mention my "wife" in the reference he gave me, which he would have to give me, since it was that I had worked for, and that I would need to get the job. And provided that there was such a nursery school, where Betty could dump her child and go out to work. I had discovered that there was such a one in Glasgow. She would be a widow then. Or divorced. It would be a change for her, from what I was giving her, but I didn't really care what tale she told.'

Brentford said, 'What happened?' and Milham stared at him as though he knew, or ought to know, already.

'What do you think happened?' he demanded. 'You've heard. You must have heard. "My" children. And what do you think Betty was thinking? Four years she had lived as a respectable housewife, and for me the nightmare was ending. I came home one night. She wept. She was sorry, she said. But she was afraid we were going to have another child.'

CHAPTER XX

BECAUSE HE was given to mild expletives, Brentford thought, oh dear. He had not forgotten that Ethel had called him at the office to ask when he would be home for dinner.

To lean over a field gate by a country lane was the kind of thing mooning adolescents did, or old men who used it to rest their elbows and had nothing to think at all.

It was a misty pre-autumn evening, though it could hardly be called a sunset. Seen from the lane where he had stopped the car, a layer of smoke lay over the town, rising chiefly from the hosts of chimney pots, with television aerials, that were crowded in the valley bottom towards the river. His view of Lockley included the Secondary Modern School, higher up the slope, in an open space among slightly better houses. The centre of the town was partly obscured, like the court-house, the police headquarters, and the old-fashioned public library, by the turn of the hill. It was not even a very good view when seen from this route home.

But if he was going to think about crime in Lockley and try to fit Milham into it...

Crime in Lockley, to Brentford's mind, fitted into several quite definite patterns. The poorer houses, in the bottom of the valley, including Lower River Street where Milham had stayed three weeks, were the start of most of it. But that kind of crime, the most simple and the most prevalent, surely excluded Milham. Milham at least as he had heard of him from Follet.

Everyone, the probation officer, the social worker, and the police, who met occasionally at the court-house, knew how that kind of crime appeared in Lockley. A house in the valley bottom was of the kind without books, where conversation consisted of blows and four-letter words, and had either a drunken father or a broken home.

Brentford could see the small houses, the crammed roofs and television aerials in the valley bottom. And he could see, higher up the slope that faced him, the Secondary Modern school, in the style of school architecture of twenty years ago. By the time the son of one of those houses was walking up the hill to the school, he had been classified, tested, failed as an entry to the Grammar School which was across the town and out of sight (quite over the horizon as far as the boy was concerned), and had his I.Q. measured by methods that depended primarily on his ability to talk the teachers' language and read the questions and write the answers quickly. No premium on taking thought, and any boy who thought there were two possible answers to any questions was failed automatically.

It must be quite an experience, Brentford thought, looking into the valley, to realise, at twelve or thirteen, the time you were just becoming aware of yourself, that you were a bad boy, somewhere near the bottom of the C-stream, and that you were nothing and you were going to be nothing, all your life. Of course, if you were big enough or fast enough, you could take it out on society to begin with by being good at football or a playground bully. But if you weren't either big or fast or clever or beautiful ... Oh, well, there were other ways the educational system of Lockley could teach boys with spirit to be the out-and-out enemies of society, and none of them, specifically, from what he had heard, applied to Milham.

He shifted his gaze and lifted his sights a little. Not all Lockley was narrow streets and cottage slums. If Milham had begun there, he had presumably moved out fairly rapidly and with considerable elevation (three weeks; Brentford rather liked that), and either taken a flat in one of the larger houses that had been split up into flats towards Fairfield, or gone into one of the new slums of miniature houses and miniscule gardens of the early suburbs. One thing was certain, and that was that he had not gone straight from a furnished room in Lower River Street to a big house by the river over the low hills to the eastwards which Brentford could see by craning his neck a little, and that hid the view of Penlee.

There were lots of reasons why the clerk-type of individual, with a fixed and settled life and wife and children, should take to crime. No man necessarily had to go to the Secondary Modern school to do it, or to join those gangs who took their girls into the shadowy part of the car-park on Saturday night and who made the constables on the beat between the coffee bars and the dance-hall—Brentford could see the roof of the dance-hall—patrol in twos. An apprenticeship to criminality was useful, but not strictly necessary. Like the advertisements, not quite legible, on the railway hoardings over there. YOU TOO can step out of this narrow rut. Betting was the highroad. Oh, for heaven's sake, man, your mind told you, take a chance; just for once in your life do something big. The big bet, the one you could not afford. Well, all the people who got anywhere had to take risks sometime, didn't they? Pity it was necessary to borrow out the petty cash drawer, if not the safe, to keep things going. And the only way out was a bigger bet next time.

Brentford looked at the suburbs, which spread across the hillsides, and at the office centre of Lockley, which was on the curve of a fold of the valley, and to his right. He toyed with the idea. The sheer boredom and dullness of a clerk's lot, adding up figures for Follet. He, John Brentford, was not at all sure that he would not have taken to crime under those circumstances. This was life, and what the great world offered. Babies' nappies and narrow rooms and a flower bed three feet by five. Everything carefully insured, including your life. And the great work and objective of your existence was making neat columns of double entries for people who were duller than yourself. Damn it, your own wife had an infinitely more satisfying existence, risking pain and death every time she had a baby, and getting through it, and watching them grow up. Were you man or mouse? Was this the greatness and glory that Drake and the first Elizabethens had dreamed of, when they made England great?

Brentford was never puzzled why such people took to crime. He was only infinitely puzzled why they didn't. But Follet had shaken him with his final words. Milham had *not* been stuck in it. He had gone away to the war, and had better offers elsewhere after that, and he had come back of his own accord, so Follet said. That was what put Brentford out of countenance altogether, and kept him hanging over the gate, looking at Lockley in the fading light when he should have been going home. It was loyalty to Follet, Follet said, that brought Milham back. Or the prospect, for which crime was not necessary, of a good house by the river at Penlee, across those hills, which was an existence which would satisfy even Brentford or anyone with a philosophic frame of mind. But those were not criminal motives. Why, if Brentford knew anything about the criminal mind, or the near-criminal mind at all, the first thing it did, if it could, and even before it sold its soul to the devil, was to succumb to the Great Illusion, and head for the Big Smoke, the city grime, and relieve Brentford and his kind of a great amount of work. You did not actually say it, least of all if you were an immigrant to Lockley yourself, as Brentford was, that Birmingham and London, and similar smoke-cancerous names, and for that matter half the Americas, were populated by Lockley's rejects. Where the devil offered a better market, if a market, money, was all you wanted out of life. So therefore, why Lockley?

Brentford shook his head over it, over Lockley that was, from his position by the gate. He had formed the impression that Milham was a bright one, one of those who might well have made a fortune had he gone into a city. So why crime? That was the conclusion that Brentford had come to. That

Milham, since he had stayed in Lockley, had not needed to take to crime at all.

Unless, for example, he was being blackmailed.

CHAPTER XXI

MILHAM HAD produced a silence by his statement that his sister was to have another child.

'Oh, come,' said Brentford.

'I tell you,' said Milham. 'I tell you simply. We were in the clear, or almost. We had everything arranged, to leave Lockley. Then Betty told me.' He paused. He looked at Brentford as though Brentford might know. 'You don't think it was deliberate?'

Brentford's silence was enough to say that it was not for him to say that. Or to comment or judge in any way on a woman who he had only known and could only see through Milham's account of her.

Their chairs were turned to the electric bar. When Brentford looked at Milham, he was in profile, eyes fixed upon the glow, but he turned to Brentford.

'You understand what it meant?'

'You must have known that your sister, here in Lockley, was behaving in a way that might get her another child.'

'Behaving, yes. But do you think, when she had had one, I hadn't seen to it that she knew enough not to have another?'

Milham still seemed to feel it, and Brentford wore an expression as though it were something they had to stop and look at from all the angles.

He could not know if Milham thought that if he looked at it too long he might see it from too many angles. There were some things they had not yet talked about.

'My sister wasn't the girl I'd first found curled up on a bed in my parents' house,' Milham said suddenly. 'I've made that clear. She no longer thought that what she had done, having her first child, was a sin for which she was being punished, out of all proportion, by an outraged vindictive and jealous God. If she had ever thought like that. She had not looked as though she thought, only long-legged and pale, three years earlier when we had been walking round Lockley with the suitcases. And don't think she hadn't fitted into Lockley, and everything else, including my frame of mind, that there was for her to fit into.'

Brentford only listened.

'We had had three years, nearly four of domestic life. In the afternoons, while I worked in the office, earning the daily bread, she would put on her hat, and her neat coat, and the baby in the pram, and walk down to the local library. She read, you see. Previously, at home, she had read only moonlight-and-roses romances. But now she read what I read. I thought it would be good for her. When we read by the fireside, she would look up from her book, rock the cradle, and say, "Do you know about these tribes in Borneo, where women don't marry and leave home, but stay in their brothers' and parents' family houses and have babies by other men?" Her big eyes would look at me innocently. It really was all new to her. Or she would say, "What does this Russian, Dostoevsky, mean, 'All things are lawful'?"'

There was something peculiarly shattering about the picture of innocence that Milham painted.

Brentford's reaction was probably highly normal. He said, 'So you blame your sister?'

'I don't know,' Milham said. 'But wait till I tell you how she actually told me she was going to have another baby. I was an idealist, remember. I still had a capacity to be shocked by simple things. To me, theoretically, the English were in fact just another savage tribe, with tabus, and a day set aside each week to pray in churches to a God who did not exist. Yet I still had a tone of surprise in my voice when I talked to Betty in the evenings about things I was finding out. Like about a churchwarden, whose accounts we did, but whose rectitude was such that he behaved with the utmost ferocity to his slightest debtor. Like the common business tricks that I discovered. But I was tolerant. You have to understand that. It wasn't people's fault if they had these superstitions, like belief in England, or Russia, or Christ, or Buddha, or the universal solution to all problems that would come with Social Credit. Poor people, I used to think. I didn't even realise that implied I felt myself above them. Perhaps, do you think, that attitude of mind was enhanced by the way I lived with Betty?'

Brentford shook his head.

'You can tell me what you like,' he said hopefully. 'You are doing the telling.'

Milham's eyes, looking at him, did not seem to be greatly comforted.

'I had just come home from work,' he said. 'It was just an ordinary night, if you can call any night ordinary the way we were. But I was pleased it would soon be over. I was thinking I would go to London. I was sorry that Betty would have to go to Glasgow, where there was a nursery school into which she could put young David while she went out to work, as a working girl, but I didn't think too hard about that. I knew, of course, that it would be quite a change from the way she had lived at Lockley. She had, in fact, lived well in Lockley. She had had to, to look in all appearances like my proper wife. There is a lot of difference between being a comfortable, leisured young housewife, and being a young woman with a baby, whether she called herself divorced or widowed, who would work all day, shop for food when she could, and then fly to the nursery to get her child, and come home to spend the rest of the night looking after it while she made meals and did the housework. But perhaps I did not see the difference clearly enough, while Betty did.'

He looked at Brentford with a definite significance, while seeming to ask him what he thought of it.

'She must have been in a blue funk,' he said. 'After all, she had experienced it before. She had told something similar to our parents once. In my case, that night, she waited until I had eaten and we had moved to the fireside chairs with our coffee, and the child was in its cot. I couldn't guess then, and I can't now, how far what she had to tell me was the result of events that were intentional. Do you know how it is when you dread a thing, and still let it happen, because you can see it is for your benefit in the long run? But it was there, and she had to screw herself up to tell me. "William," she said. "We can't change it now; this is something that is going to happen. I am going to have another baby".'

He looked at Brentford solemnly.

'I am afraid my reactions were quite orthodox,' he said, 'and not at all enlightened, and exactly what you would expect. Within five minutes I had reduced her to tears, of course. But she must have been expecting that. What she may not have been expecting, and what I think is a little odd, when I think of it now, is the way I went on and on.'

Milham frowned, and looked earnest, though he had a slight air of incredulity though talking about himself.

'I saw it in a very ordinary way,' he said. 'You'd be surprised how ordinary. What I found myself saying, though I had not really thought of it that way before, was, "Not me for Joe Muggins this time." I was a little shocked by that. It was obviously unfair. Betty had not asked me to look after her and solve her problems for her first child. But none the less that was the line I took, while she wept and looked at me with surprise, and then with a look like the ones she must have given my parents the first time. I raised my voice. To Glasgow she was going, I said, and to Glasgow she would go. "Or Siam or China, for all I care." I had had enough. My life was not to be wholly ruined by my sister. I had to live my own life. Somehow, the feeling seemed to build up in me. I became desperate and called her names, obscene names, such as she could not have imagined would ever pass between us, and which made her cover the child's ears. She was a bitch, a whore. It was a dreadful scene. Her look of surprise remained. She gathered up the child and ran off into her bedroom.'

It was not for nothing that Milham had fixed his eyes on Brentford.

'Around midnight, finding her door unlocked, I went into her room to renew the contest.'

Brentford listened expectantly to the bedroom scene.

'You can't guess what it was like,' said Milham. 'Even I, in a way, was shocked by it, though knowing her I was prepared a little. But I had not seen her in that nightdress before, transparent like a halo, with the bedside light behind her, arranged to shine on her golden hair. It was like a set-piece from the silent film days. Only something, somehow, had slipped past the censor. It looked like the grand seduction. As it appeared in a highly ingenious but not very experienced woman's mind. Only you should have heard the way she talked.'

He seemed to wonder how to convey the sense to Brentford.

'I admit I was overwhelmed a little. I am not sure quite why I had gone in there. To attack her physically perhaps. But that wasn't something I could risk, even if she was my sister, with her in that bed like that. I mean, I would be lost entirely. She pointed to the bed. "Sit here with me, Bill." I remonstrated. "We can't go on like this. Just look at you!" I said. "Now, Bill," she said. "Just come here and talk sensibly." If anything had been arranged to make sensible talk impossible, it was what she had done, but she said talk sensibly. "It won't do!" I suddenly said, outraged. She looked up at me innocently, as though everything were not so obvious through her transparent nightdress. "But that's it, isn't it?" she said. "What do you mean?" I said. "Well, if I went away," she said, as though there were no thought of that. "But you must!" I said. "There'd be talk, wouldn't there?" she said. "I mean someone would have to help me to have the baby, wouldn't they? And they ask questions, don't they?" I stared. "And we have been living together, night after night, like this, haven't we?" she said.'

Milham looked sad. 'I think my face was something like a fish,' he said. 'And I did then what I should have done in the first place. I went back to my room, and thought.' He looked at Brentford.

'I see,' said Brentford.

'You don't,' said Milham. 'You can't. Not on one telling.' He seemed convinced. 'I was still a very young man. I had my life before me. You can't realise.'

'You had rather put your head in the noose,' Brentford said. 'Perhaps this is why brothers don't usually do it, cover up their sister's mistakes by acting as man and wife.'

'I saw it on a kind of gaudy scale,' said Milham.

He did indeed look at the electric heater as though he saw something in the glowing reflections of its distorting mirror.

He spoke earnestly.

'I have told you how I saw life,' he said. 'Innocent people. Even around us there in Lockley. Credulous people, all over the country. I don't know if you can understand all this. The innocent pity of innumerable people, all living their little lives. Living according to moral standards that were virtually accidental. But keeping them very badly, and blaming themselves for sin. Gods and demons. All believing their country was the greatest, and that their way of life alone was right, irrespective of which it was. Being cheated, and cheating in turn. Monogamy or polygamy according to the fashion of their place and time. Not reasoning. Not even knowing, ninety-nine-point-nine per cent of them, what reason or logic was. But living their lives traditionally, and so without them. I had felt superior; you have to understand that. I'd been out of it, and somewhere up above it, because I knew modern science and mathematics. You see, I knew that the stars were suns, and that there were galaxies and stars beyond them. Our portion of the universe was incredibly tiny. Even if there were a God, he could not be concerned with us. I had grown up to know all this, to see it. Yet not one thousandth of one per cent of the people on earth knew it. Not to feel it, as I did, as common knowledge. You don't know. You don't know the extent to which I, with a half-baked education, but because I had at least some education, because I had educated myself despite the schools I went to, had seen myself as being above, apart.'

Brentford felt mildly concerned for Milham, who appeared moved.

'I think you are dramatising it a little,' he said.

'I am not! I assure you. I was only human too. It was an awful feeling. I didn't know where I was for a while, sitting in my bedroom, thinking. All kinds of childish ideas moved in my mind. Perhaps I had done something awfully wrong by living with my sister and calling us man and wife. I had sinned in some way, and I could not say what. All kinds of fanciful ideas became true to me. Betty, my sister, had sinned. That had been the beginning. She had become a Fallen Woman. Only now could I realise how fallen. But I, by touching pitch, had become defiled. There were the incongruities of half a dozen moral standards running around in my head. I think if my mother and father had turned up then, bringing a priest with them, I might have listened to them. Except that they would still not have been able to talk my language, nor have known that other standards were possible, except the one. I felt absurdly lonely, grieving for the lack of some intellectual mentor I had never had. Then that feeling passed. Like a kaleidoscope, I changed again.'

Milham held out a hand, as though demonstrating a grave temptation.

'I became a Machiavelli. All life, I suddenly saw, was evil. I had had evidence enough of that at work. I knew Lockley businessmen's ethics, even if they were churchwardens. No matter what they did on Sundays. Probably the priests themselves, in their pulpits, did not believe, not really or practically, in their miracles and after life. Not in the way they knew how to drive a car. Life was all a pretence, designed to fool the multitudes and to support the gross, inflated body of a wealthy church. Make-believe, like the politicians' stories, which they must laugh about at international conferences, where, as a statesmen, they could not possibly believe in the kind of jingoistic nonsense that was strictly for home consumption. But it was not people who did not believe, and who said they did not believe, that got on in this world. It was the hypocrites, the ones who maintained a pretence, as savage and self-seeking as it was vulgar. The showmen and the sanctimonious bastards. Old Follet, for example, for I put him in that class. I was nothing if not thoroughgoing. Learning itself, I thought, rising to its pyramids in the universities. What kind of a searching after truth could there be, when the scholars from a Christian university met those from a Moslem one, and both remained unshaken in the faiths demanded of them by the sponsors who endowed their colleges? You wouldn't think, would you, that a young man's brain could contain such wealth, and such a variety of thoughts and revelations, just because his sister told him she was going to have another baby?'

'And had said, implicitly, that if necessary she would name him as its father,' Brentford said.

'Yes, there was that,' said Milham, gloomily.

He remained quite still, half sitting and half lying in his chair for a lengthy moment.

'Evil won,' he said. 'I have to confess to you. I would not, believe me, if there was any way, without confession, that I could explain what happened later. But perhaps you would see it anyway, since Betty was using me, under that intellectual statement of "all things are lawful", to bring up her children. Why not? Why not be evil and enjoy it? It was only a matter of degree, after all. If other people were bad, I could be worse. There had been an error in the intellectual thinking on which I had based my life. I did not believe in God or conventional morals. I have been clear about that. I was a freethinker, one of those idealistic, mildly liberal-minded young men. You will still find them, though they are mostly aged forty or fifty or sixty now, among the men of good will in the vaguely academic circles of any town. But there is an error in their thinking. They don't believe in God or all the myths, as they quietly think of them, of the Christian church, but they have still retained the love, the sympathy and the pity, that was taught to them, through religion, in their childhood. They fail to see that there is no need for that. Intellectually, they are adult, but emotionally they are still children. Only I grew up. It seemed to me that I grew up, emotionally, in a single night.'

Brentford did not reply at once. He was not sure if Milham had become guarded in what he was saying, or if there was some actual difficulty about it involving as it did, 'confession', or if he claimed his sister had corrupted him.

'What do you mean?' he said.

Milham was very still.

'That must have been what Betty wondered when she found me quite normal and outwardly composed next day at breakfast,' he said. 'I can see now, though I could not see then, why it made her more nervous than all my shouting and raving of the night before. She tried, two or three times, to revive the subject of our conversation the previous night. "Bill, I want to say—" she said over the breakfast table. A look of mine froze her. She tried again. "Bill, I'd never harm you. Really—" My eyes must have come round to her, asking her a silent question, for she said, "It's only I wondered if I could lie well enough, tell a story well enough, if I was on my own." She seemed to be pleading, yet the substance of what she said showed she had not recanted. Looking at me, she suddenly went pale. "Bill, say something!" she said. I got up to leave the table to go to work. As I passed her, she drew back and flinched. It was her own movement that made me suddenly snatch and grab her arm above the wrist. She screamed, and fell to the floor. I stood over her. Then I stood back: I had not hurt her. "Bill, please!" she screamed. I did not raise my voice. Her guilt was obvious. "Things are going to be a little different, you'll see," I said. She wept, remorsefully. "We'll do it your way," I said. "But things will be a little different now." I went to work, walking to the office and thinking, but leaving her there weeping on the floor.' He thought. 'I wept a little.'

Milham's gaze dropped, as though he could see his sister there on the floor between them and the electric bar.

'Things were different,' he said. 'I haven't known it personally, not in any other young man, of intelligence and with everything in his favour, and a universe in his mind, that he has set out to defeat the world that betrayed him, and to be deliberately and methodically bad before.'

CHAPTER XXII

BLACKMAIL, BRENTFORD thought.

He was considering it as he put the car away. While he had been listening to Follet, he had been sure that Milham had intelligence. But such a man could not defeat a blackmailer. If only he could discover what Milham had been blackmailed for. In a way, it increased his problems instead of solving them. But he thought of it. He thoughtfully closed the garage door, looked at the garden in the twilight, and then went in, into the cottage.

He glanced at Ethel standing by the stove as he passed through the kitchen. She had her back to him and was dealing with a pan, which was what she usually found to do when she heard his car, but it crossed his mind that for someone doing that she was unusually smartly dressed. As he went through without turning, she remarked, 'You're late.'

She had been out to the Red Cross, he remembered as he went to the living room. He did not think she usually dressed like that for the Red Cross. In the living room, he switched on the light and partly drew the curtains. 'You know I always say I'm sorry.'

Her voice came from the kitchen equably. 'I phoned you at the office.' He was glad it was equable.

'I went to see a man.'

'What man?'

'Follet of Follet and Milham. I didn't know if he would be in.'

He turned to speak to her in the kitchen, but found her coming in with two bowls of soup. It was faster service than she usually managed, and he raised his eyebrows at her. She smiled as though that kind of thing was easy to anyone who was thoroughly competent, and they went to the table and sat down.

'Is the case going well?'

'No.' He was surprised by the definiteness of his own answer, but perhaps, he thought with mild appreciation, anyone who could produce a meal on time, without knowing what time ought to be told at least a little of the truth.

'Would you like to tell me about it?'

'Not much.'

'Not even when I'm interested?'

It was good soup. Perhaps it was that which made a difference. 'I went to see Follet to talk to him about Milham,' he said. 'It was probably a little rash.'

'Rash in what way?'

'It's pretty obvious that he'll phone Milham, isn't it? Tell him the police have been inquiring about him. I told him a nice story about how it was better for his firm if he didn't alert Milham until I spoke to him, but you know what that means. Only that he'll tell Milham not to say he told him.' Brentford found himself convinced of it on second thoughts.

Ethel broke a piece of bread while giving him flattering attention. 'And is that at all important?'

Was it? Brentford was unsure.

'It depends on what Milham does. If he packs a suitcase and leaves a note saying "Fled the country" it's all in order. The worst thing he can do is phone someone, say the Chief Constable, and say calmly, "I hear you have been making inquiries about me. I am surprised, but can I be of any possible assistance? I'd be glad to help" That would be awkward since I'm fairly sure Parker has kept the Chief in ignorance that this case is even going on.'

'I see,' said Ethel.

'You don't,' said Brentford. She could not since he had not told her. 'Not even Parker would actually want to get Simpson sacked. The Chief would listen to Parker with growing consternation. "Why wasn't I told?" Parker's only possible answer would be that he didn't want to run with tales to the Chief about Superintendent Crosston. Which is just what the Chief would want him to do. And about Tapman and McIvor. Parker's position is liable to become untenable. I doubt if he will be really nice to me.' He hoped Ethel would grasp why he did not usually tell her about office politics.

'Poor John,' Ethel said, and collected up the soup plates. She took them to the kitchen and made cheerful sounds from there. 'Your Chief Constable always seems such a nice man,' she said.

'Is he?' said Brentford to the kitchen door.

'Well he is, isn't he?' Ethel's voice held slight doubt. 'Such a moral man. Making speeches about Prevention of Crime, Relations of the Police with the Public, and Clean Up T.V. That's what they appoint them for, isn't it?' Rattling the refrigerator door, she seemed to suggest that everyone would try to get a Chief Constable who would wash whiter than the next man's.

'It isn't quite like that,' Brentford told the kitchen. 'Speeches within the force, as well as outside. "The prevalence of the Abominable Crime." Very moral, of course. The importance of keeping an eye on men who dress in a certain way. Every man is expected to do his duty. Then he goes out and pays particular attention to the physical appearance of young constables on the beat as though he suspected them. It can be unnerving.'

A slight laugh from Ethel indicated that she realised that this seemed a night for revelations. She came in with two dishes of something done in aspic. 'Sex worries him?' she said. 'That kind of sex?'

Brentford looked at the aspic which was one way of producing a dinner on time without knowing when. 'All sex worries all Chief Constables,' he said, getting away from personalities. 'It is a particular hazard of spending your life in a disciplined and largely male force that also makes moral claims. But it is not so much that.' He watched Ethel sit down. 'It's that he worries other people.'

Ethel looked unusually thoughtful. She produced a new version of the lunch-time salad without apology. She seemed to hesitate a moment. 'Would it do any good,' she said out of the blue, 'if your Chief Constable knew there was something, shall we say sexually notable, about your Mr. Milham?'

Brentford had picked up his knife and fork. He put them down again. He looked at Ethel and considered how a general conversation had suddenly taken a plunge into the particular.

'Notable?' he said. 'Milham?'

She was busy moving things around the table. It might have been chance, or mere perversity, that she did not look at him.

'Answer the question, John.'

'Yes,' he said in a careful voice. 'It would make a difference. It is unkind. But if Parker could tell the Chief that Milham was a sexual deviant, the question of inadequate proof of murder might be largely academic.'

'I don't think people should be like that, do you?' she said, concerned.

Watching her eat, he said, 'Does it occur to you that you might not be like this?'

She had been to the Red Cross, he thought. He could even remember asking her—not that she seemed likely to take too much notice—to keep her ears open. Then she phoned the office.

She ate placidly. 'Though I'm not sure it would be in the way you think,' she said.

'That's nice, that you know so much,' he said. 'While I don't.'

'I don't know,' she said. 'I only think.'

Presumably, he thought, she had some reason to think. He looked at Ethel's face and hair and wondered if that followed. He wondered if it was conceivable that she was just guessing, like she tried to make it appear she was.

'What is this?' he said.

'You're the detective, John, not me,' she said.

'I don't know,' he said. 'I don't see why I should be a detective with regard to my own wife. It might be thought unnecessary. Some people might think so.'

It gave her thought while they ate the aspic.

'I thought we might go out tonight, John.'

That was fine, he thought. He watched her getting up to remove the plates again.

He had forgotten one or two things. In addition to going to the Red Cross and phoning him at the office, she was also dressed in a way that he now realised was preparation for going out, and dinner had been on time, when to have it on time must have been almost quite impossible.

'In connection with William Milham?'

She stacked the plates gravely. 'In connection with land,' she said. 'Do you know Frazer, the Penlee architect? I had a word with Lucy Frazer, his wife, today. I don't think I'd quite realised who she was before. She gave me some information about building land in Penlee.'

They had talked about Follet, Milham, the Chief Constable, sex, Milham again, and now about land in Penlee.

'There is no building land at Penlee. You aren't allowed to build.'

Ethel took time out from the plates to look at the clock. She was not in a great hurry, just a moderate one.

'You could on this. The plans were already passed.' She glanced at him. 'I did say to Lucy that we might possibly go round to see them.'

Somehow, from her attitude perhaps, as she stood by the table, he derived that then she had phoned him at the office.

'Where?' he asked.

'Where? Where what? Oh, you mean the Frazers?'

'Yes.'

'At Penlee.'

He wondered how he had guessed that it might be that or something like that. Like a Greek play, he thought, where you knew the end before the beginning. Who said a man's dinner table conversation with his wife should be like that? But perhaps it was not, he thought as she began to move calmly of towards the kitchen, except with Ethel.

He could be equally enigmatic. He got up and headed on across the room. He said, 'I've got to make a phone call.'

CHAPTER XXIII

'It isn't easy to be thoroughly evil,' Milham said seriously 'Oh, we all think it is. We travel through our lives in an imagined glow, of virtue and self-congratulation. "I don't steal from the petty cash," we tell ourselves. "And only last Sunday when my neighbour wanted to borrow the garden shears, I passed them across the hedge, though I knew he could buy his own." '

He looked at Brentford as though he felt a concern for him

'You should try it yourself, Inspector. It's the only way you can cease to confuse evil with mere stupidity, the way you policemen and judges do. Wake up one morning and tell your self that you will be wholly bad that day. Selfishness and self interest will rule your actions. Do you know what will happen? By evening you will find you have done no differently from any other day. The difference will be that you have met that stranger who is yourself.'

He went on looking at Brentford for a moment, and then looked around the room where they sat, and at the garden door by which they had entered, the glass in which was black with the night outside. His story was coming nearer, he seemed to say, as it was bound to come nearer as he went on with it. Then he looked back at Brentford.

'What I did with Betty,' he said, 'was to bring her here, to Penlee.'

For a moment Brentford looked back at Milham and wondered if he had heard correctly. 'I thought Penlee had been built almost entirely in the last twenty years,' he said. He too looked at the room in which they sat. 'This time of which you are speaking is before the war?'

Milham nodded, resting his elbow on the arm of his chair and looking at Brentford. 'It was because there was virtually nothing here that our move from Lockley to Penlee before the war was most effective. I was early, you see. I had heard something at a business conference that I attended, or rather to which I took a set of accounts from Follet's.'

There was something in his look which said that that was not all it was.

'When I say I brought Betty here, to Penlee in those days, when there were heavy woods along both the rivers, and a narrow lane running down here, to the fisherman's cottages on the point, I don't mean she came willingly,' he said. 'I have told you the kind of girl that Betty was. She liked to wear her pretty clothes, go to the library, and then push a pram up High Street, looking at shop windows, until she came to the café, where I knew she often had afternoon tea with other young housewives, but where I had not known she also met her men friends.'

Brentford considered Milham. 'I am not sure whether you are saying you did this as some kind of land speculation or business deal,' he said, 'or as something to punish your sister. Was it to make money, or as revenge for moral blackmail?'

Milham had looked at the garden door again, and this time Brentford too looked at it, thinking of the verandah just outside it, the garden and the woods, through which they had come when entering the house.

Milham and his sister and Penlee, he thought, and wondered how closely their stories were connected. He began to have a feeling about that, a presentiment.

'You haven't taken my talk about evil sufficiently seriously,' Milham said. He turned back from the garden door without haste. 'Perhaps you aren't accustomed to it, even as a police inspector.' He looked thoughtfully at Brentford. 'I imagine when people confess to you they admit "I did this or that". But they don't normally tell you, I imagine, that they did it with the deliberate aim of so altering their character and view of life that they were worse than the next man.'

His eyes narrowed, looking at Brentford.

'There was something else, as well as business and revenge, you see,' he said. 'By moving Betty out into the country, which this place then was, I could live a much freer life in Lockley. Have you thought of that too? For four years I had striven to look like a domesticated young man, little David's father and Betty's much-married husband. But I now saw that even in business, because of the way businessmen look at things, that was not wholly to my advantage. And if I intended to change my character in that respect, and live more in the style of the instigators of the Penlee development plan, who were liable to betray their wives occasionally, it was better to do it with the wife not right on the doorstep.' He looked at Brentford as though Brentford might guess what he meant by that.

'I see,' said Brentford; and Milham, this time, did not contradict him or say that Brentford did not see at all.

On the contrary, he seemed to think that Brentford had understood more than he had actually said. 'People do see things,' he said irrelevantly. 'They are quick to grasp a point like that.' But his eyebrow moved. 'Except the people most concerned. When I told Betty that the Calwen Row flat was too small for us, and that we simply had to go into the country, much as she regretted it, she thought at first that it was for purely financial reasons.'

Brentford waited a moment then said, 'What did you move into? How did you do it, move to Penlee before Penlee was built?' He watched Milham look more thoughtful in response to his factual question.

Milham quite visibly considered what he should say about this part of his life. But he was, though careful when he spoke, as factual as Brentford had asked him to be.

'I turned up at the Calwen Row flat with a car one day. Betty didn't understand at first. It was a little time after I had threatened her, when we had talked of her second child. Perhaps she thought that that had quite blown over.' His expression made it clear it had not.

'I went in and told her, "Come and look at my car." She

looked a shade foreboding. "How did you get it?" We were in the street then. "On credit," I told her. "I have also bought a country cottage and quite a bit of land." She began to understand then.'

He looked at Brentford as though it was something that Brentford might or should appreciate.

'I told her, "The two things go together." I mentioned that I'd had a talk with Follet about the addition to our family. I had talked to him of our need for a bigger house. "And, to be big enough, and if we were to afford it, it would have to be in the country," I told her. "He helped me to get a mortgage." She stood looking at me. She knew I had never done a thing like that without consulting her before. "Get in the car and I will take you to see the new house," I said. She was even a little reluctant to come to see it. I had to dress and fetch young David.'

To judge by the particularity and clarity with which Milham told his story, he remembered it in detail, although he said it was only a symptom of other things.

'Betty had not been down the river valley to Penlee before,' he said. 'I saw her looking about her as we went, at the open and then the wooden country, which, although it was not so far from the town, looked miles away from anywhere. "What about main water and electric light?" she suddenly asked me. I said, "There's a well and oil lamps, and from now on that is all we can afford." I was surprised she made no answer. When we reached the fishermen's cottages you spoke about, and drove past them, I saw that her expression was tinged with horror. From the point, we drove up this river, over quarter of a mile of what was then an unmade, rough woodland road. There was a woodman's cottage at the end of it, on more or less this spot, and when I stopped the car, Betty looked at it. "I don't like it," she said, and then, "Bill, you can't expect me to live in that."'

Milham had moved his eyes from Brentford when he had referred to the spot where the house was, and he looked at the surroundings of his present house again, and at the garden door. When he resumed, it was methodically, but while looking at a corner of the carpet, speculatively.

'I told Betty that the tumbledown cottage was only temporary,' he said. 'While we stood in the circle of trees looking at the overgrown garden and the roof, I said that if what I had heard on my inside information was true, we would sooner or later be able to sell a portion of the land, and build a house here. She did not seem to think that that would compensate for the problem of bringing up children in such a place and drawing water from a well.'

He glanced at Brentford as though surprised.

'When we looked inside, she found it much worse, it seemed. She cried out with horror when she saw beetles in the kitchen. For some reason the cottage interior seemed to move her to a great emotion. But it was not only that. She pointed out of the window, to the view of trunks of trees. "And I will be a prisoner!" she said. "I'll be tied down here to the children unless you take me somewhere in the car." I expressed astonishment. "But that's what you want, isn't it, for me to look after you? That's what you wanted when you decided to have a second child?" She stared at me, then she began to cry, not silently, but with loud complaints.'

Milham looked as though he wondered if Brentford understood his sister's reaction to her first view of the cottage.

'It was no better when we moved in,' he said. 'She asked me why I had cut down on the household expenses, why I didn't take her out more, and why I kept her short of money. For a long time, though always as though it were a new horror, she was asking me why I kept her short of this and that, and most of all of clothes. It was a constant plea. My reasonable answers, that the car was a new expense, and that she hardly needed pretty clothes in a cottage where, as she said herself, she never saw anyone, seemed hardly to convince her. She seemed convinced that I was doing these things to her purposely, with some frightening intention, and as a result, instead of getting used to the cottage, for a long time she seemed to hate it more.'

He looked thoughtful, with the detached, expository air of a man telling a story of an unreasonable woman.

'It affected her a little in odd, unexpected ways,' he said. 'She began to see something sinister in even the simplest things.

Even natural phenomenon, which she should surely have got used to, even though she was not accustomed to living in the country. She would come across the head of the stairs and appear in my bedroom in moonlight, dramatically in her nightdress at dead of night. "What is that noise?" I had to tell her to go to sleep, and that it was only the sound of wind in the trees. With the wind in another direction, it would be, "What is that lapping sound?" It was the sound of wavelets, I had to tell her, of water in the river. But she needn't be afraid. The river had always been like that, and we were well above it. A third time when she appeared in my bedroom, in the early hours of the morning, I could not hear anything. "What is it now?" She was staring out of my window, with the faint light behind her, in her nightdress again, against the stars. "It is the silence," she said. She was annoyed when I told her she was unreasonable. For a time she conducted a woman's campaign against me. Making a plea of the inadequacies of the cottage kitchen, she saw to it that none of my meals were on time, and all of them were spoiled. The result was that, since it suited my convenience when doing other things, I stayed away from home a night or two. That terrified her, apparently, and she spent the nights she told me, barricaded with David in the farthest bedroom.'

Milham stopped speaking and looked away reflectively, as though he could end for a while at that point, and Brentford said, 'What other things?'

Milham looked up at him as though that were a pertinent question, and thought a moment.

He spoke as though he were talking of something different and entirely new. 'What do the police think of it?' he asked, and thought what he was going to say. 'The fact that it's quite well known that there's always an inner ring of businessmen in a town like Lockley?'

Brentford tried to think what he meant. 'An inner ring?'

'Solicitors,' Milham said with a glance. 'Surveyors, county councillors, even sometimes an accountant. The kind who, when they die, always leave far more than they could possibly have earned in their whole life in fees.' He gave Brentford a frank look. 'You can't spend all your time, apart from headline

cases, chasing motorists. Even if they have killed their wives
and children and wrecked their cars, even your people must
doubt sometimes one would imagine, the utility of prosecut-
ing them in the way you do.'

Brentford was not willing to indulge in the public's favourite
sidetrack. 'What are you saying,' he said, sticking strictly to
the point, 'about this Lockley inner ring?'

Milham moved himself uncomfortably in his chair. 'Only
that over the years I had become aware of it. That all the real
money in the town was concentrated in a few hands. And that
working for Follet, Follet being what he was, was not the ideal
springboard to get into it.'

Brentford could not say anything to that. He intimated that
Milham would have to tell him.

'Mostly friends of your Chief Constable of the time,'
Milham said, still looking at him in a particular way. 'You
know how it is. These most respectable of Lockley men are
usually on the Watch Committee. Your Chief Constable of the
time was very strong against vice and prostitution. There were
three women in Lower River Street he used to have brought in
to see him every Saturday, and the Watch Committee upheld
him in his moral line.'

Mentally, Brentford had a slight swimming sensation when
sitting in Milham's room in Milham's chair. It was only temporary, but it was as though the hard realities of life had bent
a little.

Milham went on as though he had not noticed Brentford's
delay or silence. 'I told you I was interested in certain people,'
he said. 'To reach Councillor Hobson and what we might call
Lockley's inner ring of businessmen, I was not so well situated
in Follet's office. Follet himself was the kind of old-fashioned
accountant who would have preferred suicide to tipping off
someone like Hobson that this or that local firm was in a state
of precarious financial health. Very proper, of course. And such
propriety could be useful, if I were not myself attached to it
and could make use of it. But I myself had to appear in a
slightly different guise. I have suggested to you that the kind
of men who would interest Hobson and his circle would be
those who might have, should we say, the slightly flattened

face of a boxer, young men in difficulties in other words, which Hobson and his people usually were themselves.'

Brentford looked at Milham as though he were doing a thin-ice act, which he was, even though the time he was referring to was so long ago.

'That is one of the reasons, just one of them, why, to Betty's horror, I used to stay away from the cottage occasionally, and not come back at nights,' said Milham. 'The other was the obvious. Almost as soon as we had moved to the cottage, I had done something I had been wanting for a long time. I have told you about the girl in our outer office, the one who had denounced me to Follet, and she, all the time I had been be-having so well, had been chipping away at me, making double-edged remarks about Betty, and pretending to sympathise with me about my too-early and expensive marriage as though she had got out of Follet what he knew about it. It was almost by the way that I got my revenge on her. With Betty out of the way, I pretended I could reveal my hand, letting her know that it was only because it was that my wife was very jealous that I had not previously been able to reveal my love for Patricia, as her name was. I was sure she was not in love with me, but then pure spite, other people's pure spite, was at this time one of the motives I liked most to work with.'

'What are you telling me?' Brentford said, temporarily at a loss, but looking hard at Milham.

'That I invented work that would take me and this girl to an hotel fifty miles from Lockley for a night. I am illustrating my new outlook on life and people. It was precisely because her motives were not love that I wanted to go to bed with her. She blushed when I came into the office on Monday morning, took deeply to religion after one night, and took to keeping a prayer-book on her desk, to read when I came in.'

Brentford stared at Milham as though he were tantalising him or being exceptionally perverse.

'One of Follet's clients was a young widow whose husband had died a year ago and whose business affairs we handled,' Milham said. 'With the car. I was able to visit her, and after business have tea with her, in her country home. "I have an unhappy married life," I told her sadly. "I suppose your wife misunderstands you?" she asked me with a smile. "No," I said. "As a matter of fact, my problem is that my wife has had a lover." Have you noticed, Inspector, that to seduce a good woman, you must assure her that her motives are very good?'

Brentford shook his head, though it was not exactly in answer to Milham's question. He had not noticed.

'She was quite shocked to hear that a young man like me was married to a woman who took a lover,' Milham said. 'She asked me if I was going to get a divorce, and I said I was thinking of it, but I was thinking of the children. I could see she was thinking of the effect of broken homes on little children. "But my wife and I have different bedrooms," I told her. "I don't think I can endure that indefinitely." She looked at me and saw that I was a personable young man, and she thought how I might be enabled to endure it. Now that became a long-lasting association that lasted for many years.'

Brentford's and Milham's eyes met, and abruptly they both fell silent, with a stare between them.

Milham moved a little in his chair, and no longer seemed wholly comfortable in it. He began to speak again, but he did so as though just dismissing, and getting out of the way, a minor matter.

'My widow was not discreet. She told her friends at a Lockley tea shop my story about Betty. The result was that one day when Betty was working in the cottage, bare-legged, in a torn skirt, with soot on her face from the stove, her hands roughened by the pails and working at the well, and wearing a blouse that happened to be so thin as to be barely decent, she found the Vicar at the door. He had come to have a serious talk with her, he said, about constancy in marriage, and virtue, and wifely duties. And he wondered, when she had heard what he was talking about, why this odd young woman in the woods should become hysterical.'

Brentford still confined himself to looking at Milham in a way that was expectant, as though what Milham was saying was not what he expected or thought to hear.

'Well,' said Milham, looking away. 'That was just one result.'

The silence came back and lasted a little time.

'I couldn't do what I wanted to do in Lockley by working apart from Follet's office,' Milham said suddenly. 'As a result, I had to drag Follet's office along with me. I hope it's long enough ago to tell you. The way I worked with Councillor Hobson and his crowd was to make information available to them from all the files. They had got it at last, the message that I was the kind of young man who might do that, for money.'

Brentford spoke solidly, 'What were you doing?' It sounded like a question that had to have an answer.

Milham fixed his gaze on a spot about a foot over Brentford's head.

'I can tell you because it never happened,' he said. 'I had worked hard to get the information. I had to appear to be one kind of young man to one person, and another to another. I'd got the gem of information first, before even I bought a delapidated cottage and an acre of unproductive woodland, that Penlee was to be developed. Hobson was to get it through the council. His brother-in-law the contractor was to get the roads and works. Two conveyancing solicitors and their special clients were to get the land that was to be turned overnight into building plots. Two builders were to be specified in the deeds when the land was sold, under a specified architect, and they, it so happened, who were to "guarantee the style and quality", were going to build at least one house for Hobson. It was a typical building development, in other words, on a basis of you-scratch-my-back-and-I'll-scratch-yours. No loose money passing around, you notice. No rude words like bribes, or cheques that could be later traced. And I was just the office boy, who, because he had been useful, and had had the effrontery to buy himself a piece of land, had had to be counted in, on the outer fringes.'

Milham's gaze dropped and reached Brentford's face.

'Most young men would have been satisfied with that,' he said regretfully. 'It was an apprenticeship, as you can see it was, to orthodox, respectable business life in Lockley. All I was expected to do was to provide information on alternative tenders and offers, and the resources behind them, from Follet's files. Then I would be in. I would be tried and tested, and one of the respected inner ring of Lockley businessmen from that time forward. Only I wasn't satisfied with that. What I was doing was journalism, if you want to call it that. I was keeping a file on the whole transaction, in the finest detail. And at a given moment, that was coming fast, I would make the existence of this file known. To put it bluntly, what I would want from everyone concerned, not to pass my file on to the police and local newspapers, was a sum of money. I could see a glorious future before me. I would leave Lockley suddenly and for ever more. The more so as my project of taming Betty by keeping her in the cottage was ultimately failing. She was no longer objecting to it. She had even begun to like it, like some maenad in the woods. I could not understand her, but I did not have to. I estimated that with a thousand here and two thousand there, I would have ten thousand in my pocket altogether, and depart for London or Birmingham, or at any rate for the fields of high finance, where I could pursue my course of evil and malevolence in pastures new. Betty could keep the cottage. I would bequeath it to her, while I entered the international world of service flats, servants minions, property tycoons and yachts, amenable girls like nymphs, and no doubt the ultimate of a villa in the south of France. And who knows? It might have worked.'

Milham stared at Brentford in a way that, in recollection at least, expressed a tortured longing, while Brentford looked back at him with a glare that simply expressed a question.

'What happened?'

Milham's face moved convulsively. The longing became hopeless, and whatever the eyes expressed it was not a recollection of tranquillity.

'War broke out,' Milham said. 'Before the Penlee plan got off the ground. Everything was postponed for four or five or six years. And it was true that Betty could keep the cottage. She kept it throughout the war, and the car as well, which she learned to drive. Because I didn't need it, you see. Not where I went. It was not the city and limousines and high finance for me. I was of military age, just an accountant's clerk, and like every hapless young man in Lockley what I faced was the call-up, with the prospect of the parade-ground, the sergeant's bellow, and certainly, if not a bullet in the head, at least the guns, the trenches.

CHAPTER XXIV

HE MIGHT have known, thought Brentford.

The headlamps lit up the hedgerows and he drove along the familiar road with a confidence that was not quite justified in the darkness. 'It is a coincidence,' he said to Ethel. 'You will forgive me if I say platitudes about coincidences.'

Ethel was relaxed in the car in the flattering poise she assumed when he drove at night. Like a parcel, he thought as he glanced her her. A woman's going-out appearance was that of a parcel insecurely wrapped. The value of the contents, such as were not already revealed, was assured by the wrappings. And after two thousand years, they still contrived to make it look as though the wrappings were coming off.

'What is?' she said. 'A coincidence?'

'That we should be going to Penlee.'

Gravely, while he took a bend that proved a little tighter than he remembered it in daylight, she considered it. While the hedgerows tilted, altered their angle, and settled down again, he thought that men should retaliate. We could wear a new style of dress, he thought, to look as though our trousers were always on the point of coming down.

He did not think it would be somehow quite the same.

'Actually, it was only because I led Lucy Frazer to talk about Penlee,' she said in a mildly thoughtful way, 'that I heard about the land.'

He used a faintly disbelieving tone. 'The reward of duty.'

'I did think that if I hadn't remembered what you said, to keep my ears open about Mr. Milham, I wouldn't have heard about the land.'

'What did happen at the Red Cross this afternoon?'

As a parting of the ways came up, which took him slightly by surprise, the signpost indication being up above the head-lamp beam and anyway pointing only backwards, she said, with an air of what the French would call snobbism, 'You know I'm no good at the she-said, I-said, so-she-said kind-of-story, John.'

Sorting out the landscape and putting it back where it belonged after a momentary indecision, he wondered, what did you do with a wife who was a liar?

'Let's just say it's convenient,' he said.

There was a mist on the stretch by the river, and they were coming on to Penlee.

'Convenient?' she did not see it.

'That I, who am hampered in this case by a prohibition against questioning Milham's neighbours, should be provided by you with a sixteen-carat chromium plated cause to have a cosy chat with them.'

'Oh, I don't know that the houses are so near as that.'

'How near?'

Her voice was innocent. 'Mr. Milham's house is on the east river I think you said, didn't you? I do know that you get to the Frazers' by a turn from the west river.'

'That's nice.'

'What?'

'To know where we're going.'

At the moment they were going, he saw with surprise, to where the west river, which they had been following, went one way, and the road the other. They circled round in some obscure way, the road ascending and the river presumably descending, until they came together again in Penlee. They had reached the woods, the bridge and the No Through Road sign, and he had not known they were as near as that.

'It's quite easy. She gave me directions.'

He distrusted women's directions. Somehow, taking the car up the hill through the woods that led over and down to Penlee, he suddenly distrusted women altogether. It was a feeling that men were liable to have from time to time.

'I suppose it does exist,' he said with coarse scepticism, 'this building plot.'

'Oh, John.' Her indignation was placid. After all, they were nearly at Penlee. 'Why should you say that?'

'Because it is a coincidence. Because I'm wondering who

would have such a plot. Why they haven't sold it. And because I met a man, Colonel Baker, today, who showed me how we might eat, as well as merely have a house to live in, if we were eventually to retire to Penlee.'

'Why,' Ethel said with supreme confidence that for her they would, 'things do sometimes work out like that. And look,' she said.

He looked. It was the first time they had seen Penlee by night, and he almost stopped the car.

It was a fraud, he thought. All Penlee was a fraud. It was only the angle of the approach road, and the way it looked down on the rivers, that gave it its air of beauty. But none the less the lights flickered away below them in three dimensions, seen through the hedges and the last of the trees, in a narrow V. They were in little horizontal groups, situated up and down the landscape, and away out on the darkness of the waters was a single light that must be a boat. Even the yacht club, in that landscape, contrived to be just a gentle glow, filling in the depths by a miniature shore-line, while the spirit, just by being no longer earth-bound by solemn flatness, seemed somehow to be released.

Penlee was a fraud in the same sense that any painting was a fraud, or any sculpture. It was no more than a way of looking at the common elements of air and earth and water; and thinking of comparisons, Positano, Portofino, from their hurried trips abroad, he said 'Venice,' quite at random.

'Don't be foolish, John,' Ethel said with her inner certainty. 'Venice is only a level island, as you quite well know.'

She might as well say that Positano was impossible for cars, and therefore impractical, or that Portofino was just kept that way for tourists. In English fashion, combining Official Outstanding Natural Beauty with narrow lanes and a complete ban on parking, Penlee could only be kept that way for residents.

'Which way?' he said.

'I think she said turn left by the cottages.'

Descending the hill and taking the turning with the landscape changing around them in the darkness, he would have preferred her not to use that word 'think'.

'Where now?' They might have got to Penlee police station, but instead they had passed that turning and were going up a hill.

'Third right,' she said. 'I'm waiting for it.'

They were liable to end up back in the woods, he thought, and after two bends in the road already, the surface was showing signs of deterioration, and the points of light around them had taken a curving downward swing. 'Ah, here,' she said, and while he was saying, 'Did you say not the east river? It looks to me—' she was saying, 'There's only one house and she said it was important not to go too far.' He put on the brakes abruptly, very conscious of the drop on one side.

When they opened the doors to look, the air seemed softer and the silence of the trees came crowding in. The house, as might be expected of an architect, was built partly out from, and partly into the hillside. He got out to look at the car again, but there was no damage. Ethel, sitting half out of the car and showing pale leg that she would not have continued to show if he had not disappointingly been her husband, was looking down and across at the curve of trees.

'That's possibly Milham's there,' she said, showing more leg and above, recklessly in the darkness, as he helped her out.

'Milham's?' he said, and turned to look over the drop where half the lights of Penlee were missing, having been eclipsed beyond the slope.

'She did say they could see from their bedroom window—' Ethel let her voice fall in the soft air and silence.

'You mean to say you spoke of that—?'

'Are you going to leave the car there?' Ethel moved away to the glow from unseen windows and the pin point of the bell-light that was the welcome of the house. He could leave the car there if he chose, she seemed to intimate. It might save someone's life.

They came together again as they followed the path through the sloping garden.

'It would be nice if you told me what this was about.'

'It's too late to talk of that now, John.'

Lucy Frazer, or the person Brentford supposed was Lucy Frazer, opened the shadowed door. 'Why, Ethel,' she said in a pleased voice. They might have been long-lost friends who had met after many years. She turned to Brentford when he came into her flood of light. 'Inspector,' she said, 'it's so good of you to give your time to come to see us. It's so very good of you.'

CHAPTER XXV

MILHAM HAD fixed Brentford with a look of pure despair that was echoed in Brentford's soul. What Brentford was desperate about was time. There was a clock on Milham's wall, quite a good clock, but, as might be expected in a room that looked cluttered as well as bare, as a room where a man lived alone always did, the clock had stopped.

Brentford made a mental calculation. Milham had taken two and three-quarter hours, he saw by looking out of the corner of his eye at his watch, to cover a period of something like five or six years. He had thirty to cover in all. That was twelve plus eighteen over four. In other words, it was going to be well after noon before Milham ended, even by methodical and uninterrupted progress, a narrative that he had begun at midnight. And, what with emotional involvement, Brentford doubted if he could last out so long.

Milham's eyes had widened. 'The blackest hour often comes just before success at last,' he said. And the change in his expression, visible on his face as he lent over the arm of his chair to Brentford, was like a dawn breaking and a sun arising.

'Suppose we skip the war,' Brentford said. 'You weren't in Lockley, were you? Supposed we skip the war?'

Milham looked at him blankly, and then as though Brentford were robbing him. 'But we can't leave out the war,' he said. To Brentford he looked like the incorrigible confronted with the impossible. 'None of the rest of my story makes any sense at all, I assure you, apart from that.'

Brentford felt rather than asked a morbid question. Did Milham's story make any sense anyway? It was a thought that came over him in waves two or three times in the night. After all, a man who claimed to have lived with his sister, as man and wife, for thirty years, and brought up three children. And who declared he was innocent of incest. To say nothing of the sister's ultimate and unhappy death. Had Milham even contemplated how such a story could be presented, with due formality, with wigs and robes, in any court?

Unfortunately, it seemed all too likely that Milham had contemplated it, and that was exactly why he was making his night-long appeal to Brentford.

'For the first two years,' Milham was saying, 'I was living between Cairo and a sixth-storey service flat on the blue-water side of Alexandria, and the best of those who lived with me was a Turkish girl.'

'Eh?' said Brentford. 'What was that?'

Milham looked at him appealingly. For the first time that night he got up out of chair. Perhaps he thought it would hold Brentford's attention better if he got up and walked around a little. Besides, when he got up, he found he had an object. He went to stand by a sideboard on which Brentford now saw, when he saw some point in seeing, there were dusty ornaments of a vaguely oriental kind.

'I told you,' he said, looking back from there at Brentford accusingly, 'In Lockley, when war broke out, with all my plans wrecked, and contemplating my call-up to the army, in which my highest ambition would probably be a post in the Army Pay Corps, I was at my wits end.'

Perhaps, Brentford thought, caught by one captivating glimpse, Milham's wartime service did have some relevance, after all.

A psychological relevance, he thought. Not that Brentford had a very high opinion of psychologists. Their methods were all right, but the plots and motives by which they explained human conduct came straight from Victorian novelettes. To explain Milham, he thought, they might need a course of later reading.

'Suppose you just tell me what happened,' he said. 'You know what I mean, man.' He had not left his chair, but he sat up in it. 'Briefly. The simple things.'

Milham looked at Brentford as though he must be innocent or insane if he thought that anything in life was simple.

'I wrote to the Ministry,' he said, with the approach of someone who had to explain things unduly to simplify them for a child. 'A branch of the Treasury as it happened. Naturally they weren't the only ones I wrote to. I had eighteen months, it appeared, before my call-up was due, to be spent in seeing people and writing letters. I was an accountant, you understand, and a patriotic man who wanted to find his right place in our war effort, who wished to do his bit.'

'You didn't just think of volunteering for the Navy or the Air Force?' Brentford too had experience of the kind of considerations that moved in a man's mind in time of war, and it could be that, if the Army had a certain reputation, it was its own fault.

'I assure you I did. The Navy, if you remember, was overwhelmed with volunteers, and the Air Force, from what I could make out by my inquiries, was as liable to use an accountant for peeling potatoes or digging latrines as was the Army. Fortunately the Treasury came through, after I think it was the eighteenth letter I wrote to someone. I had discovered the secret of success by accident. Faced with a form that had space for the names of referees on it, I had put down the local Conservative M.P. on it.'

'You knew your Conservative Member of the House of Commons?'

'Not at all. I had met him once at a Lockley civic function in the Town Hall, but have you ever met a politician who said he didn't remember names or people? Asked by someone in the Treasury if he supported my application, he phoned back to his Lockley agent, who told him that Follet's, my employers, were positively the most respectable, and that was enough for him under the heading of Local Knowledge.'

Brentford had a sinking feeling that that was the way things were done in Whitehall in time of war.

'But why Egypt? Why Cairo and Alexandria? And whatever possessed the Treasury to send you there?'

'Someone had to go.' For a moment, Milham's expression was noble, like that of a man who, as he said, had done his bit. 'It was put to me at the interview, and after what I had seen of unfamiliar London in the blackout, to say nothing of the interior of the Treasury, I promptly volunteered.' His expression became solemn. 'As you can guess, with Alexandria occupied by the Navy, and all the fighting in the Western Desert, there was a lot of accounting between the British and Egyptian governments, and I was sent to various places.'

Brentford thought of Milham, what he knew of him and his state of mind, doing the accounting with Egyptians.

With the Egyptians of the old regime, he remembered. They still had the monarchy, while the small boys in the streets asked strangers if they would like to meet their sisters.

'I admit I was astonished by Alexandria,' Milham said. 'The blue-eyed sailors on the British Fleet that was riding there, and all the brothels down the alleys of the port area that was round about. It seemed to me so fitting, and so unchanged since Roman times. It was true that the awful battles with Rommel in the desert were going on not far away, but when I descended from the troop ship, a civilian with the nominal rank of Captain, you would not have known it in Alexandria. I headed across to the wide roads and spacious buildings of the modern business section, and was given cool drinks by what I took to be slave girls in modern dress, a view which I later found to have an intricate accuracy which was uncanny, but when I asked my duties there was no one who seemed to know. I was told by people who had their own preserves that I had better create my own establishment. I therefore visited all the Egyptian and British departments I could think of, told them that I had been sent by the Treasury to examine their accounts, and the following day, in the suite I had taken in my hotel, I began to receive the presents.'

Brentford sought to meet Milham's eyes. 'It wasn't really like that?' he said.

Milham met his eyes. 'It was really like that,' he said. 'From the British officials in white shorts who sat drinking in all their hotels and terraces, to the Egyptians in their sumptous apartments with their boys, their abject downtrodden clerks, and what I have described to you as slave girls. Admittedly the civilian officials, as opposed to the services, wore long whites instead of shorts. And the Egyptians received me kindly because, seeing me as a newcomer from the

Treasury, they hoped to make new demands from me. But Alexandria, you must remember, is a place where the old stories in Greek plays, about a donkey and a woman for example, have always been performed on demand for tourists. The Navy's system of marking off the brothel area, except for a few inspected places, as out of bounds, was far from water-tight. The officers' combined club and brothel for recreational leave from the western desert is quite well known. All these separate parts of Alexandria have always been, as it were, insulated yet interconnected. I made errors to begin with as was natural. When I asked the Egyptian friend I made "How do I get a girl?" I didn't expect her to be delivered by a taxi at my flat next morning, thirteen years old, like Cleopatra in a bathrobe, and find myself in full possession, with what I regarded as full responsibility, as after an outright purchase of so much toenails, hair and eyebrows and other parts, but not a word in common.'

'No,' said Brentford from his chair, but the word was like a groan.

'Yes,' said Milham, not insistent but factual and explicit. 'You can't just tell a girl like that "You're free; you can go away," you know. She would never have been sold if it hadn't been for the probability of starvation in the first place. It was all a misunderstanding. I wondered at myself in those incompetent days, "Now I've got one, how do I sell a girl?" But, Treasury officials or not, it taught me one thing, that wealth is purely relative, and what you can do with money doesn't depend on how much you have. Any American or British millionaire was a pauper compared with me. The value of wealth, in any place, depends on what other people will do to get it.'

Brentford looked wide-eyed at Milham who was standing by the sideboard. 'I ought to caution you. This may be over twenty years ago, but if you misused government funds like that, I can still arrest you for this, you know.'

Milham shook his head a little sadly. 'You're too late. I was found out at the time, after two years that was. It was over something that happened in Cairo. We got a new military commander, whom you must remember, a Puritan with a narrow-minded streak, who made certain inquiries, and mine was one of the heads that began to roll.' He looked pained. 'I did make a sacrifice for my country, you see. I was sacrificed. As though Egypt could be altered overnight. It never was, but we had what was called a shake-up.'

'When you say you were sacrificed—?'

'I was sent to India to be precise, on a dangerous ship to Calcutta, dangerous just because Japan had entered the war. Calcutta, as you know, is a step beyond Alexandria. The city is even bigger and more remote, and at any given time there are a hundred thousand people literally living and starving on the streets. They call them professional beggars.'

Brentford was not happy about Milham's way of expressing the realities of Eastern life. Like most people who lived comfortably in the Lockley area, he liked to think that all such things were always made up by journalists to make a story, and that the world was such, with decent people living in it, that if the stories were true then obviously they would not be allowed to happen.

Resting his elbow on his sideboard with its eastern ornaments, Milham looked him in the eye again. 'After the war, the newspapers were full of photographs, you remember. The picture would be of emaciated creatures, and the caption, 'Belsen'. There was some pretence made that it shouldn't be allowed to happen again. But it was happening again. It is still happening. They pick them up every day, too weak to move, in the Calcutta streets.'

Brentford spoke more sharply. He did not know what Milham was trying to do, but he was not going to allow it. 'What were you doing there?'

'I told you. I was being punished. They didn't waste time sending people to jail at that time. Besides, you don't send a Treasury official to jail. I was put to work as a kind of clerk, at a depot as they called it, which was literally an army dump, a hundred miles north-west of Calcutta, and I stayed there for the rest of the war, in the Indian plain.'

Brentford was glad they were talking about the end of the war at last. He still had not seen what relevance all this had to Milham's later life at Lockley, unless what he had said about the nature of wealth in Alexandria meant that he had felt that to become a millionaire in the west, when he came back, would be an anti-climax.

'You just stayed there, and then came home?'

Milham looked at him for a moment, and nodded.

'I had what they called a bungalow to live in. I was the only member of the civilian staff. I used to look out of my windows at midday and see the flat horizons heavy and luminous through a cloud of dust. In the foreground I would see an old woman taking up a cake of cow-dung to bake and use as fuel. In the background was the wire, a sleepy sentry, and the two or three people who would always camp there, not in any real hope of anything, for we were too distant from the battle to have troops or movements, but because of what we had and they had not.'

'So you came home?' said Brentford.

Milham kept his eyes on Brentford and spoke perfectly evenly.

'Our officer, a man called Gorling, shot one of those people once. He was pilfering, he told me, but it would not have mattered if he had not been, as he carefully explained to me. In the city, when you gave a beggar two annas for a bowl of rice, it was possible that you gave someone something. Depending on the currency situation, the food might be imported. But in the country, where we were, you could have no such illusion. To give food to one person was to take it from another. There only was a certain amount of food, and the number of people alive was fixed by it. You could cure malaria or typhus, and no more people would be alive. Or you could set up a machine gun and mow down a thousand, and what you would have done would be to save the lives of a thousand children, who would otherwise have died through sheer starvation. Gorling had a word for it. He said we were in a place that was beyond good or evil.'

Brentford stared back at Milham, who had nodded when he had asked him if nothing had happened in India and if he had just come home.

'I became friendly with an Indian doctor who ran a hospital,' Milham said. 'It was a place of huts in a compound near a village bazaar ten miles away, and he had a different point of view. What he wanted, when I first met him, was for me to steal some sulpha drugs or penicillin for him, and to persuade me, he took me round his hospital. After all, we, the military authorities, had penicillin when no one else had. He showed me the emaciated bodies in the wards and the families who sat outside and round the thatched huts waiting. "These people will die," he said. I affected Gorling's bravado. "They will die anyway," I said, "or someone else will." He took me by the sleeve and stopped me, his brown eyes looking into mine. "You do not understand," he said with the over-friendliness of the Indian babu. "You are my friend, and I ask you to do this for me, not them." He was right, I did not understand. "For you?" I said. He told me, "I was born a Hindu, and I am a selfish man. I do this for me, not them." ' Milham paused. ' "For me, not them," ' he said.

Brentford did not ask him again if he came home after that, for he had done so twice, and in any event he could see that Milham was going to tell him.

'The way I got back from India was like this,' said Milham. 'I got a letter from Betty one day; saying she was in dreadful trouble, which she did not specify, and I must come home. I would probably have been there another year, since the war with the Japanese was not ended, apart from that. But I sent the letter to my Chief since it was the kind of letter that got you compassionate leave, and it was an open secret that if you got compassionate leave at that time you were not sent back to the east again. I was able to hitch a ride on an Air Force transport, and after some formalities I came back to Lockley. I had a discharge in effect, and I never heard about Alexandria or anything else again.'

Milham moved. He came back to his chair as though he preferred to be near Brentford for what he had to tell, and he sat on the arm of it, looking at Brentford for a moment.

'When I came home, I arrived back at Lockley station with a suitcase. As I stepped out onto the platform, it reminded me inescapably of how Betty and I had arrived there so many years before. It even looked the same, and all Lockley looked the same, with white clouds sailing overhead in an English sky. I looked at the waiting room, and the ticket barrier, and then out at the Lockley streets that hadn't changed at all since before the war. And there was my car waiting outside the station, with Betty waiting in it. I went to it and opened the door, and we looked at one another, and I got in. "What is this trouble, Bet?" I said. She looked at me as though I had become a stranger and said, "I'd sooner tell you when we get back to the cottage, Bill." So we started home.

'It was a strange drive. On the way out of town, she pointed out to me the few changes that there were. Then, on the road to Penlee, she showed me a bomb-crater in a field. The road has been widened in a few places, and, talking like strangers, I asked her why. "Look," she said when we came down into Penlee. A few trees had been cut down on the south-facing bank. There was a new strip of road, and a quay, already disused, that had been constructed for the D-day preparations. But what she pointed out were a few red-and-white surveyors' poles. "The development has started," she said, and glanced at me. "You're late. They're starting to develop Penlee." She looked away and said, "There have been quite a few things going on here." I felt I understood them.'

Milham lifted his head and said 'I don't know if you realise that when a man serving out east, who had been away a long time, got a letter saying that his wife was in some kind of trouble, there were not usually too many guesses about what that trouble was. But this wasn't quite new to me. When we arrived at the cottage, and I admired the kitchen garden where Betty had been growing food for herself and the children through the war, I began to feel I had been through all this before. She asked me to come into the cottage, and looked afraid.'

He shook his head.

'We went into the kitchen, and she went round the table, putting it between me and her. "Bill, there has been a man stationed near Penlee, on coast defences. He only left a week ago." She had practice, I thought. The first time, she had had to tell our parents. The second time, she had had to tell me. "He used to come here sometimes," she said. "When he was here, he used to stay the night." I did not say anything. "Bill," she said. She was pleading with me. "I loved him. It was different this time. He's married. I didn't think he'd go back to his wife. If I was having his child too, why should he?" She looked at me in helpless fear, and I knew what she was suggesting. That I should say that the child was mine, and that the birth was premature.'

Milham watched Brentford.

' "Come here," I said. It took me a minute to persuade her to come out from round the table. Even then, when she did come, she looked as though she expected me to hit her. When she came near enough for me to reach out and touch her, she looked as though she were about to endure something awful that was inevitable. I kissed her on the forehead, and she looked pale and sick. "We've managed this kind of thing before, Bet," I said. "We will again." She stared at me. She fell into one of the chairs by the hearth. She looked as though I had hit her, and she was collapsing. She would not have done that if I had hit her. She looked at me now more than ever as though I were a total stranger. And then she began to cry.'

CHAPTER XXVI

THERE WAS something that was not quite right, thought Brentford. He was not sure what Ethel had got him into, but at least the interior of the Frazers' house looked normal, and the atmosphere, apart from the fact that Lucy Frazer seemed to think that the Brentfords were doing her a favour, instead of she them, had all the appearance of being that of an ordinary social call.

'You should come in the daytime,' Frazer said, standing with him in front of a large but fully and somewhat gaudily curtained window, 'and then you can see the view.' A big, domesticated, smooth-suited man, Frazer had a slight tendency to sell his house as he demonstrated and explained it. He switched on lights in various places and showed Brentford the high fidelity installation in the corner. 'What will you have to drink, Inspector?' They had reached the cocktail cabinet now, and Frazer did seem to be occupying the time, to a slightly unnecessary extent, with talk and action.

'Gin,' Brentford said with the over-weight he usually put on the word, since people normally expected him to take whisky; and he was pleased to see Ethel and Lucy Frazer appearing after a five-minute gap, the explanation of which had been that Ethel had had to put away her coat.

'John is quite interested in the land, Gerald,' Lucy Frazer said, speaking to her husband but looking at Brentford with a conspiratorial air that told him that she and Ethel had been talking about him. She looked slightly as though Ethel had told her that he snored in bed and other details, and yet she had an air of reserve, as though Brentford should not judge her too harshly yet. She looked around her room as though to see that all its four walls and its floor and ceiling were properly in place, and said, 'Now why don't we all sit down and have a drink?'

Frazer was already seeing to it. He went on seeing to it none the less. 'Oh, yes, the land,' he said with a somewhat pre-occupied and vague air.

His need to ask Ethel and Lucy what they were going to drink allowed Brentford the opportunity to look around a little on his own account, without being shown what he ought to see.

There were some Scandinavian chairs along the wall, the wall that was not almost entirely filled by the picture window, but the fireplace and the rest of the furniture had more of an ordinary domestic-and-homely Penlee look. A photograph in a frame, echoed by a portrait on the farther wall, conveyed the fact that the Frazers had a daughter who was not bad looking. Brentford resisted a temptation to be fascinated by the architect's Scandinavian chairs. They had curved plywood petals like flowers, and, really to fulfil their form, he had a tendency to think that you should sit upside down, like a bee, in them.

Not that the chair he had actually taken was uncomfortable, and Ethel was saying, 'At that price, I think we should be very interested, but perhaps you might tell John how, as a building plot, it comes about that it's still for sale'.

They had launched immediately and easily into talk about the land. If it were the important subject of the evening, Brentford would have expected it to be led up to, with a general talk about houses and prices and what it was like to live in Penlee.

'Do you know our chapel preacher, Lambkin, has been after this plot on more than one occasion?' Frazer spoke to Brentford directly, as though there were some things to be disposed of, and he proposed to dispose of them efficiently. From his position by the cocktail cabinet, he waved a hand at the window curtains. 'You know where it is, out there between us and the Milhams'? What Lambkin wanted it for first, when he first tried to get it, was to build his chapel on it.'

It was then that Brentford had a sense of stronger things impending. He had not known where the land was, nor had he known that names like those of Lambkin and Milham were in any way involved in it, but he had a distinct memory of Lambkin in the hot, close atmosphere of the glass-fronted office of the Penlee police station, and he remembered, almost as a direct vision, Lambkin's occasional obscure glances that seemed to represent a particular fear, and also his statement that, due to his poverty, he could not live in Penlee.

Brentford looked at Ethel, who looked back at him mildly, with an air that suggested that she had put on a show for him, and that, instead of looking critically at people's furniture, he might sit up and pay attention to the opening act.

Lucy Frazer was the kind of woman who liked to help her husband to tell a story. 'It wasn't that we really *minded* if Mr. Lambkin built his chapel there, despite what Mr. Milham said,' she said. 'It would be in his view more than it would be in ours, but it would mean people and cars coming past along this road, and you do understand, don't you, chapel people.' She drew Brentford's attention to the portrait on the wall. 'You see, Petty does have a tendency to sunbathe in her bikini on the lawn, and particularly on Sundays, and there have been times when we have caught her without all of the bikini on.'

She smiled at Brentford as though she felt sure that Brentford knew what girls felt about the hard lines of no sunburn that were left by their bikinis, and similar matters, and Brentford nodded back to show that he quite felt the social dilemma that had confronted the Frazers, who, morally speaking, didn't really mind the chapel.

'You mean that you and this Mr. Milham actually had some talk about this?' He looked from Lucy to her husband indiscriminately as he asked the question. 'About Mr. Lambkin's proposed purchase of this land and his plan to build the chapel here?'

'Milham came over and wanted to know if I would put up money with him to buy the land and keep Lambkin out,' said Frazer bluntly. 'I told him I'd give him moral support, but for the rest, I just couldn't spare the money.'

'Besides, we didn't think Mr. Milham was only concerned about the view. It is fairly well known he is an atheist,' said Lucy on a cool note.

'The only way I came into it was this,' said Frazer. 'After Milham bought the land to keep Lambkin out himself, there was the fuss about the chapel by the people around where it is at present. They more or less brought about the ban on further private building. You can see Milham's position. He'd naturally hoped to sell the land again, after Lambkin had built the chapel elsewhere. In case he got stuck with it, he came to me, since I'd said I would give him moral support, and asked me to get plans for a bungalow drawn up and passed before the order that would stop any building on the land came into force. He knew he'd be all right then.'

Brentford took the opportunity to sip his drink. Oh, Lambkin, he thought. You didn't tell me you were already squabbling with Milham three years ago. He glanced at Ethel again, to ask her if she knew she was ruining his case against Milham, in so far as it was supported by the word of Mr. Lambkin, but she just looked back at him in a way that told him he ought to wait a while.

The social atmosphere seemed to go a little more wrong, too.

Lucy Frazer was looking distinctly uncomfortable. It was as though a thought had come to her which she felt she should, but could not, repress. She looked at her husband. 'Of course if the Inspector really wants to buy this land from Mr. Milham, it could be distinctly difficult and awkward,' she said.

Brentford went back to his look at Ethel. A thought had come to him, too. He could see that it would be awkward, at the same time as suspecting Milham of murder, to negotiate with him on any reasonable basis about the purchase of a plot of land. And no doubt Ethel could see it. But how did the Frazers know?

All Ethel did was to open her eyes a little wider. She might have led him up the garden path quite literally, by not telling him who owned the land, she said in silent semaphore. But that was exactly it. It was exactly things like the origin of this unexpected attitude of Lucy's that she hoped that he would find out.

It was all highly unsatisfactory.

Frazer seemed to override his wife's objections. With a look at Brentford that said he could only deal with one thing at once, he said, 'That was where I really came into it. When Lambkin tried to buy the land again, and made his approach through me, saying he wanted his name held back, and I was only to tell Milham that it was "a client".'

Brentford looked around the assembled company and then came back to Frazer.

'Lambkin tried to buy the land again?'

'To build the bungalow for which Milham had had the plans passed,' Frazer said. 'You can see how it was. He'd built his chapel, and wanted to live near it, but prices were too high, and to buy and build on the one remaining plot with planning permission was his only hope.'

Like ours, thought Brentford, though he could see their chances growing distinctly slimmer.

'You say you were not to say his name?'

'That's right. After the earlier business, Lambkin took it that Milham must have a thing against him. He had, too. When Lambkin's name had to come out, after months of negotiation, Milham just turned him down. He told me he wasn't going to have his land bought from him with his own money.'

Brentford felt he knew the answer, but he said, 'What did he mean by that?'

Lucy Frazer intervened again. 'I don't know that what Mr. Milham had against Mr. Lambkin was the same thing the second time as it was the first.

'Mrs. Milham had joined the chapel by then,' Frazer said. 'Of course, I don't know what the relations were, financial I mean, between her and Lambkin.'

The atmosphere of the room seemed to have grown sticky somehow. Brentford noticed that quite a number of the drinks were standing around untouched.

He tried to think of some remark he could make without revealing his own prior knowledge and concern for the case, and failed.

'That is Mrs. Milham who was found drowned in the river recently,' Frazer said. 'Suicide, they said it was.'

Lucy Frazer was looking thoughtful, too. She was content to wait until Brentford's eyes came round to her, but then she said, 'Of course, we don't know the relations between Mr. Milham and Betty Milham either.'

'That's why we thought we'd deal with it this way,' Frazer said. 'After all, he has been our neighbour for fifteen years, and you don't like—you know.'

CHAPTER XXVII

BRENTFORD LOOKED at Milham, who was back in his chair again, and then got up. He did what Milham had done. He went to the sideboard, and this time he really looked at the ornaments. With his hand, delicately, he disturbed a thin layer of dust. They included an ebony elephant, a carved head that had probably come from central Africa, and a small but well-polished Buddha. He touched the Buddha with his fingers, and felt its smoothness. And then he turned back to Milham, looking across the room.

'No,' he said. 'I don't believe it.'

It was the first time in the night he had made a remark of that kind.

Milham looked surprised. He did not know what to do for a moment. He found it unreasonable, as was clear. Brentford had not said he did not believe him when he had told him how he had come to live with his sister as man and wife.

For that matter, Brentford had not said he did not believe him when he had told him how the second child was born. He had only said, 'O, come'. And this, he seemed to suggest, was relatively simple and straightforward.

'But you know it is true,' he said, looking back at Brentford. 'You surely know it as a fact already, that I have lived here in peace with Betty from the end of the war.' He thought for a moment. 'Well, lived here, for twenty years.'

Brentford could not deny simple facts like that, he seemed to suggest, or they would get nowhere. They would not be able to talk at all.

If the facts were so simple.

Brentford looked at the ornaments again. He looked at the Buddha, and then at Milham. He seemed to explore a connection between the two. 'What I find hard to believe,' he said, 'is this reformation, if you call it that—this change of heart.' He regretted to have to say it, but it was there.

Milham looked gloomy, as though he were wondering what evidence there could be for a change of heart. He looked as though he were going to ask Brentford if he wanted an attestation from a lawyer.

The way Brentford looked at him said he knew his difficulty. He did not deny it. 'Twenty years,' Brentford said. 'Just like that. After the way you treated her before the war.'

He put the Buddha back in its place again.

'Betty didn't believe it either,' Milham said quite slowly. 'She asked me what was I going to do, and I said "Nothing." I meant it, too. The day after I came home, I walked down through the woods, and sat on the rocks by the river bank, and threw stones into the water.'

As activity, at least it was purposeless.

'In time, I began to write to accountancy firms up and down the country,' Milham said. 'I told Betty. I needed to know what salaries I was offered to show to Follet. Then the postman on his bicycle brought replies to the cottage on a morning I was out. Betty took the letters to the kettle and steamed them open. She burned all the best ones. In case I didn't do so well with Follet, she took no chances. Or she thought I was playing some awful trick on her.'

It had not been a wonderful beginning, Brentford thought, for Milham's post-war life.

If it had been a sentimental reconciliation, it had lasted for an hour, an evening. There was a suggestion of truth in that. In the books Brentford read, people said one thing then stuck by it. In life, they said the opposite another day.

In fact, Brentford looked round the room, which undeniably existed as evidence of what Milham had rather doubtfully called his peaceful life since the war. The curtains at the window and the loose covers on the chairs had not been professionally made but had been run up on the sewing machine in the corner, almost certainly by the sister. One way or another, it was a fact to be faced. Whatever else Milham had done, he had stayed.

Like the French Existentialists, Brentford thought. He wondered if Milham, like himself, had tried to read the French Existentialists. They too had had experiences in the war. And then, according to the characters in their novels, they did things that were totally inexplicable afterwards, which did not need any explanation, since they were just evidences of the arbitrary human will.

An English court would need a lot of convincing about that, and Milham did not look like a French Existentialist.

'I felt responsible for Betty,' Milham said, looking at him. Perhaps he did think an explanation was necessary. 'Not only responsible for how she was going to live. I felt responsible for what she had become.' It was something he offered, to someone who had to have a motive.

'I'm glad you didn't say you just felt responsible for how she was going to live,' said Brentford, considering returning across the room. 'Because you could have treated her as an unfaithful wife and sent her alimony while you lived in London or Birmingham.' He offered the dry, unhappy, facts.

Milham did not look too happy about the comment, or his explanation. He looked at Brentford hopefully. 'You could see it as a psychiatrist might see it,' he said. He made another offer. 'From my childhood, I must have had a deep unconscious love for my sister. Deep because it was incestuous, and unconscious because it was never consummated. Before the war, there were complications. Afterwards, there weren't, so you could see my love in all its horror or its beauty.'

Brentford looked at him as though he were slightly mad. He was sorry he could not help it.

'Yes,' said Milham, relapsing. 'Psychiatrists do seem to get their stories from novelettes.' And he seemed to suggest that if that explanation did not work, and he himself was extremely doubtful of it, none did.

Brentford crossed the room.

When he reached his chair, he sat on the edge of it. He leaned forward so that he and Milham, though separated by six feet, seemed to put their heads together.

'Didn't you think anything about what you were doing?' He used the tone of voice of a slightly too-reasonable schoolmaster. That too was unavoidable.

'No,' said Milham. He tried to act the schoolboy, but failed. 'All the thought came later.'

It was something. He had thought, apparently. But it was not at the time, but later. Perhaps years later.

Brentford might well have asked what good thought was, if it only came much later than the event it was supposed to explain. It was questionable if it could be called thought, under the circumstances. It was worse than the estentialists' existence preceding essence. But he did not ask. He did not even put any irony in his tone. He just said, 'You got on all right, without thinking?'

Milham looked slightly alarmed for a moment, as over dangers long past. 'Oh, yes, I think so,' he said. But he did not let it go at that. After a moment, he looked tentatively hopeful, as though he had thought of something.

'I walked round Penlee, you see,' he said. 'In the woods, and on the roads. I wasn't doing anything. I was just looking. Then I went back to Follet. I was surprised how they welcomed me at the office. It must be true, that absence makes the heart grow fonder. From the way the girls looked at me when I came in, I thought they must forget the bad things. And Follet, too. When he had me sitting in his office, he gave me a sideways look. "I hear Hobson and the contractors are developing Penlee," he said. It hadn't occurred to me until then that what he really wanted me to do was to get Follets into that. I went along to Hobson's. "Well, I don't suppose that we can really hold it against you," he said, "we on the Council, that you were defending us in the war." So I told him. "I feel I've become a little old now," I said, "to be an office boy." "Yes," he said, "I can see that. I suppose we'll have to find a different place for you." Then I hadn't been back a week before my widow called me at the office. There is a kind of impulsion that makes you do what people expect you to do. "I hear you're back in town," she said. "When are you coming along to see me?" But it wasn't like before the war. I was in.' Milham looked surprised. 'I wasn't an outsider any more. I was in.'

Looking at Milham's surprise, Brentford wondered profoundly what Milham meant by the statement he was in.

'You mean you played ball?' He spoke distinctly.

Milham was puzzled. 'Played ball? Well, I suppose you can call it that. They expected me to be part of the normal business life of Lockley. And so I was.'

Brentford too contemplated the effect on a man of what people expected him to do.

'We developed Penlee,' Milham said. 'First we bought the land with the bank's capital, and hung on. Then we put up the best white villas, to make it a select residential neighbourhood, on the south-facing bank above the water. Then we put up the bungalows to make it popular.' He did not say why he said that, or what it had to do with anything, he just explained, 'Hobson said that was the way to do it. An extra five hundred above the cost price on each of the hundred bungalows. Fifty thousand pounds. It took me a little time to catch up with the post-war world, but it was the way.'

'What did you have to do with it?' Brentford said.

'I suggested that the wartime D-day quay would be a good place for a yacht club, to add to the amenities.'

Brentford swallowed a little. Earlier, he had contemplated the fact that Milham was not regarded as an acceptable member of the yacht club. Now he contemplated the fact that he had invented it. That too was truth.

'Look,' he said. He paused, and tried to think of some form of words that would express his feeling that all this was unbalanced in some way, was not quite right. But was it? Was it not too, exactly, right? And was that not the trouble? 'But this went on for years. It must have done. What did your sister think of all this?' he said.

Milham, five feet from Brentford as they leaned towards one another from the edges of their angled chairs, looked despondent, as he usually did when his sister was mentioned. He could not help the anguish.

'She lacked faith,' he said. 'She was like that. That was the way she was. When the white villas went up, around the point between the rivers, she said, "When are you going to build our house, like you said you would?" Living with her from day to day was like that. "Why can't we build now?" she said when I explained about the delay. Then, five, no, six years after the war, when we could look out of the cottage windows at breakfast and see a start being made on these foundations, she looked at me across the corn flakes and said, "When it's finished are you going to sell it?"' Milham looked at the room around him as though that had been incredible or inconceivable. Except that it was there.

'You mean after all that time, after five or six years, she still wasn't sure that you were going to stay, that she thought you might go away?'

Milham looked at Brentford regretfully.

'She said she didn't understand me,' he complained. 'Just because I used to walk around Penlee, through the woods and along the rivers. She said I wanted to sell it all, which wasn't true. She even complained because I only went out to see my widow or some other woman two nights a week. I lacked passion, she said; I wasn't sufficiently in love with them. And she could hardly talk. Once we got the house built, she didn't go out to men friends any more. She had three children, and she suddenly announced to me one day that that was enough.' His eyes widened and he looked doubtful. 'Or perhaps she did become reconciled about then, two years after the house was built. The way she looked at it was probably that my feet were set in solid concrete.'

158

They both paused then. Examining Milham, Brentford noticed in him a slightly startled air of having got somewhere.

It was as though Milham himself had not realised, until he told it, how true what he had just said had proved to be, and how near it had been to being ultimately complete and final.

Except that Brentford noticed that Milham's next expression was one of nostalgia, of the kind that people felt for something that had happened a long time ago. He said, 'And then?'

Milham's face became long. He moved back in his chair a good six inches. He looked glum beyond any immediate or obvious reason. 'I began to think,' he said.

It sounded fatal.

'Think?' said Brentford.

Milham made a gesture. 'One day on a grassy bank in a glade, in the woods,' he said. 'With one of my new neighbours' sixteen-year-old daughter beside me, lying with her head in a nest of her hair among the daisies, her blue eyes looking up at me, her knees up, and her skirt fallen back around her waist.' He was explicit.

'So that's why you went walking in the woods.'

Milham's expression did not change, and his tone was even. 'No, you mistake me. The meeting in the woods was pure chance. I went walking in the woods, and so did she. Only I just went walking. She went walking with one young man or another, if you call it walking. I don't know what happened that day. The young man had to go home, or they had a row. They were young and irresponsible, so perhaps he didn't come. So she and I met in a glade and she said, "Hi", and I said, "What are you doing on my land?" and she said, "Do you think you own the whole of Penlee?" and we both sat down. It was like that,' he added, 'except that I was nearly forty.'

Brentford shook his head. 'An interesting beginning. To thinking.'

'The thinking began because I didn't have a contraceptive. She seemed to think I would.'

They sat there thinking of the phases and nature and times of life.

'I am not clear,' Brentford said, 'on the extent of your reformation.

'Nor was I,' said Milham. 'That was the trouble.'

He did not question Brentford's doubt. He had enough of his own. 'However incredible a man of my generation found it, if any girl was asking for it, this Christine Tankerton was. I could only imagine these young men of hers must have been boy scouts who always came prepared. I was out of touch. I don't know if it was the conversation in which she more or less invited me to remove her light summer clothing. She had heard about me, she said, not hinted. I had a certain reputation, don't ask me how. She wondered what it was like with an older man. What do you do, with blue eyes looking up from a nest of hair among the daisies, curious and full of interest? I found I thought, why not? You'd have to have a different mind. It was more or less just in time, knowing that there must be a catch in it somewhere, that I asked her if she had taken precautions for this kind of thing, and she said she hadn't.'

Brentford stared at Milham. But Tankerton, he thought. What held him was the name. He had known he was important.

'She relied on the boys,' Milham said. 'Daddy wouldn't give her money for contraceptives. I didn't get so far as asking if she'd told him what she wanted the money for. I was morally paralysed by the fact that she seemed incapable of saying no. Even after this delicate conversation about the facts of life. My salvation, I thought, might be if she would only keep her knees together. Then I thought of Betty, and how she got her first baby from a married man, and what I had thought of the man at that time. It didn't work. I had a strong contrary feeling that this girl positively ought to have a baby. For the benefit of the body politic, to keep her out of circulation. I raised my eyes to heaven, and engaged myself in a contemplation of the universe, and other things.'

'This is keeping me in suspense,' Brentford said.

'It must happen once in the life of every man,' Milham said. 'Possibly even in yours.'

'You didn't?'

Milham looked at him with due solemnity. 'I decided I loved her too much,' he said.

He saw Brentford's expression.

'No,' he said. 'Seriously. I mean there ought to be girls like that. Of that spirit and catholicity. Their enlivening effect is quite tremendous. I was twenty years younger if I was a day. I very much wanted—well, you can imagine the anatomy of what I wanted. But instead, I went walking in the woods with her. There was much conversation about whether she should be dressed or she shouldn't, and whether she looked better with or without, that kind of thing. Even when she said she had to go home, I went on up the slope. It lasted, the euphoria. Even when I came out at the top of the slope, I looked out over the view of Penlee and the rivers and I found that my thoughts, quite solemn now, were moving with unaccustomed force and clarity.' He looked steadily at Brentford. 'I reviewed my present life,' he said.

Brentford saw a little of what was to come. 'The way you were living since you had come back from India?'

Milham looked at him steadily in silence for quite a lengthy period.

'If I tell you that there are certain basic truths that are proclaimed by all great religions, you will almost deliberately misunderstand me,' he said. 'You will think that I am saying that religions are true, and that there is "something in them", and I am not. What I am doing is talking about certain simple, logical and basic truths that have been exploited by religions.'

Brentford wondered what was coming, and what conceivable meaning it could have in Milham's story.

'For example,' Milham said with an air of explaining plain straightforward sense to a little child. 'If a thing is to please you, you must begin by endeavouring in some way to love it. There is nothing occult about this, and it presumes only that you would like to live a pleasant life. I explained it to myself by thinking of a graceful statue I would like to have made of young Christine without her clothes. I would find it delightful, I did not doubt, but the delight could not be in cold stone. It must come from me. But what applied to a statue must also apply to all our neighbours, to Betty, to Betty's children, and also to old Follet. To enjoy them, to take pleasure in their company, even if I were the most selfish man in the world, it would still be necessary to love them sufficiently to excuse their faults. It was a question, I suddenly saw, of what love is. Love is a state of being pleased with a thing. And it amazed me suddenly, it astounded me, that all the people, religious leaders and psychologists, all those who use words like "love" so frequently, had never taken the first elementary scientific or dictionary step, which was to define their terms. For if they did, then it was the simplest logic that if a man wished to live a happy life, and enter "the kingdom of heaven" in fact, then the one essential was that he should love the world around him.'

He gave Brentford his steady look and nodded as though what he was saying should be obvious to anyone.

'It was my first glimpse of it,' he said, 'standing there in the trees on the hill and looking down on Penlee, in one of those great cohesive moments of life when the understanding of all things seems complete, and all things seem to come together. My mind seemed imbued with infinite knowledge, and at the same time with total understanding. It ranged over all science, including the intangible nature of the physical universe as it appears in all modern studies. It included philosophy, and I remember thinking quite clearly that the ancient Greek who said, "I think, therefore I am," should have been better at introspection, and should have said, "I feel; I fear and desire, therefore I think". I remember thinking that what was wrong with our university professors was their belief in objective thought, while in fact all they knew, or scientists could discover, was how to accomplish their own desires. But most of all I remembered my own experience, in Alexandria and other places, and saw that to hate a thing could only bring the one who hated pain, or at most one blinding flash of pure destruction, while to despise the world was itself to be bored by it. Simultaneously, I reviewed all scientific knowledge, and saw that while scientific theories change, what remained was the actual experiments and the instructions how to do things, and, at the same time, I knew what my Hindu doctor had meant, in his Babu English, when he had said, "I don't save these children for *them*: I save them for *me*." ' he smiled at Brentford.

But even as he did so, he looked a shade uncertain.

Mad, Brentford thought quietly.

For the first time for some time, he looked at Milham carefully, from his greying, receding hair to the tips of his slightly pointed shoes. Without too much effort, he could imagine himself writing it in his report. 'At this point in his story, Milham appears to have gone a little crazy.'

He knew what he was going to say. He said it. 'This was just something you thought?' he said. After all, he knew what sense and facts were.

Milham's eyes opened wide. He looked alarmed. 'This was me making my peace with the universe,' he said. Then if possible his eyes opened a little wider. 'You have to see that,' he said. He looked an appeal at Brentford. 'Because this was when I realised. That Betty had begun to go off her head,' he said.

And he looked at Brentford as though he quite believed it.

CHAPTER XXVIII

BRENTFORD DID not know. He did not know what it was that Frazer did not like to do about a neighbour of fifteen years. He looked around the room, at the Scandinavian chairs, at the window curtains, and the Hi-fi in the corner. But from the atmosphere in the room he could almost guess.

The Frazers were nice people.

What did nice people do, when they thought or felt, or possibly even knew, something about their neighbour? In Penlee? What they did not do, quite obviously, was to walk down to Penlee police station, and talk, or lay a formal complaint, to someone like Constable Hebble.

Looking at Frazer, who was looking at him dubiously, but rather with the air of one businessman to another, and at Lucy Frazer, who looked embarrassed, and at Ethel, who had been used to make contact with him through the Red Cross (which was surely very appropriate), Brentford wondered if it would have made any difference, after all, if Simpson, or even he or Parker, had sent six-foot policemen around in Penlee to knock on doors, and ask about the Milhams. Probably door-to-door policemen would have been treated like vacuum-cleaner salesmen, and been told that the inhabitants did their business elsewhere.

'You see, I'm not sure,' Frazer said.

It was no wonder that the atmosphere of the room was sticky and that drinks were standing around undrunk.

'Perhaps if I knew what you were unsure about,' said Brentford. He tried to be helpful. 'I believe the Coroner did return a verdict of "suicide".'

Ethel did what she could. But she was acting according to some rules of her own. She confined herself to picking up her drink and playing with it. At least that looked natural, and even that, Brentford considered, was a little help.

'I didn't know much about it until I read the inquest report,' said Frazer, excusing something.

'That's fairly usual,' Brentford said with calm gravity, 'unless you attend.'

But Frazer must have been too busy to attend the inquest.

'He was reported as saying he didn't get up,' he said in a sideways way. 'Until his usual time to go to the office. On the morning that his wife died.'

Brentford raised an eyebrow. 'You mean he did get up?'

Frazer looked a little helpless. He found it awkward.

Both men's wives helped them. At least that was what Brentford assumed it was.

Lucy Frazer made a wifely intervention. She spoke to Brentford. 'Gerald has a weak bladder,' she said. 'You know how it is these early autumn mornings. He's wakened by the dawn chorus of the birds, and then he lies awake. I tell him to go to the bathroom.' She looked at the curtains of the room. 'When he comes back, he sometimes looks out through the bedroom window curtains.'

Frazer too thought that was a natural action. He could go on now. 'He was up,' he said with certainty. 'He was dressed and crossing the lawn, heading down towards the river. The only trouble is that I can't be absolutely certain what day it was.'

Brentford looked at Ethel. So this was what she had brought him to, his look implied. It was almost perfect evidence, quite enough to occasion much more direct inquiries, if only on a charge of perjury, except that it had a fatal flaw. But Ethel would not accept his glance. He might think he knew what he was doing, the way she looked away implied, but she was doing something else.

Brentford had to accept that. He was suddenly aware that Lucy was looking restive, as though she might break in again with something different. Which was all very well, but for the moment he had to stick with what he had.

'Surely if this happened on the day that Mrs. Milham died, you'd have thought of it, on whatever occasion it was you heard of her death?' he mildly inquired of Frazer.

'That's it.' Frazer shook his head. 'I know I was thinking of other things when Ralph Peterson came into my office and said, "Do you know they pulled a neighbour of yours out of the river this morning, a Mrs. Milham?" But I should have thought of it. Like you, I think I should. But you see I didn't. Not until I read the inquest report. And then I thought it was so.'

It was tantalising. Brentford's picture of Milham up and following his wife to the river, at the time he had said he was not up, was the kind of thing that had hanged many a man in the past, when the execution of the accused was helpfully final.

There was even a kind of law about it in Brentford's opinion. People rarely read such details as the inquest report within a week or two of the actual crime or accident, and when they did read them there was something in the average, extrovert human memory that tended to bring things together, on a certain day. People remembered it was fine that day, or something like that. And, because it was Penlee, he had to come up with Frazer.

'You can't be more sure of it? Look, perhaps you can remember you did think of it, when who-was-it, Petersen, told you. Suppose you were to think a little.'

'Convince myself that I did think, you mean, by reconstruction? You know I can convince myself what I could think and should think. But I don't think that would be fair, do you? Like thinking it was fine that morning, when over half the days were fine.'

Frazer was a much too complicated personality to be useful in a law court. He was probably the kind of man who read a particular advertisement a thousand times and then bought something else. And Ethel was looking at Brentford as though asking how low he could sink.

'John,' Lucy Frazer was saying. 'Inspector.'

Life would be simpler if you could keep wives out of it, Brentford thought. There was much to be said for the purdah and bedroom system as practised in Moslem countries. He looked at Lucy not quite as perfectly politely as he might have done. 'Have you something to tell me too?' he asked.

Ethel gave him a warning glance. Whatever it was that Lucy had to say, it was a far more fragile flower than that. And Lucy seemed to retract a little.

'Not evidence,' she said. She looked worried. She looked around the room as though wondering how she could say what she might say. He was puzzled by her attitude. 'It can hardly be true. I've always thought that, even when I've wondered, that it could not be true.' She looked at her husband.

Frazer too seemed to find it difficult to help her. 'Personally I've never believed it,' he said. 'I find it hard to believe it now. Even if what I think is true, and it was that morning that I saw old Milham up.'

'It's just one of the things,' said Lucy, 'that makes us doubtful, and has made us doubtful for ten years, when we look across towards the Milhams'.'

Brentford thought about it. Ten years, he thought. If it was anything, it was news that was ten years old. He wondered what it was that could be valuable, and not be told for ten years. It sounded like a contradiction.

Ethel broke her rules. It was possible that it was something that was visible to no one but Brentford. She looked up and said, 'Lucy, you'd better tell him about the children.' Then she looked at Brentford.

Lucy Frazer looked at her, and Brentford. It was something about which she had to be sure she had the green light. She saw she had. 'It was when their Jenny used to bring their Caroline to play with our Petty,' she said.

'This is something that children said?' said Brentford.

She nodded. That was it. What she was reporting was what the neighbours' children said, ten years afterwards.

It was neither truth nor hearsay nor supposition in other words. It was something else again.

'You know how they talk,' she said. 'Modern children. Carolin and Petty were in the nursery and I was in the kitchen. It was nothing to hear them talking about babies in their mummies' tummies.'

Was it? Brentford didn't know. He looked hopefully at Ethel.

'I made a point not to check them,' said Lucy. 'We all do that. But when Caroline said to Petty, "My mummy and daddy aren't really married," I thought I ought to interfere.'

Brentford swallowed. 'I think I might.'

Lucy found him a more understanding man. 'I went and told Caroline,' she said. '"That's not a nice thing to say, Caroline," I said, "and you mustn't say it." But she said, "It's true. My brother David says so." So you see. It was when Jenny, the older girl, came to collect little Caroline, I thought I ought to have a word with her.'

Brentford looked at the Frazers' wallpaper. It had a nice pink tone.

'These are just the things they said?' he said. 'Ten years ago?'

Lucy Frazer had decided in her own mind he was someone she could talk to.

'I've always remembered exactly what she said,' she said. 'You would too. I mean the Milhams only live across the way. When you see them, or someone speaks of them, or times like that.'

Brentford tried to imagine it, in connection with the Frazers' wallpaper. If you were Lucy Frazer, he thought. And you couldn't speak of it because it was what the neighbours' children said.

'I took Jenny aside when she came,' Lucy said. ' "Your little sister had been saying things she shouldn't," I told her. "What's that?" said Jenny. "She's been saying your mummy and daddy aren't properly married," I told her. "It's not a nice thing." '

Lucy's voice took on an unbelieving note.

'Jenny was ten or eleven,' she said. 'She took it in her stride. "Oh, David and I told her not to say that. You see my mummy is really my daddy's sister." '

Brentford sat up at that point.

He looked at Ethel, who looked back at him quite freely now. He could even see why Ethel had applied her self-made rules, even knowing as she did of Lambkin's allegations and the puzzle, which had seemed a puzzle, of Mrs. Milham's sin.

' "Now Jenny," I said,' Lucy Frazer said. ' "That's worse than your sister said, and I won't let either you or Caroline play with our Petty if you say things like that." Of course Jenny was sorry then. "Oh, Mrs. Frazer," she said. "We won't. It was only when David had to go away to school he told me that if I found out, as he had done, I was not to say it, and I told Caroline." ' Lucy looked in a *distrait* way at Brentford. 'These children,' she said. 'I saw that quite obviously it was just a children's story. But it makes you think.' She waved a hand to the window as though to invite him to see the distance to the Milhams'. 'And then, ten years later, these other things—'

It was not easy for either Brentford or Ethel to think what to say to her.

'Now Mrs. Frazer,' he said. And he showed his empty glass to Frazer. He risked an impoliteness. 'Do you think,' he asked, 'that we might all have another drink?'

It might be, Ethel's eyes said. They were working away to him like a signal station, engaged in their private semaphore. I've never heard anything of the kind round Lockley here before, have you? Then she looked a kind of appeal at him: now, wasn't I right to bring you here?

CHAPTER XXIX

BRENTFORD CHOSE his words with care. 'As long as ten years ago, the balance of your sister's mind began to be disturbed?' he said. 'That is your story?'

Suddenly, outside the garden door, they could see the first signs of dawn. As yet, it was no more than a lessening of the absoluteness of the darkness. But things were no longer quite the same, when, perhaps without knowing quite why as yet, they were both aware of passing time.

Milham was leaning forward in his chair and Brentford was sitting upright in his, but what Brentford thought, exactly, was that soon it would be the hour when Betty Milham, dragging herself out of bed for reasons only she knew, had started her walk down by the river. And the same care Brentford had used in choosing his words was apparent in their actions as Milham put his hands on his knees and Brentford watched him.

For a moment Milham looked at him in a new way. Unexpectedly, he said, 'I think you know why I am telling you all this.'

Brentford absorbed the new sense that the night might soon be ending.

'I can guess,' he said.

They both seemed to know what they meant by that. Milham looked as though Brentford should know now why he was claiming his attention.

'You wouldn't have known anything was happening to Betty ten years ago,' he said. He looked specifically at Brentford. 'I didn't know it. I'd—what? Made my peace with the universe? The change in Betty, at first, was she seemed to become more normal.'

He defied sense deliberately, his eyes said.

Brentford thought about Milham's contention that while he, because of the life they were living, had had to have a revelation that some people would describe as religious, to bring him to a more certain and balanced and tolerant frame of mind, his sister had first shown a failure of adjustment by more evidence of normality.

'I don't see the meaning of that. I think you know I don't.' He lifted his head to Milham, and Milham went on.

'I am telling you the facts. At this time, Betty became more like everyone else in Penlee. I would come home unexpectedly early in the afternoon. I would find her in the garden, wearing a pair of gardening gloves, and weeding her pretty flowers. And they were pretty. In summer, this house was surrounded by gorgeous blooms that she had grown. Then she would go out, to meet the children coming home from school, she said. When she was delayed, I would look out up the road and see her talking across the hedge to some other Penlee wife and mother, smiling and talking politely as though they had mutual subjects of absorbing interest. Her attention was devoted to her garden and her children and her home, but not in isolation. As though, as an original inhabitant, she felt it was a part of the Penlee that was new and had grown up around her.'

Meeting Milham's eye, Brentford said, 'It would seem to me that you were far more unbalanced, with your episode with Christine Tankerton, and your wandering in the woods.'

Milham said, 'You remember that Betty was the girl who eloped with me, not knowing where she was going or where she was going to live? She was the one who, in our Calwen Row flat, pointed out to me that our way of life was that of some pagan tribe discovered by anthropologists, in somewhere like Sumatra. In her maturity she had lived alone in the cottage and had a love affair with some man I never knew. All her children were illegitimate, and I, her husband, was her brother.'

He was deliberate and explicit.

Brentford was silent, not agreeing, but seeing little, a fraction possibly, of what Milham meant.

'I'll tell you the next thing,' Milham said. 'Another summer, eight or nine years ago. Penlee was almost as it is today then, and I looked out of this door here and saw Betty with the two younger children, the girls, on the garden path. She had dressed them in new coats and dresses and white cotton gloves and put prayer books in their hands, so that they looked innocent and pretty as a picture. She was sending them off to the new Penlee Anglican Sunday School that had opened, and when, after she had seen them off down the road, I asked her why, she was a shade evasive. She said it would teach them their social manners.'

Brentford saw more of what Milham, on looking back, had found significant. It was one thing to see it, and another to be convinced by it. He made it very clear.

'There are few women, coming to Penlee from another life, who would not do something of the kind. A retired prostitute, living in Penlee with children, would very likely do the same thing.'

Milham looked at Brentford as though it were he who was evading something. 'Betty had not retired She still lived the same life in my house. With her, it was not something that was in the past.'

Brentford thought of Milham paying the bills and bringing up the children. 'Can you tell me something clearer, some decisive action, something you yourself observed and thought important at the time it happened?' He wanted that.

Milham looked at him a moment, and said, 'Do you know Tankerton, Christine's father?'

Brentford thought of what he knew of Tankerton, interviewing him in his office, the vision he had of him driving his motor yacht down the Penlee river and scattering the smaller fry. He remembered what Tankerton had said of Milham. Since hearing of Milham's meeting with Christine in the woods, he had guessed the reason.

He said, 'Not really.'

'Tankerton is a modern materialist,' Milham said. 'He can see physical objects, and nothing at all beyond them. His wife had left him three years before this time. She had complained Tankerton was neglecting her, so he had bought her a big new house in Penlee, then neglected her the more to work to pay for it. Tankerton is the kind of man who sees a way of life in a place like Penlee, decides he must have furniture just like the Jones's, works all his life to get it, and spends his old age in an

echoing house sitting in a circle of beautiful, empty chairs.'
He looked carefully at Brentford.

Comparing what Tankerton had said of Milham with what
Milham said of Tankerton, Brentford thought there was no
comparison in terms of calculated viciousness. He wondered
why.

'What has Tankerton to do with your sister Betty?'

'This is what you asked me, an incident and Betty's behaviour in it. It was over a year after my meeting with Christine in the woods when Betty answered the door one evening
when I was out to find Tankerton there, red-faced and bluster-
ing, demanding to see me and refusing to believe that I was
out.'

While the grey light outside the garden door grew and became cold and drab as seen from the lighted room, Brentford
watched and waited. Time was moving now.

'He said Christine was pregnant and I was the father,'
Milham said. 'He didn't behave in the customary way for
Penlee. He pushed past Betty at the door and went into the
house to find me. Betty knew about Christine. I had told her
about our meeting in the woods, and she had seen with her
own eyes how often the girl went there in the evenings, with
one young man or another, and came out looking rumpled.'

Brentford gave Milham a hard look.

'I myself had seen Christine once since then,' said Milham. 'I
had passed her, driving in the car, and waved to her. She had
put her nose in the air, turned to her boy friend, and refused
to see me. And this is about Betty, not about myself.' He
looked back, denying what Brentford thought.

'Go on about your sister.'

'Tankerton was furious and incoherent. Betty told me about
it when I got home. Have you seen those religious paintings
with people in the foreground, turning their eyes to heaven,
where there are angels with pleased expressions, while some
martyrdom of imaginative ferocity goes on in the middle
distance? Betty was like those people.'

'You are telling me about that, how she looked and spoke to
you?'

Milham shook his head. It was not that.

'In some way I could only just imagine, she had cornered Tankerton in the living room, and got his story out of him. To the surprise of no one in Penlee but himself, Christine had told him that evening she was pregnant. After his wife's desertion, it was a blow to him. Who knows what goes on in a mind like Tankerton's? He had showered all he had on Christine, and as a result she had turned out even more high-powered than his motor-cruiser, and had run aground. He had reverted to a primitive rage when she had told him in their home, and he had put Christine across his knee, tucked her skirt up and pulled her pants down, all of which Betty was able to tell me, and attacked her with sadistic fury with a plastic belt. He had expended his rage, I gathered, before he had even got round to asking her, while still holding her across his knee, and applying the belt at intervals with accuracy, "Who is the man?" It had worsened his temper how long Christine had held out, while he tortured her in a way that he, being he, would not even know was naked jealousy and sadism that in fact it was.'

Brentford thought of Tankerton in his office, and his house behind the yacht club. 'What has this got to do with your sister?'

'You know what Betty was. You know her history. What I am telling you is what, almost invisibly, she had become. You would think she would have sympathy for Christine. And she had in a way. She understood Christine's mind, it seemed. She was able to understand, from what Tankerton said, that he had been applying his belt where it would be most effective and asking for "a man". Christine could not commit herself without further repercussions just because she knew that the truthful answer would be in the plural, not man but men. It would be only under some particular agony that she would say any name at all, and when it came, it was my name that she yelled out. And Betty understood that too, she said. She attributed quite a lot of thought to Christine in that position. To name me, an older, married man, would both make her look more innocent and stop her father trying to produce a shotgun marriage that she knew, though he didn't, could not be brought about. And as for injury to me, she would not care for me, so Betty said, just because of what I had not done in the woods that day. It was her revenge.'

Brentford looked at Milham constantly as he produced his analysis from his sister's mind. He spoke abruptly. 'What did she do?' he asked.

'It is what Betty did that I am telling you. She could have temporised with Tankerton. Admittedly she wanted him out of the house before I came home. But she had no need to do what she did, which was to tell him in detail all about his daughter, what she had been seen doing, and that other people, such as the Frazers, could confirm it in every detail. She even used Tankerton's sadism quite ruthlessly, picturing for him Christine laughing at him at home, because he thought he had done enough with his belt and she had successfully got rid of him. She got Tankerton out of our house by sending him back to Christine to undress her properly this time and do things that were medieval. And when I came home, Betty told me all this in a detached way, like the people in the religious paintings, saying that Christine was a bad girl, especially to have mentioned my name, and that she should be the one to suffer. To me, who was imagining what Christine was enduring in her father's hands even then, it clearly seemed for the first time that Betty had taken leave of her senses in some way, as religious people do, blinding themselves to what is actually going on because of some abstract or moral principle which they say that they believe in.'

Brentford looked at Milham, at his fiftyish, greying hair, his grey suit, and his slightly pointed shoes, and imagined him saying what he had just said in court, claiming it as evidence of his sister's madness. He waited until Milham himself looked up at him. He was a little colder.

'And this is one of your main points?' he said. 'As it must be, from the time you have expended on it? You are suggesting that this, this complete normality of your sister's actions, as other people would see it, was evidence, in her, of something like an incipient madness?' He was careful about it. It was the way he looked at Milham that suggested that, to one who was himself mad, as he had actually thought that Milham was, it was the rest of the world that looked that way.

Milham looked back at him and saw his point. Milham spoke in a different voice. 'You know that that is exactly why I have to tell all this to you. The whole story. To convince you. For there is very little I can point to in the next five years. Betty herself began to go to the Anglican church occasionally at one time, about six years ago. I sat with her on the verandah outside here one evening, while the shadows spread across the trees from behind the Frazers' house and the sun set over the river view. I asked her why she did it, why this church-going, and she was silent for a long time while the darkness spread below the woods. Almost the only light below us was the reflection of the sky in the pool below the village before she said she thought it was "time we became respectable." "But you can't be respectable," I told her. "This dressing up in hats, and going to sit with the other people in the pews only makes you seem respectable. It's based entirely on the fact that they don't know who you are, and don't know who I am, and don't know who your children are. It isn't anything real, for you to do it that way. It's just a fraud."'

Brentford sat still, looking at the pale, drab light that was growing outside the misty glass outside the room, but he made a hissing sound between his teeth. 'You told her that?' he said. It was something he saw, in one way.

'I didn't know what I was saying,' Milham said. 'I didn't even wish particularly to prevent her going to church, if that was what she wished. It only pained me to see her indulging in such self deception, when her life was her life, as I thought, and could not be changed. Because Lambkin, with his doctrine that confession was a way out, was not here then. He was only someone who appeared in the district and went collecting from door to door from time to time, saying something that I doubt if even you, the police, believed, that he wanted the donations to build a chapel.'

Brentford thought about the story that had come right to the times he knew. 'Your sister was going to the doctor, Dr. Hargreaves, for her nerves, before she ever joined the chapel.'

Milham looked at him as though to say, so that was something that Brentford knew.

'Yes. That was after I had pointed out to Betty that this respectability, this ordinary absorption into the suburban life of Penlee, which she was making so much her own life, was based upon a fraud. I hadn't known what I was doing when I said it. You have to understand that. But she became visibly more reserved, and less free to talk to other women across their garden hedges. She took to wearing the hats she had bought for church, and clothes to go with them, for everyday. It gave her a pathetic look, as though she now had to strive and make a point of her respectability, and it was within a year or two of that that she began to walk around the village muttering to herself. The housework was not done so well, and she began to neglect the garden. I had to persuade her to go to Dr. Hargreaves, but perhaps you know that.' Anxiety shot across his face.

Brentford did not know it. He only knew that Milham had gone on seeing Dr. Hargreaves about his wife after she had ceased to attend the surgery and joined the chapel that Lambkin had built instead. But it made a perfect dovetail between the story that Lambkin had told, and what Brentford had found out, and what Milham had been telling him through the night. A perfect join.

Milham looked at the dawn outside and said, 'With your permission, I would like to break off a little while at this point. If you are willing, we might go to the kitchen and make ourselves a cup of coffee. I think we need it.'

Brentford nodded, but they did not get up at once. They sat where they had been and looked at the growing dawn outside for a little time. The light must have been like that, Brentford thought, at the time he had thought of, when Betty Milham had dragged herself out of bed in that same house, though without the electric bar they had used, and washed and dressed, and gone out, perhaps through the garden door.

'You see, I quite obviously can't stand trial,' said Milham. 'I am virtually bound to be convicted. A judge, I am sure, would tell the jury to disregard the fact that Betty, the woman I lived with, was my sister, not my wife. Judges are good. He would tell them to cast out of their minds the fact that I was an atheist, a freethinker, and that Betty was a religious and repentant woman. But my defence would be that my sister was unbalanced. And men are men. Juries are very often stalwart, God-fearing men. They would see me as unbalanced, and Betty as my victim. If you once charged me, I will be prosecuted, and I will be convicted. That is why I have had to speak to you and try to convince you. That is why I have kept you up all night.'

They sat on for a moment longer. 'All right,' said Brentford. 'We'll have that cup of coffee.'

They were getting up. 'I killed Betty,' Milham said. 'I killed her by words, by mistake, by the things I said. But I didn't push her in the river.'

Brentford stopped. He looked at Milham. 'Who said you pushed her in the river?'

CHAPTER XXX

WHEN BRENTFORD and Ethel left the Frazers' house, their hosts left the porch light on while they found their way down the path to the garden gate. They said goodnight, and they had already talked before they left the house, with more confidence than any of them truly felt, of future meetings.

When they reached the gate, Brentford called back to Frazer, 'All right. We can find our way now.' They said, 'Good night,' 'Goodnight,' again, and the light went out.

They paused and waited, since, just outside the garden gateway, they were plunged in near-total darkness. The lights of the village were below them and too far away. The ground was rough, and the car was not so near as the Frazers had thought that they would have left it.

But they were content to stand together in the soft night looking out over Penlee and waiting until their eyes had become accustomed to the transition. Brentford thought that Ethel would be bound to say something about what they had heard in the house, and then, when she did not speak, he marvelled quietly at her ability not to say it.

'Do you think we really want to live here?' he said.

'I am not so sure as I was,' she said, looking at the night view of Penlee. But she could say it as well as not say it. 'I'm not quite so sure they are our kind of people.'

They began to move then, towards the car. As they went, he thought what she meant. The Frazers had known what the children had said about the Milhams for ten years, and not made any move. Ethel and he, had they been faced with a similar situation, would not necessarily have done anything either. But they would have found out the truth. At the end of ten years they would have been able to say, "It is true", or "It isn't". He took Ethel's arm as they moved towards the car with the view below them. It was the difference between manners and a sense of responsibility, he thought.

They stopped, quite mutually and together. The point of a lighted cigarette was glowing in the darkness between the hedge and the car. It moved, from face level to waist level, and came a pace towards them.

A controlled voice that sounded carefully calm said, 'Excuse me. Are you by any chance Detective Chief Inspector Brentford? My name is Milham.'

They went forward. The man joined them, and they stood in a little semi-circle in the roadway beside the car.

'I am,' said Brentford. Not without point, he added, 'This is my wife.' It made it not an easy meeting.

They paused for a moment while they all thought of what the presence of Brentford's wife meant.

'I have been trying to get in touch with you,' Milham said. He spoke like someone who had decided in advance exactly what he was going to say. 'When I inquired about you at your headquarters, they suggested I communicate with you at the Frazers here.' In the darkness, they could make out his profile and the fact that he made a gesture towards the house.

'I had hoped that if you wished to speak to anyone you would speak to me. I left a message.'

'I believe you have been making some inquiries about me. I would be glad to help you in any way I can.'

There was a slight sound from Ethel, hardly an exclamation and more a recognition of what Brentford had said he thought might happen. Brentford did not reply.

'Would you like me to call in your office tomorrow morning?' Milham said. 'Or would you like to come to my place to talk tonight? I would prefer that.'

Brentford moved. He took Ethel's arm, and moved her towards the car. He said. 'Do you think you can drive the car home?' It was a request, a demand almost, rather than a simple question, which she resisted.

'I could,' said Ethel, who was perfectly competent to take the car down the twisting road. 'But I don't think that I wish to.'

Brentford left her and went towards the car. As he did so, he said, 'I'll turn it round for you.' She had to go.

When he had turned it, and got out and held the door open with the courtesy light on for her to get in, they could see she was biting her lip and looked reluctant. 'Be careful,' he told her. 'There may be some mist beside the river.'

'Be careful—!' Ethel said. As she adjusted herself in the driving seat and he closed the door, she could be seen looking at him in a slightly wild way.

'I can always phone for transport home,' he said. 'But I expect I will go to the office after I've been with Mr. Milham. Don't be surprised if I'm not home by morning.'

Ethel looked at him as though there were times when she had to hate him, though her face was dim now in the lights from the dashboard. She let the clutch in, and the car spurted away from them with a little crunch of gravel.

Brentford and Milham stood watching its lights, to see it safely on its way down the curving hill. 'I hope she'll be all right,' said Milham. 'It wasn't my intention to give you any trouble.'

'We sometimes can't help it,' Brentford said. 'As you should know, as a married man.' They turned and started for the footpath through the woods that ran between the Frazers' and the Milhams' houses.

Driving between the house lights in the Penlee lanes, Ethel thought that the Penlee police station must be somewhere there. But she did not look for it at all carefully. She had decided it was not that she wanted. It was not enough.

There was mist along the inland river stretch. It was not danger to herself or the car she worried about as she drove through it. It was the chance pedestrian who would be walking on the wrong side of the road, with his back to the traffic, wearing something dark or grey. Her mind refused to calculate just how fast she could go and not hit him if he happened to be there.

She did not put the car in the garage, but left it in the drive and ran into the house, fumbling with her key and going straight to the telephone.

Parker was infinitely reassuring on the line, considering the time of night it was. 'I see, Ethel. Yes.' His voice came out of the receiver. 'Even if it is Penlee.'

Her voice rose insistently, 'The circumstances are peculiar.' A little tartly, he replied, 'I think I understand that.'

He concluded the conversation on a more urgent, comforting note. 'You leave it to me, Ethel. I'll see he has help on call. Now you get a good night's sleep.' She understood what he wanted, and got off the line.

In his dressing-gown, at the other end of the wire, Parker replaced his receiver and looked at the clock, the time.

Brentford, Parker thought distinctly, was the kind of policeman who would not merely go for a midnight walk with a murderer, and talk to him in his own house, but let him make a cup of coffee for him, then drink the coffee. Parker looked at the phone again.

Presumably not merely Ethel, but Brentford too could use a phone. So Brentford already had help on call, which was what he had promised Ethel. Parker went to bed.

CHAPTER XXXI

I T W A S daylight, though the sun had not yet risen, and there was a silver light in the sky that betokened its arrival behind the woods, while the mists were rising from the rivers and drifting away across the trees, when Brentford and Milham stepped out through the garden door. They left the door open to air the stale room to which they had not wished to return after they had had the coffee. For a while they just walked, looking at the dew on the lawns of the garden and the still, quiet and misty landscape of the village and the rivers, fresh in the air and light of dawn, with dewdrops on all the flowers in the garden beds, as they traversed the length of the garden, and turned, and walked the path again.

They were reluctant to begin again the conversation they had broken off, but which had to be concluded. They had a clear view of time now, and knew they had plenty of it before the country around them came to life, and curtains were drawn back and doors were opened, and people went about the normal business, as they would certainly believe it was, of every day.

It was a point that was in Brentford's mind.

'You can see the chapel from here,' he remarked. It was possible just to see it, a peak that was probably its small bell-tower, though it required a little guess and imagination to believe it at that hour, in the clump of trees down in the village.

Looking in the other direction, at right angles to the village and the point, Brentford could also see the Frazers' house across the trees, with a gable of roof and one touch of colour, tiny, from the bedroom curtains. But it would be a vain fancy, he thought, to think that anyone might be looking out on that morning, to see him, if for example he were to find cause to wave.

'Lambkin has been a success here,' Milham said. 'More so than churches like the Roman Catholics. Secret confession must give people the feeling that they come alone to God, and that isn't quite right for Penlee. When you think of it, it is Penlee that people like Betty truly need to confess, if it is to be useful, to give them a feeling of belonging.'

They seemed to have returned to their subject without too much difficulty of transition.

'You think Betty was attracted to Lambkin's chapel just because they had confession?' Brentford said.

Milham looked at a flower bed as they passed it. Perhaps he was thinking that it had been planted by his sister's hand.

'I don't doubt it, after I had pointed out to her the falsity of sitting with the respectable people in the Anglican church. Of course the English church says it welcomes sinners, but I think Betty felt it when I pointed it out, that the people who go there would be horrified if they knew what she was, sitting there among them; and without confession, the church offers no way out.'

Brentford wondered if it was time, and decided it was, to tighten their talk a little.

'I believe you told your Inspector Simpson that you tried to stop your Betty going to the chapel.'

Milham took it, if not in his stride as they walked, at least as something that was bound to come.

'I had to,' he said simply. 'I saw a kind of horror of inevitability when Betty joined the chapel. It was clear that after what I had told her, only a confession that all Penlee would hear would give her that sensation of a return to normality and respectability, that for her was the spiritual sensation of belonging.'

He turned his head to glance at Brentford.

'As you may know, for the past year or so I have been engaged in negotiations to take over our firm, Follet and Milham, in its entirety, from Follet. It has been delicate. If Betty were to confess all she could confess, it would not merely make it impossible for me to run the firm, it would mean complete financial ruin. I saw Dr. Hargreaves, and tried to persuade him that Betty was unbalanced in her chapel-going, and that he ought to intervene and warn her. He did not know what was at stake, of course.'

Milham looked around at his house and garden as though it had been that which was at stake, the physical basis as well as a way of life.

'He adopted the usual blind medical attitude,' he said. 'That religion would be good for Betty and soothing for her "nerves". The more I spoke of mental symptoms, which I had looked up with intention in a text-book on psychology, the more sure he said he was that a blind faith of religion would be good for her. The more I wanted him to threaten her with insanity unless she pulled herself together, the more he was inclined to let well alone.'

Approaching the shrubs and bushes at the end of the path

away from the house, at a point where they were hidden from the Frazers', Brentford thought that Parker had been right when he had suspected that the husband's complaints to the doctor about his wife had been invented. As a point against Milham, he found it very damning.

'So your sister was not insane at all,' he said, 'although at the inquest you allowed it to be more or less said she was?'

Milham paused when they reached the end of the path, and did not speak until they were heading back towards the verandah and the house again, with its open garden door. Down in the village there was a brightening of the light on the houses near the river point, and it seemed that the sunlight would strike there first when it rose through the mists up the eatern river valley. The pause gave what Milham had to say a little weight.

'It was true what I told your Inspector Simpson, that I had a fierce argument with Betty on the night before she died. I had to stop her going to the chapel at all costs. I tried to do what I had done before, to change the way her actions and thoughts were moving by pointing out their illogic to her. In the room in the house in there, I told her I had already done everything I could to prevent her going to the chapel, including opposing the building of the chapel itself and refusing Lambkin when he wanted to buy the land. But I could see she was becoming more deeply involved in it, including giving Lambkin money, and so I must speak plainly. What she was trying to do was futile, I said. In trying to reconcile herself and become a respectable part of Penlee, what she was likely to do, if she confessed herself, was to bring such ruin on us that we would be driven out of Penlee altogether, and be forced to leave the district. Betty's response to that was irrational. She attacked me with her nails.'

They were coming very near the time now, Brentford thought as they walked down the garden path. No longer talking of slow developments that had taken years, they were dealing with the events of the night before the fatal morning.

'She attacked you?'

'She looked at me in a wild way and said what did it matter. That was all I had ever thought about, money and how we were going to live and what we were going to do. I was responsible for everything that had ever happened to her, she said. She worked herself up. "If it hadn't been for you, I would have had my first baby in a home, and been reformed." She was screaming things like that. I was sitting in my chair, but she got up and her hair was wild, disordered, and she looked like an old woman raving. "I'm going to confess," she told me. "I've told Mr. Lambkin that I will. You've always been able to stop me doing what I wished before, because we've had to bring up the children, but now the last one is away from home, and I can do what I like at last." I told her, "I forbid you to go near that chapel again, or you don't come back into this house." I was trying to make her see, physically, the effect of what she was proposing to do upon herself. I tried to make her see what kind of a respectable part of Penlee she would be if she were locked out of the house, and she must suddenly have seen I meant it, for she attacked me and flung herself upon me. That is what I call madness, when people for religious or emotional reasons or any other refuse to see the facts of logic. I took her by the wrists and shook her. I slapped her face. "You will not go to the chapel in the morning," I told her, and pushed her out of the room and sent her up to bed.'

They were in the throes of it now, Brentford thought, hearing how Milham's voice was stumbling. He was a man of astonishing control and coherence when under the stress of deep emotion, but none the less he was weaving a little and had begun to walk more quickly, unconsciously, as they walked to and fro on the path in the clear morning light.

Brentford looked up at the Frazers' house, and thought of the telephone he had seen in Milham's living room, and the distance to the Penlee police station, which would be down then up. He tried to do a calculation, touching Milham's arm as he did so and drawing his attention to the Frazers' house.

'You were seen up next morning,' he said, and watched Milham stop walking abruptly along the path.

He had every cause to watch Milham. The very fact that he had stopped walking, unless he denied it immediately, was a confirmation of Frazer's half-belief that he had seen him up.

Milham did not deny it. He stood between the lawns and

the flower beds looking about him in a haunted way. But there was no exclamation of wild distortion of the features either. Milham seemed to look about him at the garden and the river curve and landscape as though he were seeing it as a stranger might.

Or, Brentford thought, as a man might who was looking on a familiar scene and saying goodbye to it for a period like fifteen years.

'Seen up?' said Milham.

Brentford felt fellow-feeling for him. It was impossible to do what Brentford was doing without fellow-feeling.

'He happened to look out at a little before this time that morning. You were dressed and crossing the lawn, he says. Why did you cross the lawn?'

They had come to the bare bones of it now, thought Brentford. There was nothing left for Milham to talk about, except the morning when Betty died.

Milham moved his head a little. He was looking at the garden plots again.

'I wakened in my room to hear her moving about the house below me. I didn't know if she would go to the chapel. I got up and dressed. I thought she might. To stop her on a Sunday evening when people would be about would be impossible. To do it in the morning when no one would be about would be ideal. I had to break her of the chapel habit. But as I finished dressing I heard the front door slam.'

Milham had not known that his sister had already confessed to Lambkin. He would have understood her outburst of the night before better if he had. Brentford did not tell him.

He spoke in a feeling way. 'Is this what you intended to tell me? It is not what you told Inspector Simpson.'

Milham turned to him with his feet crunching on the gravel of the path. He gave Brentford a direct look. 'I lied to Simpson. You will see why I lied. But I had thought and intended to tell you this. It is what seemed necessary to me when I heard you had begun to make inquiries.'

There was no way now of ever telling whether that was true or false.

But Frazer's observation had served its purpose, just as had

Lambkin's story, even though one was uncertain and the other was incomplete, and Brentford was content with that. He knew too well how little a man being questioned could guess about the evidence that the police said there was against him, and that was why he felt his fellow-feeling.

Unless Milham made some unexpected move, that was. He watched his hands.

'I went down and out and across the lawn.' Milham showed him with a gesture to the garden. They were on the spot and almost at the time. 'There is a short cut down through the woods to the river road there if you don't mind a little mud. I knew what I had to do. I had to appear in the lane ahead of Betty. I had to head her off, use force if necessary, and bring her home.'

It had been good psychology, Brentford thought, saying nothing. A woman caught and prevented in a defiant act was that much less likely to do it a second time. He watched Milham who met his eyes and spoke in a way that had all the possible indications of being the simple truth.

'I arrived down in a rush in the lane before her,' Milham said slowly, 'and Betty stopped. You know what that lane is like down there, with the woods on one side and the river on the other. I said, "Betty, you must come home." She tried to get past me on the woods side, and I went that way, so she went away towards the grass of the river bank. I thought she would get past me, so I grabbed at her. It was no more than that. I can show you the place. When I caught her coat, she swung her handbag and hit me in the face. It only caused me to close my eyes, but she wrenched away from me. When I opened my eyes, her handbag was on the grass and she had gone over the edge of the bank and was falling into the water.'

Brentford saw that in the cool morning air, a slight sweat had broken out over Milham's face.

'You tried to rescue her?'

'I climbed down the bank. I am no swimmer. If your men had searched my house that morning, they would have found my muddy suit. The water seemed four or five feet deep only one yard from the bank, but the bottom seemed to be soft mud, and Betty seemed to be floundering and drifting with the current. I saw her white face looking up at me, and I made a grab at her. I can't guess if it really happened. As I grabbed, she seemed to push herself off, away from me, into deeper water. I wish I needn't believe that, but the impression was unmistakable.'

'You called out for help?'

'I was trying to get her myself. The river mud is soft. You can hardly stand in it. I scrambled up the bank again, and looked around for anyone to call to. By the time I had seen there was no one, and looked back for Betty, I could not see her. I was standing on the grass, with her handbag at my feet. I did call out, once, and I began to run for help. Then I stopped. I found myself doing an awful thing. I had gone back, and I threw her handbag in after her. It was only after I had done it that I realised both what I was doing and why I had done it.'

The light had brightened over the houses on the point at Penlee, and the first sunlight, shining mistily down the valley, was touching there. There was no movement on the roads that they could see, but there was smoke from one or two chimneys and the Frazers' curtains had drawn back while they were not looking. They were just two men standing on a garden path, and had anyone seen them they would have wondered what they found to talk about at that hour.

'You could still have gone for help then,' said Brentford. 'You could have reported the accident.'

'You forget that I could not explain my presence on the river bank there. Except by the truth, that I had gone to stop Betty going to the chapel. That meant I would have to admit there had been a struggle. That meant there would be charges, probably of manslaughter. I thought it out suddenly, as though it just came to me as a realisation, as I stood on the bank in streaming clothes.'

'You couldn't face the charges?'

'Not without too much coming out. A police investigation of such a crime is always far more thorough than that of a simple suicide, without any suggestion of foul play. Why did I wish Betty not to go to the chapel? Or were those really my motives? I could imagine you discovering that Betty was my sister, and just how much cause I had to stop her chapel-going. I looked up and down the road again. I looked at the bank and saw I had brought some mud up with me when I had climbed it. I removed the mud. Then I went back into the wood before anyone came along. I took most of the mud off myself with grass in the woods. Then I went home, to change my suit and see that the clock said I could still go to the office at my usual time. You know the rest. My worst moment was when the police came to me as I arrived at the office, to tell me Betty had been found in the river. I had to pretend sudden shock and grief. It sounds heartless, but it was terrible just because I had to suppress the real shock and deep aching grief I felt inside. A murderer has to act tragedy while feeling tragic. I had not known that.'

So it was out now, Brentford thought, looking down at his foot, with which he drew a line in the gravel. While doing that he could keep an eye on Milham's hands and watch for any sudden shifting of his weight onto the balls of his feet. And it was unlikely now that Milham would ever change again his story of what had happened on the river bank.

He would have no cause to do so, unless an eye-witness could be found, which had never been likely. And Milham's point about a murderer having to act tragedy, even an accidental murderer such as he claimed to have been, was a valid one. Few people would realise the difference between having to act a part in a controlled way and giving way to grief. It was one of the many things that had to be found out by observation or experience that gave his version the sound of truth.

'Inspector,' Milham said.

Brentford lifted his eyes to his face without haste, changing his attention as he had to watch the eyes.

Milham's eyes met his, not appealing exactly, but saying wordlessly what he had spent the night in saying. 'I was innocent,' Milham said. 'I think if you have heard my story, you will realise that I was innocent in intention. Yet a jury must convict me. You know why. They will not be able to get past the charge of incest. I have gone out of my way to tell you all this even before you came to me, because I know that my only chance is to escape prosecution, and it is up to you what you report about me.'

Brentford met Milham's glance, and he saw the truth of his contention. Fifteen years in prison was what Milham faced.

Brentford could see what prison would mean to Milham. Discomfort, close quarters, bad company. Prison did not affect all men equally. The drabness, the ugliness, and what to Brentford always seemed the worst thing, the constant smell of urine and the utterly inadequate sanitation, would affect Milham while many hardened criminals would not even notice such things. And prison would not do Milham any good. On the contrary, he judged Milham to be one of the type whose mental deterioration would be severe as the years went by. By the time he came out, he would be senile at sixty-five. It would be a great expense to the taxpayer, and not even the people who felt that murder demanded vengeance would have the same satisfaction on sending a man to prison as they had had when there had been the death penalty, the hangman's noose, and the cat.

'I am sorry, Milham,' Brentford said.

'You mean you are going to charge me?'

'You are unlucky in me in a way. A younger man would have been harder to convince and talk to, but he might not have made up his mind so clearly, as I have had to do, what is his province and what is that of parliament and the courts.'

Milham still stood as he was.

It was only an almost indefinable difference, the difference between the stance of a free man, among his own possession and in a place where he belonged, and that of a man who already felt he was to some extent in custody. It was in that way that the fifteen-year prison sentence came slowly close to Milham.

'I would prefer death,' said Milham.

Brentford knew he would. That was why he had thought what prison would mean to him, and why he was watching him so carefully as they stood on the narrow path in the morning, with the sunlight now casting the shadows of trees around them.

'You chose to take a chance on being able to talk me out of a prosecution instead.'

'Suicide is not a crime in this country.'

'When you have been apprehended, it is incumbent on me to keep you alive for trial. It is my duty to prevent you.'

For a fleeting moment, Brentford thought Milham was going to try to bribe him. His eyes went away to the plot of land, a clearing with a track to it, between and below the place where they stood and the Frazers' house.

It happened then, while Brentford was thinking that surely Milham knew that they could not even get away with that. Perhaps if Brentford had not been distracted by that one thought, he would have been a little quicker.

Milham's long-legged frame seemed suddenly to uncoil as he stood by Brentford. He sprang sideways first, and then he began to run, first across the flower-bed, and then down across the lawn. Brentford moved, but he was too late, he knew. To be in time, he would have had to catch Milham by his wrist just an instant before he made his move. As he had been thinking, but as he had unconscionably hung back when it came to the time to do it. Brentford reached the edge of the path, then stopped there.

Milham crossed one lawn, leapt down from a terrace, and was on his way across another. Brentford saw his direction and carefully noted it. It was to the same slight gap in the woods, marking a track that ran diagonally down to the river, such as the children of a house might make, that Milham had shown him when he had told him how he had gone to meet his sister. From it, Brentford glanced up at the Frazers' house, but saw that there was no one at the window.

It was possible that that affected the speed with which Brentford went along the path back to the verandah and the open garden door, but he did not think so. Unlike Milham, Brentford was not actually built for running, and he reached the room where they had spent the night, and the telephone he had seen there, soon enough.

After all, he thought as he sat in front of it, Milham would not get much further than hiding in the woods, if escape was his intention. And also, he thought, picking up the receiver and dialling carefully, he, Brentford, had done his job. To take his case from remote and absurd suspicion, to the point where the man he was questioning in connection with a death suddenly cut and ran, was a fairly competent piece of work for any Chief Inspector.

It was just that he would have to make sure, as he would by his report, that Parker and the Chief Constable looked at it that way. He could fairly say that Milham went before the word 'arrest' had been even mentioned.

'William Milham now wanted for questioning in connection with the murder of his wife.' He was careful how he phrased it to the Lockley desk. 'No, I don't know where he's heading, but alert the local force and tell Constable Hebble to meet me, with his car not his bicycle, at Penlee Point.' He looked out of the window at the scene of woods and rivers. 'Yes, I think you would be right to put out a call immediately and set up road-blocks.'

He was wise, he thought, not to tell Lockley that he thought he might find Milham, with Hebble's assistance, more or less where his wife had been found, in about an hour. He clicked the phone's receiver-rest and began to put in a call to Ethel.

If Milham decided to do that, he thought, looking out at the woods. He would be under no necessity to do it when he discovered he was not pursued. Milham had been given a choice, which was one of the reasons he had not pursued him. There would have been no point in driving him into the river.

'Hello, dear,' he began into the phone. 'I'm sorry about last night, and I'm afraid I'm going to be held up this morning . . .'

THE PERENNIAL LIBRARY MYSTERY SERIES

Delano Ames

CORPSE DIPLOMATIQUE   P 637, $2.84
"Sprightly and intelligent."

—*New York Herald Tribune Book Review*

FOR OLD CRIME'S SAKE   P 629, $2.84

MURDER, MAESTRO, PLEASE   P 630, $2.84
"If there is a more engaging couple in modern fiction than Jane and
Dagobert Brown, we have not met them."   —*Scotsman*

SHE SHALL HAVE MURDER   P 638, $2.84
"Combines the merit of both the English and American schools in the
new mystery. It's as breezy as the best of the American ones, and has
the sophistication and wit of any top-notch Britisher."

—*New York Herald Tribune Book Review*

E. C. Bentley

TRENT'S LAST CASE   P 440, $2.50
"One of the three best detective stories ever written."

—*Agatha Christie*

TRENT'S OWN CASE   P 516, $2.25
"I won't waste time saying that the plot is sound and the detection
satisfying. Trent has not altered a scrap and reappears with all his old
humor and charm."   —*Dorothy L. Sayers*

Gavin Black

A DRAGON FOR CHRISTMAS   P 473, $1.95
"Potent excitement!"   —*New York Herald Tribune*

THE EYES AROUND ME   P 485, $1.95
"I stayed up until all hours last night reading *The Eyes Around Me*,
which is something I do not do very often, but I was so intrigued by the
ingeniousness of Mr. Black's plotting and the witty way in which he spins
his mystery. I can only say that I enjoyed the book enormously."

—*F. van Wyck Mason*

YOU WANT TO DIE, JOHNNY?   P 472, $1.95
"Gavin Black doesn't just develop a pressure plot in suspense, he adds
uninfected wit, character, charm, and sharp knowledge of the Far East
to make rereading as keen as the first race-through."   —*Book Week*

Nicholas Blake

THE CORPSE IN THE SNOWMAN P 427, $1.95
"If there is a distinction between the novel and the detective story (which we do not admit), then this book deserves a high place in both categories." —*The New York Times*

THE DREADFUL HOLLOW P 493, $1.95
"Pace unhurried, characters excellent, reasoning solid."
—*San Francisco Chronicle*

END OF CHAPTER P 397, $1.95
". . . admirably solid . . . an adroit formal detective puzzle backed up by firm characterization and a knowing picture of London publishing."
—*The New York Times*

HEAD OF A TRAVELER P 398, $2.25
"Another grade A detective story of the right old jigsaw persuasion."
—*New York Herald Tribune Book Review*

MINUTE FOR MURDER P 419, $1.95
"An outstanding mystery novel. Mr. Blake's writing is a delight in itself." —*The New York Times*

THE MORNING AFTER DEATH P 520, $1.95
"One of Blake's best." —Rex Warner

A PENKNIFE IN MY HEART P 521, $2.25
"Style brilliant . . . and suspenseful." —*San Francisco Chronicle*

THE PRIVATE WOUND P 531, $2.25
[Blake's] best novel in a dozen years . . . . An intensely penetrating study of sexual passion. . . . A powerful story of murder and its aftermath."
—Anthony Boucher, *The New York Times*

A QUESTION OF PROOF P 494, $1.95
"The characters in this story are unusually well drawn, and the suspense is well sustained." —*The New York Times*

THE SAD VARIETY P 495, $2.25
"It is a stunner. I read it instead of eating, instead of sleeping."
—Dorothy Salisbury Davis

THERE'S TROUBLE BREWING P 569, $3.37
"Nigel Strangeways is a puzzling mixture of simplicity and penetration, but all the more real for that." —*The Times Literary Supplement*

Nicholas Blake (cont'd)

THOU SHELL OF DEATH   P 428, $1.95

"It has all the virtues of culture, intelligence and sensibility that the most exacting connoisseur could ask of detective fiction."

        —*The Times* [London] *Literary Supplement*

THE WIDOW'S CRUISE   P 399, $2.25

"A stirring suspense. . . . The thrilling tale leaves nothing to be desired."

        —*Springfield Republican*

THE WORM OF DEATH   P 400, $2.25

"It [The Worm of Death] is one of Blake's very best—and his best is better than almost anyone's."   —Louis Untermeyer

John & Emery Bonett

A BANNER FOR PEGASUS   P 554, $2.40

"A gem! Beautifully plotted and set. . . . Not only is the murder adroit and deserved, and the detection competent, but the love story is charming."   —Jacques Barzun and Wendell Hertig Taylor

DEAD LION   P 563, $2.40

"A clever plot, authentic background and interesting characters highly recommended this one."   —*New Republic*

Christianna Brand

GREEN FOR DANGER   P 551, $2.50

"You have to reach for the greatest of Great Names (Christie, Carr, Queen . . .) to find Brand's rivals in the devious subtleties of the trade."

        —Anthony Boucher

TOUR DE FORCE   P 572, $2.40

"Complete with traps for the over-ingenious, a double-reverse surprise ending and a key clue planted so fairly and obviously that you completely overlook it. If that's your idea of perfect entertainment, then seize at once upon *Tour de Force*."   —Anthony Boucher, *The New York Times*

James Byrom

OR BE HE DEAD   P 585, $2.84

"A very original tale . . . Well written and steadily entertaining."

        —Jacques Barzun & Wendell Hertig Taylor, *A Catalogue of Crime*

Henry Calvin

IT'S DIFFERENT ABROAD   P 640, $2.84

"What is remarkable and delightful, Mr. Calvin imparts a flavor of satire to what he renovates and compels us to take straight."

—Jacques Barzun

Marjorie Carleton

VANISHED   P 559, $2.40

"Exceptional . . . a minor triumph."
—Jacques Barzun and Wendell Hertig Taylor, *A Catalogue of Crime*

George Harmon Coxe

MURDER WITH PICTURES   P 527, $2.25

"[Coxe] has hit the bull's-eye with his first shot."

—*The New York Times*

Edmund Crispin

BURIED FOR PLEASURE   P 506, $2.50

"Absolute and unalloyed delight."

—Anthony Boucher, *The New York Times*

Lionel Davidson

THE MENORAH MEN   P 592, $2.84

"Of his fellow thriller writers, only John Le Carré shows the same instinct for the viscera."   —*Chicago Tribune*

NIGHT OF WENCESLAS   P 595, $2.84

"A most ingenious thriller, so enriched with style, wit, and a sense of serious comedy that it all but transcends its kind."

—*The New Yorker*

THE ROSE OF TIBET   P 593, $2.84

"I hadn't realized how much I missed the genuine Adventure story . . . until I read *The Rose of Tibet*."   —Graham Greene

D. M. Devine

MY BROTHER'S KILLER   P 558, $2.40

"A most enjoyable crime story which I enjoyed reading down to the last moment."   —Agatha Christie

Kenneth Fearing

THE BIG CLOCK P 500, $1.95

"It will be some time before chill-hungry clients meet again so rare a compound of irony, satire, and icy-fingered narrative. *The Big Clock* is . . . a psychothriller you won't put down." —*Weekly Book Review*

Andrew Garve

THE ASHES OF LODA P 430, $1.50

"Garve . . . embellishes a fine fast adventure story with a more credible picture of the U.S.S.R. than is offered in most thrillers."
  —*The New York Times Book Review*

THE CUCKOO LINE AFFAIR P 451, $1.95

". . . an agreeable and ingenious piece of work." —*The New Yorker*

A HERO FOR LEANDA P 429, $1.50

"One can trust Mr. Garve to put a fresh twist to any situation, and the ending is really a lovely surprise." —*The Manchester Guardian*

MURDER THROUGH THE LOOKING GLASS P 449, $1.95

". . . refreshingly out-of-the-way and enjoyable . . . highly recommended to all comers." —*Saturday Review*

NO TEARS FOR HILDA P 441, $1.95

"It starts fine and finishes finer. I got behind on breathing watching Max get not only his man but his woman, too." —Rex Stout

THE RIDDLE OF SAMSON P 450, $1.95

"The story is an excellent one, the people are quite likable, and the writing is superior." —*Springfield Republican*

Michael Gilbert

BLOOD AND JUDGMENT P 446, $1.95

"Gilbert readers need scarcely be told that the characters all come alive at first sight, and that his surpassing talent for narration enhances any plot. . . . Don't miss." —*San Francisco Chronicle*

THE BODY OF A GIRL P 459, $1.95

"Does what a good mystery should do: open up into all kinds of ramifications, with untold menace behind the action. At the end, there is a bang-up climax, and it is a pleasure to see how skilfully Gilbert wraps everything up." —*The New York Times Book Review*

Michael Gilbert (cont'd)

THE DANGER WITHIN P 448, $1.95

"Michael Gilbert has nicely combined some elements of the straight detective story with plenty of action, suspense, and adventure, to produce a superior thriller." —*Saturday Review*

FEAR TO TREAD P 458, $1.95

"Merits serious consideration as a work of art."

—*The New York Times*

Joe Gores

HAMMETT P 631, $2.84

"Joe Gores at his very best. Terse, powerful writing—with the master, Dashiell Hammett, as the protagonist in a novel I think he would have been proud to call his own." —Robert Ludlum

C. W. Grafton

BEYOND A REASONABLE DOUBT P 519, $1.95

"A very ingenious tale of murder . . . a brilliant and gripping narrative." —Jacques Barzun and Wendell Hertig Taylor

THE RAT BEGAN TO GNAW THE ROPE P 639, $2.84

"Fast, humorous story with flashes of brilliance."

—*The New Yorker*

Edward Grierson

THE SECOND MAN P 528, $2.25

"One of the best trial-testimony books to have come along in quite a while." —*The New Yorker*

Bruce Hamilton

TOO MUCH OF WATER P 635, $2.84

"A superb sea mystery. . . . The prose is excellent."
—Jacques Barzun and Wendell Hertig Taylor, *A Catalogue of Crime*

Cyril Hare

DEATH IS NO SPORTSMAN P 555, $2.40

"You will be thrilled because it succeeds in placing an ingenious story in a new and refreshing setting. . . . The identity of the murderer is really a surprise." —*Daily Mirror*

Cyril Hare (cont'd)

DEATH WALKS THE WOODS   P 556, $2.40

"Here is a fine formal detective story, with a technically brilliant solution demanding the attention of all connoisseurs of construction."

—Anthony Boucher, *The New York Times Book Review*

AN ENGLISH MURDER   P 455, $2.50

"By a long shot, the best crime story I have read for a long time. Everything is traditional, but originality does not suffer. The setting is perfect. Full marks to Mr. Hare."   —*Irish Press*

SUICIDE EXCEPTED   P 636, $2.84

"Adroit in its manipulation . . . and distinguished by a plot-twister which I'll wager Christie wishes she'd thought of."

—*The New York Times*

TENANT FOR DEATH   P 570, $2.84

"The way in which an air of probability is combined both with clear, terse narrative and with a good deal of subtle suburban atmosphere, proves the extreme skill of the writer."   —*The Spectator*

TRAGEDY AT LAW   P 522, $2.25

"An extremely urbane and well-written detective story."

—*The New York Times*

UNTIMELY DEATH   P 514, $2.25

"The English detective story at its quiet best, meticulously underplayed, rich in perceivings of the droll human animal and ready at the last with a neat surprise which has been there all the while had we but wits to see it."   —*New York Herald Tribune Book Review*

THE WIND BLOWS DEATH   P 589, $2.84

"A plot compounded of musical knowledge, a Dickens allusion, and a subtle point in law is related with delightfully unobtrusive wit, warmth, and style."   —*The New York Times*

WITH A BARE BODKIN   P 523, $2.25

"One of the best detective stories published for a long time."

—*The Spectator*

Robert Harling

THE ENORMOUS SHADOW   P 545, $2.50

"In some ways the best spy story of the modern period. . . . The writing is terse and vivid . . . the ending full of action . . . altogether first-rate."

—Jacques Barzun and Wendell Hertig Taylor, *A Catalogue of Crime*

Matthew Head

THE CABINDA AFFAIR   P 541, $2.25
"An absorbing whodunit and a distinguished novel of atmosphere."
—Anthony Boucher, *The New York Times*

THE CONGO VENUS   P 597, $2.84
"Terrific. The dialogue is just plain wonderful."
—*The Boston Globe*

MURDER AT THE FLEA CLUB   P 542, $2.50
"The true delight is in Head's style, its limpid ease combined with humor
and an awesome precision of phrase."   —*San Francisco Chronicle*

M. V. Heberden

ENGAGED TO MURDER   P 533, $2.25
"Smooth plotting."   —*The New York Times*

James Hilton

WAS IT MURDER?   P 501, $1.95
"The story is well planned and well written."
—*The New York Times*

P. M. Hubbard

HIGH TIDE   P 571, $2.40
"A smooth elaboration of mounting horror and danger."
—*Library Journal*

Elspeth Huxley

THE AFRICAN POISON MURDERS   P 540, $2.25
"Obscure venom, manical mutilations, deadly bush fire, thrilling climax
compose major opus.... Top-flight."
—*Saturday Review of Literature*

MURDER ON SAFARI   P 587, $2.84
"Right now we'd call Mrs. Huxley a dangerous rival to Agatha Christie."   —*Books*

Francis Iles

BEFORE THE FACT P 517, $2.50

"Not many 'serious' novelists have produced character studies to compare with Iles's internally terrifying portrait of the murderer in *Before the Fact,* his masterpiece and a work truly deserving the appellation of unique and beyond price." —Howard Haycraft

MALICE AFORETHOUGHT P 532, $1.95

"It is a long time since I have read anything so good as *Malice Aforethought,* with its cynical humour, acute criminology, plausible detail and rapid movement. It makes you hug yourself with pleasure."

—H. C. Harwood, *Saturday Review*

Michael Innes

THE CASE OF THE JOURNEYING BOY P 632, $3.12

"I could see no faults in it. There is no one to compare with him."
—*Illustrated London News*

DEATH BY WATER P 574, $2.40

"The amount of ironic social criticism and deft characterization of scenes and people would serve another author for six books."

—Jacques Barzun and Wendell Hertig Taylor

HARE SITTING UP P 590, $2.84

"There is hardly anyone (in mysteries or mainstream) more exquisitely literate, allusive and Jamesian—and hardly anyone with a firmer sense of melodramatic plot or a more vigorous gift of storytelling."

—Anthony Boucher, *The New York Times*

THE LONG FAREWELL P 575, $2.40

"A model of the deft, classic detective story, told in the most wittily diverting prose." —*The New York Times*

THE MAN FROM THE SEA P 591, $2.84

"The pace is brisk, the adventures exciting and excitingly told, and above all he keeps to the very end the interesting ambiguity of the man from the sea." —*New Statesman*

THE SECRET VANGUARD P 584, $2.84

"Innes . . . has mastered the art of swift, exciting and well-organized narrative." —*The New York Times*

THE WEIGHT OF THE EVIDENCE P 633, $2.84

"First-class puzzle, deftly solved. University background interesting and amusing." —*Saturday Review of Literature*

Mary Kelly

THE SPOILT KILL P 565, $2.40
"Mary Kelly is a new Dorothy Sayers. . . . [An] exciting new novel."
—*Evening News*

Lange Lewis

THE BIRTHDAY MURDER P 518, $1.95
"Almost perfect in its playlike purity and delightful prose."
—Jacques Barzun and Wendell Hertig Taylor

Allan MacKinnon

HOUSE OF DARKNESS P 582, $2.84
"His best . . . a perfect compendium."
—Jacques Barzun & Wendell Hertig Taylor, *A Catalogue of Crime*

Arthur Maling

LUCKY DEVIL P 482, $1.95
"The plot unravels at a fast clip, the writing is breezy and Maling's approach is as fresh as today's stockmarket quotes."
—*Louisville Courier Journal*

RIPOFF P 483, $1.95
"A swiftly paced story of today's big business is larded with intrigue as a Ralph Nader-type investigates an insurance scandal and is soon on the run from a hired gun and his brother. . . . Engrossing and credible."
—*Booklist*

SCHROEDER'S GAME P 484, $1.95
"As the title indicates, this Schroeder is up to something, and the unravelling of his game is a diverting and sufficiently blood-soaked entertainment."
—*The New Yorker*

Austin Ripley

MINUTE MYSTERIES P 387, $2.50
More than one hundred of the world's shortest detective stories. Only one possible solution to each case!

Thomas Sterling

THE EVIL OF THE DAY P 529, $2.50
"Prose as witty and subtle as it is sharp and clear. . .characters unconventionally conceived and richly bodied forth . . . . In short, a novel to be treasured."
—Anthony Boucher, *The New York Times*

Julian Symons

THE BELTING INHERITANCE   P 468, $1.95
"A superb whodunit in the best tradition of the detective story."
—August Derleth, *Madison Capital Times*

BLAND BEGINNING   P 469, $1.95
"Mr. Symons displays a deft storytelling skill, a quiet and literate wit, a nice feeling for character, and detectival ingenuity of a high order."
—Anthony Boucher, *The New York Times*

BOGUE'S FORTUNE   P 481, $1.95
"There's a touch of the old sardonic humour, and more than a touch of style."   —*The Spectator*

THE BROKEN PENNY   P 480, $1.95
"The most exciting, astonishing and believable spy story to appear in years.   —Anthony Boucher, *The New York Times Book Review*

THE COLOR OF MURDER   P 461, $1.95
"A singularly unostentatious and memorably brilliant detective story."
—*New York Herald Tribune Book Review*

Dorothy Stockbridge Tillet
(John Stephen Strange)

THE MAN WHO KILLED FORTESCUE   P 536, $2.25
"Better than average."   —*Saturday Review of Literature*

Simon Troy

THE ROAD TO RHUINE   P 583, $2.84
"Unusual and agreeably told."   —*San Francisco Chronicle*

SWIFT TO ITS CLOSE   P 546, $2.40
"A nicely literate British mystery . . . the atmosphere and the plot are exceptionally well wrought, the dialogue excellent."   —*Best Sellers*

Henry Wade

THE DUKE OF YORK'S STEPS   P 588, $2.84
"A classic of the golden age."
—Jacques Barzun & Wendell Hertig Taylor, *A Catalogue of Crime*

A DYING FALL   P 543, $2.50
"One of those expert British suspense jobs . . . it crackles with undercurrents of blackmail, violent passion and murder. Topnotch in its class."
—*Time*

If you enjoyed this book you'll want to know about
THE PERENNIAL LIBRARY MYSTERY SERIES

Buy them at your local bookstore or use this coupon for ordering:

Qty	P number	Price
_____	_____	_____
_____	_____	_____
_____	_____	_____
_____	_____	_____
_____	_____	_____
_____	_____	_____
_____	_____	_____
_____	_____	_____
_____	_____	_____
_____	_____	_____
_____	_____	_____
_____	_____	_____
_____	_____	_____
_____	_____	_____
	postage and handling charge	$1.00
	_____ book(s) @ $0.25	_____
	TOTAL	[ ]

Prices contained in this coupon are Harper & Row invoice prices only. They are subject to change without notice, and in no way reflect the prices at which these books may be sold by other suppliers.

HARPER & ROW, Mail Order Dept. #PMS, 10 East 53rd St., New York, N.Y. 10022.

Please send me the books I have checked above. I am enclosing $_____ which includes a postage and handling charge of $1.00 for the first book and 25¢ for each additional book. Send check or money order. No cash or C.O.D.s please

Name_____

Address_____

City_____ State_____ Zip_____

Please allow 4 weeks for delivery. USA only. This offer expires 11/30/84.
Please add applicable sales tax.